Hooking

A Bachelor Auction, Secret Princess, Hockey Romance

Ella Haines

LIBRA LIBROS LLC

Contents

Warning: This book contains content such as **explicit language, steamy sexy times** (sometimes in public), and more. You need to be able to suspend disbelief enough for a 'secretly royal' plot line. *If* you have triggers – please see the Author's Note page or Content Warning at the end for more details.

This is a work of fiction. Names, characters, places, and incidents are the product of the author's imagination. Any resemblance to actual persons, living or dead, events, or locales is entirely coincidental.

It warrants repeating: this is a work of fiction. Made up. Fabricated. Not real. **Suspend your disbelief and just enjoy the ride.** Some things may/will be inaccurate: the nuances of foreign policy, the intricacies of running a *fictional* foreign country, a princess living undetected abroad. For the most part, I try to be as accurate as I can—I research, collaborate, and reach out to professionals. But at the end of the day, this is fiction, and sometimes I just want to tell a fun, far-fetched story and need to draw a line in the sand to make that happen.

Just go with it and enjoy the story in the spirit it was intended.

www.EllaHaines.com

First edition May 2024

Cover designed by Get Covers

Edited by Des at Imagination Pen Editorial

Proofread by Markups by Mackenzie

ISBN 978-1-956865-46-2 (Paperback)

ISBN 978-1-956865-45-5 (Ebook)

Published by Libra Libros LLC

Springfield Cyclones: Roster & Coaches

Team Roster

Teemu Werner, #45, Goalie
Brian Thompson, #30, Goalie
Henrick Langstrom, #5, Defenseman
Patrick Conley, #6, Defenseman
Ilya Sergechev, #33, Defenseman **(C)**
David Kasselbeck, #29, Defenseman
Benjamin Wilder, #21, Defenseman
Max Van der Beek, #25, Defenseman
Dale Cartwright, #27, Defenseman
Paul Owens, #22, Defenseman
Bobby Davidson, #17, Right Wing **(A)**
Ian Novac, #19, Left Wing
Ty Daniels, #37, Center
Jason Miller, #99, Right Wing
Mitchell Collins, #2, Left Wing
Tommy Kolbeck, #77, Center
Pavel Savic, #87, Right Wing
Christian Rudiger, #46, Left Wing
Jonathan Chamberlain, #88, Center
Vladimir Savic, #18, Right Wing
Derrick Bergeron, #42, Left Wing
Evan Frazier, #49, Center

Duke Grammar, #53, Goalie

Coaches

John Montgomery, Head Coach
Dennis Savuk, Assistant Coach
Casey Spencer, Assistant Coach
Scott Zachar, Assistant Coach

Author's Note About Content Warnings

See list of content/trigger warnings here on my site at www.EllaHaines.com/Triggers

The list is also found at the end of the book through the table of contents

WARNING: will possibly contain plot spoilers by nature of disclosing – proceed as you are comfortable

Gentle Reminder About Suspending Disbelief

For those who tend to overlook the copyright page (guilty!), here's a gentle reminder:

Within this story, you will encounter elements that stretch the boundaries of reality. Now, sure, many romances do that. How many Billionaire, Cowboy, Hockey-playing, Second-chance, Meet-cute, Alpha, Best Friend, Cinnamon roll Heroes are out there anyway?

As readers, we generally know that we have to suspend disbelief to enjoy these types of romance stories. Even so, in this book, I'm asking you to not scrutinize the 'hows' of Ashley's circumstances.

***

The acceptance of Ashley's entire situation—her attitude/thoughts, education, language proficiency, successful evasion of media detection, ability to live alone in a foreign country, etc—**is crucial to enjoying the story.**

Some things will be inaccurate or far-fetched: the nuances of foreign policy, the intricacies of running a ***fictional*** foreign country, the plausibility of a princess being allowed to leave her patriarchal homeland, etc.

But, in order to enjoy this book, you should accept the fictional setup and be open to the notion that certain plot elements were feasible and unfolded beforehand to render it all 'possible'.

***

If the above-mentioned items seem like they'd be DNF-worthy for you, then this is probably not the book for you.

But if you're willing to accept the premise of it all and want to dive into a tale of royally forbidden love, then I hope you enjoy the journey!

Blurb

When Royalty Meets the Rink, Will Love Prevail?

***

Ashley Winters has lived her life trapped in a world of expectations and responsibility. As her father pushes for her return to a life she's desperate to escape, Ashley impulsively bids on a sexy hockey player at a charity bachelor auction. Maybe one last wild moment will trick her heart into believing she has some sense of control in her spiraling life of duty and responsibility.

***

Ty Daniels, a hockey star haunted by past betrayals, finds himself at a crossroads with the mysterious bidder from the auction. His time spent with Ashley ignites a spark neither can deny, but he's been lied to before and something about her.... Well, she's hiding something. He just doesn't know what. With their hearts entangled, a world of romantic promise opens up, but it's shadowed by potential repercussions neither could have foreseen.

***

Can their love endure once the truth comes to light, or will the weight of their contrasting worlds deny them their shot at happiness?

Chapter One

September 26, Sunday

Ashley

Ashira Wazir, don't be stupid. Father is getting seriously pissed. You dodged his calls again today. You need to answer your fucking phone when we call or....

Ashley read the start of her brother's text and rolled her eyes, tucking her phone back into her glittery clutch.

Seriously?

Like Idris had never dodged a check-in phone call? Or two hundred?

Hell, her brother was the one who would sneak her down to the kitchen for snacks if dinner was gross and she didn't eat. He bought Ashley her first pair of jeans and snuck them into a drawer in her bedroom. Idris was the one who made their tutors teach her how to shoot guns, play cards, and swear in four different languages.

When did he get so uptight?

Apparently, her three years of 'respite' in the States had changed him as much as it had her.

What would everyone think of the changes in *her* when she went back in a few months?

Ashley sucked in a breath and tried not to panic. Her brief stint in the US came with more conditions and promises than any one person should make in their life, but she was confident she could at least get out of one or two of the 'commitments' that she made. There was no way her father would make her stick to *every* allowance that she made in order to get her short sabbatical here in the States.

Right?...

Ashley took a sip of her diminishing wine glass and watched all the empowered women chatting around the great hall.

What she wouldn't give to be freed of her familial expectations and responsibilities.

Scratch that. Not just familial. A *nation's* expectations and responsibilities.

What she wouldn't give to have this life forever.

To be heard. Seen. Respected.

Much better than a trophy wife. Property. An alliance bartering chip.

A broodmare to be admired, yet not truly desired...

Ashley downed what was left in her wine glass. Closing her eyes, she could feel the alcohol's warmth spreading in her belly.

A little liquid courage never hurt anyone.

Usually.

There was movement beside her, and Ashley opened her eyes to find the lovely waiter who she seemed to have on speed dial. He presented her with another tall glass of wine and a wink.

The staffing tonight was on point.

Ashley wondered if they'd consider moving to Dariqat. She could use some efficient people like this around when she went back. Or maybe she could hire some of the guys from her security team—those fellas knew how to *disappear*. She sometimes went months without even seeing one of them in person, the only reason she knew they still kept tabs on her was that her father still received fabricated reports/updates on her activities. They were *supposed* to be on her 24/7. Fortunately, she had managed to convince the intimidating, yet undeniably handsome, owner of the security company that such intense surveillance was unnecessary. His clear distaste for her father's expectations had worked in her favor, granting her a small degree of freedom once they established a routine.

Ashley took the offered glass and murmured her thanks with an appreciative dip of her chin.

The constant supply of alcohol was a great strategic move by the bachelor auction organizers; a guaranteed way to ensure a flurry of high-priced and reckless bids during the auction.

Ashley took a deep inhale over the glass, closing her eyes as she let the aromas register. Her nose was hit with a delightful mix of fruity notes, perhaps the lusciousness of ripe blackberries, a hint of plump currants, and the depth of dark cherries. Swirling the wine gently, new layers unfolded – delicate hints of vanilla or cedarwood – tangled in among the fruity bouquet.

Wow. Good stuff.

She took another sip, acutely aware of the buzzing sensation already coursing through her veins.

Well, it looked like she was bidding on a hunk tonight.

Which was totally fine because Ashley had already spoken with the event coordinators and made sure there was no media coverage at the event. There was a time and place for what her dear brother referred to as 'being stupid,' and being near the paparazzi was definitely not one of them. Idris really needed to give her more credit—she had managed to stay under the media radar for this long; she wasn't a fool, after all.

"Damn, this wine is perfect," gushed a tablemate from across the way, who was admiring her own full glass.

Lexie Galloway, heir to the Springfield Spartans—the local professional football team—was placed at Ashley's table.

The auction planning committee probably thought it made sense to put two heiresses at the same table, given that's what Ashley put on her ticket as well.

'Heiress.'

A creative interpretation, not an outright lie.

But tonight, the two women were just like everyone else—attendees at this auction featuring the sexy bachelors from the Springfield Cyclones—the city's resident NHL team.

Why they decided to create a new hockey team right next door to the Boston Bruins...Ashley would never know. But they did the same with the other sports teams, too. Football. Baseball. Hell, there was even a soccer team.

However, it seemed like it worked. It felt like all of New England jumped on board to support the new professional sports teams. Everywhere in the city, Ashley was bombarded with Springfield sports paraphernalia, so the sports market analysts chose correctly. The area apparently *could* support another team.

Who would have guessed.

Ashley didn't do the whole '*sports thing*.'

But drooling over the gorgeous, muscular, alpha athletes?

That she could do.

Ashley surveyed the opulent room and issued friendly smiles when she made eye contact with other passing guests. Spectacularly decorated tables were adorned with meticulously decorated centerpieces, each attendee had an assigned table with a custom wood-burned name plate that matched the wood-burned table number. A registration table and a small coat check station greeted guests in the front hall. The tantalizing smell of an extravagant dinner being prepared made her salivate. A small but elegantly dressed band played near the front of the room, next to the stage. Celebrities, athletes, and the wealthy mingled, their laughter floating through the air amidst the lively tunes from the string quartet.

The night was in full swing, with clinking glasses and excited chatter filling the exquisitely decorated ballroom. The scent of flowers mixed with the sharp tang of various alcoholic drinks and gourmet hors d'oeuvres. Guests socialized and flirted, their anticipation palpable as they networked before dinner was served and the auction commenced.

"I think my nipples are going to slip out," Jen, the fit beauty across from Ashley and next to Lexie, whined, as she fidgeted in her seat, trying to adjust the top of her dress.

Well...*that* was a mental image. Ashley hid her amused smile.

Another woman, seated on the other side of Lexie, leaned across her plate and scrutinized Jen's chest. She tilted her head, staring at her friend's breasts. "Maybe. It does look a little precarious. Did you at least put on nipple covers?"

"No!" Jen squawked, her cheeks reddening as she continued to fidget with the cups. "Lexie said it was guaranteed not to slip!"

Both women turned to Lexie, who merely waved a regal hand. "I said it was guaranteed *to* slip. How do you think I landed that prince last year?"

Ashley's eyebrows shot up and she chuckled into the mouth of her wine glass.

"You're such a troll," Megan laughed and turned away, her eyes wandering and coming to rest on a group of professional football players gathered across the room.

The professional football players exuded undeniable charisma and exuberance, showing their support for their professional hockey counterparts who had been "volun-told" into participating in the auction.

Megan's gaze turned distant as she quietly remarked, "We should help plan another auction where we include *all* the athletes. I think the other teams' bachelors, combined with these current hockey hunks...could probably eradicate all poverty in Springfield."

If the men knew their mere show of friendly support had sparked the idea for a spin-off auction, their loud laughter and jokes might have been tempered. Ashley hid her grin.

"Oh, don't forget princes. We should invite some princes," Jen chimed in.

Lexie's pierced and sharply waxed black eyebrow raised in thought. "Hmm, I could give him a call I guess..."

"Ashley, do you know any eligible bachelors we could call?"

She jerked and forced herself to choke down the latest sip of wine.

"Um..."

"We need some really ritzy ones if we're going to outdo this. What have you got for contacts?"

"Well, I know a few—"

"Great!"

"...but they're all somewhat controlling, ego-maniac schmucks."

The trio across from her donned matching expressions of disappointment.

Lexie pursed her lips together and narrowed her eyes. "Yeah, that was my experience with my prince. Or...at least the latest one."

Megan elbowed her. Jen just chuckled.

Lexie sighed dramatically before twirling her jet-black ponytail. "Totally worth it though...he was a *beast* in the sack."

Ashley couldn't stop her laugh—she knew this too well. "Girl. For real. But thank God they're assholes though. Can you imagine if they were sweet? The beasts are much easier to handle. It's the gentle ones you have to watch out for. Those are the ones who will steal your heart and leave you broken. With the man-whores, at least you know what you're getting."

The auctioneer stepped up to the podium and the microphone squealed, prompting Ashley to wince. The man started shuffling paper in front of him in preparation for the big event.

"Gah! I forgot my paddle and it's about to start! Jen, come with me!" Lexie leaped up from her seat and grabbed Jen's arm, almost causing the dreaded-and-awaited nip slip. Jen frantically pulled at the neckline of her dress as she navigated her way out of her seat.

Megan looked down at her phone and mumbled something about checking in with her babysitter as she turned away from the table, covering one ear to hear the phone call with the other, essentially leaving Ashley alone.

Fine by her—she was used to it.

Ashley was handed a new wine glass from the friendly waiter, and she gave him a saucy wink.

Woah. Winking at waiters?

Maybe she was a little further gone than she thought.

This shit was going to hit her hard when she finally stood up.

She didn't really come here tonight for a date: she'd only bid to make sure no man was left standing to crickets—and to help a good cause.

Maybe she'd even get a nice dinner out of it.

But it's not like Ashley was ever going to be able to do something like this ever again.

So. *When in Rome*.

Feeling the buzz really start to settle in, Ashley lifted her wine glass and gave a whoop at a pause in the speaker's intro speech.

People looked over to her and she gave them a regal nod while trying to suppress the silly smile that wanted to erupt.

Yeah, definitely drunk. She grinned and took another large gulp of wine.

Ashley's toes were starting to tingle in her stilettos.

She started inventorying the men waiting in the shadows of the stage.

Wow, they were seriously gorgeous.

Ashley looked down at the sheet that came with her paddle and read the bios.

Bachelor Number One: Bobby Davidson.

Was that the man standing closest to the far left of the stage? If so, his beard game was *on point*.

Why didn't the bio sheet come with pictures of the men?

Ashley made a mental note to tell Lexie that her bachelor auction's sheet needed to include pictures of the studs so the mares could make a well-informed decision.

She laughed into her wine glass; her childhood riding instructor would have appreciated that one.

Lexie and Jen swooped back into their chairs while Jen was hissing something furiously at Lexie, but their words were drowned out from the auctioneer's voice coming through the speakers.

Ashley tucked a strand of her dark hair behind her ear and looked up at the stage where a little, old lady was escorting out the first hockey player in an expensive blue suit.

Wow.

This guy was handsome as hell.

Ashley was 'sowing her oats', as Americans liked to say.

At least while she was here in the States.

Back home in Dariqat, she never would have been able to get away with her...exploration.

Hell, her father might even have the men killed if he found out they were touching his precious princess.

Thank God for the special visa her brother had managed to get for her. Even if it was only temporary.

"Let's give a warm welcome to bachelor number one, Bobby Davidson!"

And so it began.

Lexie's paddle was up and down so many times that Ashley worried that the candles at the center of the table were going to go out. The alcohol was really hitting her now, and just to egg Lexie on, whenever the auctioneer would get to the 'going twice' part of his bit, Ashley would shoot her own paddle up.

Lexie laughed across from her, offering Ashley a salute.

Eventually though, they were outbid by a dark horse: a brunette fox in a pink dress. By Bobby's relieved grin and wink to the woman, Ashley figured they were an item...or at least had planned his last minute 'purchase.'

Lexie sighed dramatically but gave Ashley an amused smile, apparently not too bothered by her loss.

As the next bachelor, a sexy mountain man named Tommy Kolbeck, took the stage, the room buzzed with more whispers.

Again, Lexie and Ashley, as well as many others, both young and old, battled for a date with Tommy. When it looked like a bunch of old ladies had won the bid, a blonde woman from the back of the hall had outbid them, again, at the last minute.

The hungry expression on Tommy's face had Ashley pivoting in her seat to see who caused that reaction, but too many heads were in the way to make her out.

More bachelors passed and a comfortable buzz was now causing Ashley to become lazy in her paddle raises. She slouched in her seat and lazily raised her paddle, simply going through the motions. Now that Lexie had found a wealthy woman across the room to battle with, Ashley was off the hook.

All of the men seemed to have plenty of bidders. No pity bids needed. She was free to sit back and just soak in the freedom of having *choice*.

Another glass of wine was handed to her.

Warning bells went off in her head; she should probably cut it off, but she had already grabbed it.

Well, *this* would be her last one.

Ashley looked around to tell the nice waiter that she needed to switch to water after this, but the helpful man was nowhere to be found. Naturally.

Seriously, this guy was more on top of shit than Pepper Potts.

"Another round of applause for bachelor number six!" announced the auctioneer, his voice booming over the loudspeakers. "Now, let's not waste any more time. Ladies and gentlemen, please welcome bachelor number seven: Tyler Daniels!"

As the crowd erupted into cheers and applause, her heart stopped.

The man's bright blue eyes were strikingly obvious, even from where she was sitting.

Hot damn.

He looked like he'd stepped out of a dream, and Ashley found it hard to tear her eyes away. Immediately, she pushed up in her seat. "Wow."

Out of the corner of her eye, Ashley was vaguely aware of Lexie arching an eyebrow at her reaction. Ashley couldn't stop her body from stiffening as she felt Lexie turn and take a closer look at Tyler.

"Me and you, babe?" Lexie asked, as the auctioneer started the campaign for Tyler.

Ashley forced out a weak laugh and shook her head.

Maybe in another life—one where she knew what to do with a *good* guy.

"No way. Do you *see* him? He has 'nice guy' written all over him."

Lexie snorted. "Yeah, but all I see is 'devilishly sexy' guy."

The bids kept climbing.

He had his hands clasped loosely in front of him...by his...

Ashley dragged her eyes back up to his face where he was smiling kindly to a bidder down front.

She turned to Lexie. "Then you need glasses. That guy is an *angel*. Just look at him. He's...commitment. Babies. White picket fences."

Megan's head cocked. "And that's bad?"

Ashley shook her head and stared up at the perfection on the stage. "Not bad. *Perfect*. Just...wrong for me."

There was silence at their table as the bids continued to increase.

"Good. More for me. Looks are deceiving. I heard he's a fucking monster in bed. I could use a distraction. Especially one that looks like him. He's like one of those candies that looks sweet but is *all* sour." With a hungry look, Lexie joined the bidding, her gaze fixed on Tyler.

Oh.

Ashley moved her eyes back to the hockey God in front of them and her cheeks started to feel hot.

Each time Lexie raised her paddle, Ashley's belly squeezed.

Like he sensed her eyes on him, those bright blues turned to Ashley, and she could see his chest expand when their eyes locked. Slowly, the man cocked his head.

Inviting her.

Challenging her.

The idea of Lexie getting a date with him…

A slight twitch of his lips teased at a smile. A temptation.

Well, it was for a worthy cause after all…

CHAPTER TWO

September 26, Sunday

Ashley

As the auctioneer acknowledged her raised paddle, her heart raced with a mixture of excitement and trepidation. Maybe this could be her final hurrah here in the States? A way to reclaim her power just one more time. Her brother's text and her father's earlier phone call this week replayed in her fuzzy mind.

Ashley's gaze traced the athlete's chiseled jaw and confident stance. Those bright eyes framed by that dark hair and his crisp, clean shave?

Yes, please.

"Two thousand!" a woman called from the back of the room, her heels clicking against the marble floor as she strode assuredly to the front.

Woah, this was supposed to be paddle bids only.

And also, he wasn't a piece of meat, *Karen*.

"Three thousand!" Lexie countered, pushing to stand, causing Ashley to turn her head.

In all honesty, it was surprising that it wasn't Lexie who had broken the no-bidding-aloud rule.

Lexie shot Ashley a wink and whispered across the table, "Coward."

"Four thousand!" Ashley countered, raising her bidding paddle with determination, not breaking eye contact with Lexie.

"Five thousand!" Lexie shot back, smirking slightly.

"Six thousand!" Ashley called without hesitation, feeling a surge of adrenaline as she also pushed to stand. Ashley turned toward the stage and saw Tyler watching her with a big smile on his face. When they made eye contact again, his expression turned sexy, and he gave Ashley a wink that made her panties catch fire.

Or would have, if she were wearing any.

"All right, we have six thousand from the lovely lady over there!" the auctioneer announced. "Do I hear seven?"

"Eight!" Lexie shouted, doubling down, her eyes narrowing as she raised her paddle. Megan grabbed Lexie's arm and yanked her back into her chair.

"All right folks, now this is what we consider a noble cause. Eight thousand dollars would go a long way for the organization. Does anyone else want to step in?" the auctioneer questioned, gesturing towards Ashley and Lexie. "Do I hear nine thousand?"

As the auctioneer egged them on, Ashley was hit again by the weight of her impending return to a life of duty and obligation bearing down on her. She grew more determined to seize this opportunity, to have the freedom of choice she so desperately craved before it was ripped away once more.

"Ten thousand!" Lexie called, her expression way too haughty for Ashley's liking.

Ashley laughed and shook her head. "You can't outbid yourself, you idiot."

"We also shouldn't be shouting our bids, yet here we are," Lexie shot back across the table, her grin sharp and gleeful.

Well, she had a point.

And with the other lady going silent on them...guess the torch was passed to Ashley.

Lexie needed a challenge—a competitor.

Oh, all right. Fine. She'd step up.

Plus, the guy was beautiful.

"Twelve thousand," Ashley shouted as she turned and faced the auctioneer with a beleaguered smile. She could feel the eyes of the crowd on her, but she didn't care. The roaring in her ears was resounding, and every time Ashley looked at Ty, she felt her insides clench.

"Thirteen!"

Ashley wasn't raised to lose. Princesses didn't lose.

"Fourteen!"

With each increasingly stupid bid, the energy in the room grew more electric, the onlookers gaping in disbelieving silence. Ashley took a deep breath, enjoying how exhilarating it felt to stand her ground and chase after what she wanted with such fierce determination. Was this one of the last times it would happen?

"Sixteen thousand!" Lexie called out.

"He's not a freaking hooker. He's not going to sleep with you for money," Megan hissed. "It's just a date. Probably a picnic or a dinner. Get a hold of yourself. If you want to spend that kind of money, just write a check, and then just ask him on a date."

Lexie sniffed and looked back at the stage. Ty gave Ashley a solitary eyebrow raise, and her heart skipped a beat, then another.

The auctioneer was giving out the final countdown. His bright eyes never left hers.

Ah, what the hell. It's not like she'd have a need for her mom's inheritance when she returned to Dariqat and was trapped there forever.

Besides, not to be forgotten, it *was* for a worthy cause.

With a deep breath, making sure she didn't seem tipsy, Ashley raised her paddle and declared, "Twenty-five thousand!"

The room fell silent, all eyes turning to her in shock and curiosity. Most were already watching her and Lexie, but now? *Now*, absolutely everyone was tuned in.

The room held its breath, waiting for Lexie's next move. Ashley could feel the heat of Ty's gaze on her, the undeniable pull for him growing stronger by the moment.

Ashley pushed her wine glass toward the center of the table and made a grab for the water. Primly, she took a sip and tried not to expose her inner panic.

Lexie moved as if to bid again, but Megan, now with the help of Jen, forcibly held her arms down.

"Who is she?" someone murmured behind Ashley, their words incredulous.

"Is she serious?" another whispered, a hint of amazement coloring their tone.

Ashley could sense the room's focus shifting to her, but she refused to let it faze her. This was her chance to seize control, to dictate the terms of her own destiny...for a while at least.

She met Tyler's gaze, her heart racing in anticipation. He was the quintessential ladies' man, and Ashley hoped he could be her temporary escape from the confines of her predetermined future, if only for a night...

"Going once, going twice," the auctioneer stammered, trying to regain his composure at the record-setting bid. "Any further bids?"

Tyler shot Ashley a sexy smirk that caused her breath to hitch.

Oh.

Okay, there was the devil in him.

Yum.

Ashley felt her pulse quicken, her skin tingle with anticipation.

"Sold!" The auctioneer's voice rang out triumphantly, his gavel coming down with a resounding crack. "To the lady in red for twenty-five thousand dollars!"

As applause erupted around her, their eyes locked, and it felt as if time had stopped. The air between them seemed to crackle with electricity, causing the tiny hairs on her arms to stand straight and her skin to tighten. His brow cocked, blues stirring with heat and intrigue. Double yum.

Ashley bit her lip while she stared up at him and his gaze turned impossibly darker. *Yup*. She had just accidentally paid for sex. It was just supposed to be a date but holy hell, by the way he was looking at her, it was going to add up to more than that.

Oh well. Prostitution was legal in Dariqat. That was her excuse if anyone judged her. Ashley was just living like her countrymen and women. Ashley wasn't aware it was illegal in the States....that was her story and she was stickin' to it.

The buzz of excitement grew again as the auction continued, welcoming a new bachelor to the stage. The laughter and chatter of the crowd mingled with the rhythmic pattern of the auctioneer's voice.

Well, guess it was time to pay up.

Fuck, Ashley hoped she could walk a straight line.

Ashley took floating steps over to the side table to hand in her paddle and write a check. A big check.

As the reality of her victory sank in, she felt a mix of elation and disbelief. It was also somewhat sobering.

Welp.

If that wasn't the best final, 'fuck you' Ashley could give her father for taking away a future lifetime of choices, she didn't know what was.

Ashley would never hear the end of it, but hell, by the look in Tyler's eyes...it was going to be worth every penny.

Chapter Three

September 26, Sunday

Ty

Ty stood at the side of the stage at the bachelor auction, while lingering laughter and applause continued to flit through the air. His gaze was locked on her, his champion, as she made her way to the winner's table with her dark hair cascading down her back in long twirls. Gorgeous.

And totally out of his league.

As she placed her bids, their eyes met, and time seemed to slow.

Battling an erection while standing under a spotlight? That was a sensation he'd never experienced before.

One that he could live without ever experiencing again.

But, on second thought, it might have had something to do with the copious amounts of alcohol currently flowing through his system.

He'd needed more than just one drink to convince himself to get up on the stage instead of running back to his apartment to grab his hiking gear, and hide out in the mountains until the charity organizers forgot what he looked like.

Ty didn't 'do' crowds.

One-on-one, he was fine. Fun. Friendly. Flirty.

Having all eyes on *just* him? No thanks.

Ironic—for a professional hockey player who had thousands of eyes on him most nights of the week.

Ty watched as she gracefully handed over her betting paddle, her petite fingers gliding from the handle.

Fuck. How did she make even that look sexy?

Well, time to pay the piper.

With liquid courage fueling his confident stride, Ty made his way through the sea of people. Her exquisite figure held his unwavering attention as she completed writing her check.

Her *really* big check.

He finally reached her side and she looked up, exhaling softly.

Projecting a confident smile that he didn't completely really feel, Ty greeted her with a tease, "I believe you ordered a hooker?"

Her delicious, bright red lips rolled tight, and the apples of her cheeks blushed on her dusky skin.

Perfection.

"In all seriousness, though. Congratulations on your winning bid," Ty said, putting a palm to his chest. "I believe you snagged the best of them all—if I do say so myself."

She playfully raised an eyebrow and gave him a haughty smile. "Well, Mr. Daniels, I do tend to have refined tastes." A small grin danced on her lips, revealing the faintest hint of her flawlessly, white teeth.

Oof, that was a sexy accent...

English? Indian? Something in between?

Whatever it was...it sounded like silk sheet and melted wax.

Fuck, she was like some foreign, mysterious Goddess come to life.

And completely nuts if she thought *he* was 'refined'.

"Refined? I'm not so sure about that," Ty chuckled. "But regardless, I'm glad you chose to slum it with a mere mortal, like me."

There was an alluring scent of roses that followed her, and Ty found himself taking in deep breaths just to get more of it. In all his travels, he hadn't hiked in any rose gardens but, *fuck*—if that wasn't next up on his bucket list now.

Ty cleared his throat. "Your battle was impressive. Not many can go toe to toe with Lexie Galloway." His heart raced within his chest, a strange excitement bubbling up inside him as he tried flirting with a little more alpha attitude than he was used to thanks to none other than good old Johnnie Walker "Let's hope our date lives up to your expectations, considering how much you paid for it."

She responded with a soft but confident voice, "Whatever you plan, Tyler, I'm sure it'll be worth it."

Okay...so the cocky, alpha vibe was working for her...good to know.

Ty stared at her, unable to think of something else that was witty and sexy. Playing hockey and being outdoors was so much easier than trying to make clever, flirty small talk.

She had just dropped 25K like it was nothing.

Ty made good money as a hockey player in the 'chel, but *damn*. He'd think twice before throwing that kind of cash down.

Even for charity.

And because she had 'paid' for the date...did that mean that if they had a nice time and things...progressed...that they wouldn't be able to 'go' any further?

Would he actually be considered a hooker if they slept together?

Ty had only been joking earlier, but now she was looking at him like she wanted to lick every square inch of him.

And his cock wanted to let her.

The laughter and chatter around them seemed to fade into the background as they locked eyes.

The tension in the air weighed on him, seeping into his bones—one bone in particular.

She seemed to sense it, too, as her eyes grew heavier.

In fact, her eyes appeared a bit glassy.

Perhaps she was 'emboldened' as well, and Ty wasn't alone in his state of intoxication?

Maybe, due to this, they were both leaning a little harder into the sexpot persona than they normally would.

"Congratulations on winning the highest bid in the auction, Mr. Daniels," she teased, her voice dripping with a sultry self-assurance.

Or...maybe she was every inch the sexpot she came off as. Fuck, was she in for a surprise.

An involuntarily chuckle escaped his lips. "Ah, thanks. It's not over yet though. I'm sure someone else will beat it in no time. I am really thankful you grabbed me, though. I thought the older ladies were going to pool their Bingo money together after they lost their chance with Tommy. I spent the time waiting for my turn by brainstorming ideas on what to do with a bunch of older ladies. I certainly wasn't prepared to entertain someone like you."

He'd been avoiding thinking of the entire auction at all—it was the only way that he could get himself to even show up tonight. If he thought too long about what he would be subjecting himself to...he would've disappeared from Springfield faster than the Road Runner.

Therefore, any planning he should have done in preparation for any eventual bids...were put firmly in the 'don't think about it' box.

Ashley raised an eyebrow, mischief sparking in her dark eyes. "Someone like me?" She put a slender hand on her hip and jutted it out. "What does that mean?"

Ty waved at her. "You know. Someone who is...well, the definition of perfection."

Her cheeks glowed pink and she blinked quickly before raising her chin. "I'm not perfect. Far from it. What kind of date were you planning for the old ladies—a nice afternoon tea followed by a leisurely wheelchair stroll in the park before nap time?"

"Something like that," Ty admitted with a grin, rubbing the back of his neck. "But now that you're the one I'll be spending the date with, I'm back to the drawing board. Gotta make it memorable."

As heat radiated between them, Ty's fingers itched to reach out and see if her long, inky hair felt as silky as it looked.

He forced his hand to stay by his side.

How much fucking whiskey had the guys plied him with anyway? He wasn't normally so...

Ashley tilted her head, her hair cascading over her shoulder. "I'm intrigued to see what you come up with. I'm sure it will be wonderful."

"Good," he replied in a low murmur. "Be patient though. Whatever I plan, I promise it'll be worth the wait."

The corners of Ashley's mouth turned up in a smile as she locked eyes with him. "Promise?" she whispered.

He stiffened.

Fuck him.

That message was clear.

And he was totally okay with that.

"Promise," Ty growled out, his gaze never leaving hers.

Suddenly, a woman—apparently the next winner—interrupted them, pushing eagerly past them so she could fill out her paperwork at the table.

Gallantly, Ty held out his arm. Ashley took it readily and Ty led her toward a darker area of the ballroom. An invisible current crackled between them.

What the hell was she doing with someone like him?

Why did she bid on *him*? The guys booked for later in the night were much more her speed. The lady-killers. The cocky ones.

Not him.

He was just...Ty.

Well, she was stuck with him now.

And if he wanted to give her the perfect date, Ty needed to know a bit more about her...outside of the fact that they both found each other attractive.

As they walked a few feet away to a more secluded area of the event hall, Ty threw out jokingly, "So, twenty-five grand, huh? Are you an heiress or a princess or something?"

As soon as the words escaped his lips, she froze.

Chapter Four

September 26, Sunday

Ashley

Ashley choked on her spit, looking at him wide-eyed.

Ty stilled, watching her with evident concern.

Way to be chill, asshat, she chastised herself.

She swallowed painfully, and croaked out, "No. Not an heiress. I just inherited some money when my mom died and I've been hoarding it all these years. This charity is a good cause. I just felt...compelled to bet on you. I don't know how to describe it. I just *needed* to."

Gone was the unflappable seductress. She clearly needed another glass of wine.

Or a nap.

"Okay." Ty watched her closely, a hint of a smile on his full lips. "Do you normally do impulsive things like that? That would be a good place to start. Like, what kind of date should I be preparing? Clearly not a wheelchair stroll. But if you're looking for something unpredictable...maybe streaking through Boston Commons? Or if not, maybe dinner at an elegant, upscale restaurant?"

Ashley chuckled at the streaking joke and looked around the fancy ballroom as she thought of her answer. "No. I'm not usually impulsive like that. I've had a...rough week. I was feeling a little panicky, so I *'acted out'*—as my therapist would call it." Ashley leaned forward and gave him a saucy wink. "That's why I usually avoid my dad's phone calls. Otherwise, I get a little stir crazy."

Ty grinned. "Oh, daddy issues. I can work with that." He chuckled.

Unable to resist, Ashley added, "My therapist already does. It's not working. Maybe *your* methods would be more...effective."

Woah, HAD she really just said that? Sure, she was typically bold, but not *that* bold.

Stupid, delicious, wonderful wine.

Then again, if he really was the lady-killer that Lexie said he was, he wouldn't be turned off...right?

Drunk Ashley wanted to see how far she could take this.

Just let all the stupid fly.

Her brother would be so proud. Ha!

Ashley walked her fingers up Ty's chiseled chest. "What would you do to work on my daddy issues?"

She realized how ridiculous she sounded, and yet she couldn't stop herself. Her hand and mouth were controlled by someone else.

Immodest, immoral, indecent—she could practically hear her father's advisors' criticisms in her head.

The assholes.

Well, she *wasn't* any of those.

Ashley was just a woman who was trying to claim independence—not just her sexual independence—in the short time allotted to her. She had a lot of life to live and squeeze into a three-year time period, and she was trying to learn, and *own*, her emotions, likes, and dislikes...before that option was taken from her forever.

Sex wasn't shameful.

And neither was the attraction that she and Tyler apparently felt for each other.

So, yeah, she drunkenly bid on an attractive man at a bachelor auction with the last of her inherited money. So, what?

There were worse things to be than a woman trying to claim autonomy over her own body and feelings.

After a hard swallow that had his throat bobbing, Tyler's smile was slow and delicious as he answered her flirty question. "Do you want my methods of addressing your rebellious streak to be with clothes on or clothes off? Because I am more than happy to satisfy any direction you want to take this." The growl in his voice caused her nipples to pebble.

Yup.

Same page.

Ashley gave him a regal perusal, making sure to pause her eyes as she inspected the zipper of his slacks. She drew her eyes back up his body and looked up at him. "I think, without clothes would be...nice."

Tyler groaned and closed his eyes. Tipping his head back, he let out a pained, "Don't suppose a quickie in the coatroom would satisfy my fee?"

She chuckled. "The *bidding* was for charity, so consider our date satisfied. And I love a coatroom quickie as much as the next person. It's a classic spot for a reason."

He brought his head back down and leveled her with a playful grin. "I agree, it's great for a quick one and done. But you..." he looked Ashley up and down, pausing on all the important parts, "were *not* made for quickies. You were made for *worshiping*." He dragged his eyes down her body and his tongue darted out to wet his lips. "And this was totally *not* our date. I'm not that cheap. I'm already thinking of ways to get you the most of your twenty-five grand. And *damn*, have I got some...creative ideas."

Ashley grinned and reached out, playing with the buttons of the crisp, white shirt under his suit jacket. "I mean, a later, more elaborate date is fine. But a quickie would certainly help take the edge off..."

"Nope. No quickies for the first time. The first time I have you, I want room and time to explore."

Ty bit his lip and snaked an arm around her waist, pulling her so the points of their hips collided.

"Oh?" she exhaled the word in a surprised breath.

Yum.

"Princess, when I first have you, I'm going to make you come, again, and again, and again." He growled out his promise into the shell of her ear.

Well, alrighty then. Maybe he really was the beast that Lexie promised.

A wave of relief washed over Ashley.

A highly sexual, alpha athlete who would undoubtedly be controlling and demanding, but also great in the sack? That was much better than a considerate, kind, sensual and sexy athlete.

Ashley could handle the former. Not sure about the latter. At least not when that athlete looked like Ty.

She inhaled through her nose, preparing to give him a flirty response—but paused; she hadn't realized how *good* he smelled until he pulled her up against him.

Hot damn, he smelled *fine*.

There was a small touch of cedarwood with traces of pine.

He smelled like the woods.

He smelled like *America*.

Like freedom.

As the Americans say: *fuck yeah*.

Ashley pushed her hips a little harder against his, "Hey, that's my line."

Ty bent down and nuzzled into her neck before giving her earlobe a gentle nip. "I think you've met your match, Princess. You can pretend to be high and mighty all you want. But when I take you, you'll be on your hands and knees begging me to give you more."

A moan rumbled out and her skin tingled.

Fuck.

Yup. That was what she needed. Mindless sex.

Ashley wound her hand up and into his hair.

"How soon am I getting that date?"

Ty chuckled and pulled away, letting his fingers dance across her lower back and over her hip.

The tease.

She loved it.

When was the last time a man had played with her? Or had been confident and cocky enough to challenge her back?

Fuck, yes.

She bit her lip.

He reached out and took her chin, caressing a calloused thumb over the plush of lip, where her teeth had pinkened the flesh. He grinned. “I need time to think of a good enough date idea. If you only wanted to fuck, all you had to do was breathe in my direction and I would have come running. Any guy here would have. But you bought a date. An *experience*. So, I’m going to give you one.” He winked.

“You promise?” Ashley confirmed once more, stepping in somehow closer, and looking up into his bright blue eyes.

“I promise. I want the ‘hooking’ part of our time to be over and done with before the real fun begins.” His big shoulders shrugged and a hint of a smile played at his lips. “But you might have to schedule in a couple of these ‘dates’, especially if we’re working through those daddy issues. As you know, therapy is not usually a one-and-done thing. Continued sessions prove most effective.” He sounded like he was repeating something he had heard a time or two and it caused Ashley to smile. He paused and inspected her face, his gaze heady “Then again, maybe we won’t hit it off.”

Ashley rolled her eyes and reached out to adjust his tie. “I think we’ll be fine.”

“Are you always so confident?”

She raised her eyes the slightest amount, like she would if she were wearing her veil, back home.

‘The eyes can say more than the mouth,’ her old nursemaid repeatedly instructed her.

Funny how she never took her own advice when chastising Ashley.

Ty's eyes darkened as he met her haughty gaze.

"I'm confident in most things, yes. Is that a problem?"

His grin turned wicked and he winked. "Nope, not at all. Be as cocky as you want. As long as you can be good and take instruction when you need to."

Be good? Yes. *Take instruction?* Only the sexual kind.

Though, if his blinding smile was anything to go by, he already sensed that, hence the tease.

"I can be good." She practically felt her nose start to grow.

He laughed at her noticeable lack of confirmation that she could take direction. "I just bet you can." He leaned down and placed his mouth right by her ear. "But why do I feel like your default setting is naughty and obstinate?"

Ashley sniffed and pulled back, her nose in the air. "Can't a girl be both? It's the twenty-first century."

Quick as lightning, his arm snaked around Ashley again and he pulled her to him, his erection pushing into her and their noses almost touching. "Princess, you can be naughty with me anytime you want. But I feel like you were going to do that anyway. Probably like most things you do."

She sniffed and raised her chin at him.

Well, he wasn't wrong.

"You've set some pretty high expectations for our date, Mr. Daniels. I sure do hope you deliver. You Americans. Hit or miss. I can never tell with you people."

His arm moved up her back and nestled into her hair, and Ashley gasped when he gave a firm tug. "One. I'm Canadian. And two, bite that lip at me again and I'll drag you into the coat closet and you can show me what else that mouth can do besides talk back." He gave another little tug on her hair that had her lips parting and a gasp gusting out.

Fuck, her skin was on *fire*.

And, well...he did tell her to–*she was just showing that she could follow directions...*

Ashley bit her lip again, maintaining eye contact the whole time.

He growled and his nose crinkled as he matched her defiant stare. "Fuck, Princess. You look like a queen and yet..."

"And yet." She agreed, pushing into him just a little bit.

He let out a short hiss of breath and gave one pulse of his hips into hers before he pulled away.

His self-control was...

Promising.

The buzzing in her skin and head was coming from an entirely different intoxication at this point.

A much better but maybe more dangerous kind.

"Okay, Princess. Enough foreplay for the evening. I have a couple of people I need to catch up with, and I don't need to be rocking a hard-on all night." He kept his voice low so the people around them wouldn't overhear. So far they'd been lucky that no one seemed to notice their brand of flirting.

"If it's that easy to get rid of your erection, then I didn't work hard enough." Ashley countered, her eyes dipping back down at the limited space between them.

Ty snapped his fingers in front of her nose. "Nu-uh. No more naughty-minx or it won't go away without help. And as we discussed earlier, the coatroom just won't do."

Ashley's thoughts wandered as she imagined what a coatroom quickie with this guy would be like. She let her eyes blaze over his lean, athletic build, taking in the strong lines of his jaw and the way his shirt clung to his toned muscles. Her pulse quickened, and she imagined what it would be like to run her fingers through his short, dark hair or trace the curve of his biceps as he was pumping into her.

He was opposed to the coatroom...but what about her place? Or his? Tonight...right now....

Chapter Five

September 26, Sunday

Ashley

Ashley felt a strange thrill course through her veins, a sensation she hadn't quite experienced before. It was exhilarating, addicting—like standing on the edge of a cliff and daring herself to jump.

But Ty had a look on his face that said that he was serious.

No more monkey business.

"Fine. No more naughty-minx tonight," Ashley finally agreed, her whine barely audible over the noise of the room.

"Good girl," Ty said, his eyes never leaving hers.

She felt herself grow wet.

Or...wetter.

Look at that—she really could be good!

Take *that,* Nursemaid Priya.

"I'll swing by your table later and we'll exchange numbers?"

"We could do that now," Ashley said, her hands already moving to pull her phone from her clutch.

He chuckled and leaned in, giving her a soft kiss on the edge of her jaw by her ear. "Yeah, but I want a reason to come see you again, later."

"You need a reason?"

Ty gave her a grin. "I don't want to seem too eager. I know how that scares man-eaters like you away."

Her body hummed.

Ashley couldn't wait to *eat* him.

Ty gave her a jaunty wink and walked away, slapping shoulders, and shaking hands with various people as he made his way to the collection of football players at the opposite side of the room.

After a moment of collecting herself, Ashley made her way back to her own table, where Jen was chewing nervously on her fingernail and Lexie was furiously texting away.

"So, I asked him to take you home. It's not a big deal," Lexie mumbled to Jen, her eyes not moving from her phone.

Jen shot her a look that implied whatever 'it' was...was actually a very big deal.

"Just don't fuck him. He's like...my uncle or something." Jen's body stiffened but Lexie didn't seem to notice. "Or do fuck him, just don't tell me about it. Whatevs."

Jen turned wild eyes to Lexie, who simply continued to ignore her.

Megan leaned across the table; her eyes bright as she looked at Ashley. "So? Did you guys hit it off? Feel any sparks?"

Ashley grinned and leaned in. Girl talk. *Yes*. She never had this until she came to the States. She would miss it.

"Only about a million."

That pried Lexie from her phone and she slapped it down on the table. "Finally! Yes. Tell us everything. We saw you two getting cozy over there." Her ice-blue eyes were gleaming with her excitement.

"It definitely looked like someone was smitten with her hockey hunk," Jen teased.

Smitten was a strong word...

In lust with...absolutely.

Ashley rolled her eyes dramatically. "It's just a date, but yeah, *yum*."

"Yeah, Ty's always been dreamy to look at. And he's just so damn sweet," Lexie said fondly.

Ashley froze.

Sweet? He didn't seem sweet. He was...

Actually...

He did.

Fuck!

He was fucking sweet!

“Lexie! You told me he was a lady-killer!”

“Can’t he be both?” The self-satisfied look on Lexie’s face made Ashley itch to throw her drink in her face.

Ashley would love sweet.

She always fell for the sweet guys in books and movies. But in real life? The cocky ones...those were the ones she could handle. She knew the score. Knew how not to get too close. Knew what they wanted and how to move on from them.

She couldn’t get her heart broken by a controlling, cocky athlete.

The quiet bookworm though?

Game over.

A cinnamon roll would break her.

Unfortunately, or fortunately, the guy her father had picked out for her wasn’t exactly a love match, so her heart wasn’t at risk. Ashley was prepared for a cold and lonely existence with him.

But with Tyler?

Fuck.

“He was devouring you with his eyes on that stage. I thought he was going to kill Lexie if she kept bidding.” Megan chimed in.

Lexie sniffed. “Why do you think I kept going?”

Ashley turned to her, her mouth agape.

Lexie smirked and looked down at her phone. “It’s for charity, lighten up.”

“Well, it’s just a date.” Ashley tried to fight off the nerves that were threatening to take over.

"Keep telling yourself that," Jen said. "We saw the way you were looking at him."

Oh, *now* Jen decided to join in? She should just go back to fantasizing about Lexie’s uncle or whoever he was.

"Not only the way you were looking at him, but the way he was looking at *you*," Lexie added with a wink. “He saw you before you even saw him, and Ty was mesmerized. I thought you could use the help. You're welcome. I call maid of honor!"

Ashley felt her cheeks growing warm again and her leg started to jitter nervously under the table. "Okay, but that wasn't cool. I'm not really set up to be here long term. What if he's amazing? What if we hit it off? You totally just set him up to be disappointed."

"And you wouldn't be?" Megan tilted her head.

Ashley waved her hand and noticed her fingers shaking, so she quickly tucked it back under the table, in her lap.

She had prepared her whole life for a 'love life' of disappointment; it didn't mean that Tyler had to suffer with her.

"Sure! I'd be disappointed too, but I know the score. I know that I'm leaving. I know that we have a one percent chance of success. He...Tyler...might not truly accept that."

"You seem to think that you guys will hit it off." Lexie watched her with narrowed eyes.

"Of course, we'll hit it off! Did you just see us? I want to climb him like a mountain goat. And he wants to let me!"

The girls chuckled and raised their glasses to her.

Gah!

"He's a great guy," Jen said quietly. "You'll have a fun time, get what you want...maybe even what you *need*...and leave here with no regrets. At least you tried."

Ashley's stomach felt sick. She hadn't expected to experience such an instant connection with Tyler. And while she looked forward to their date, a small knot of apprehension twisted in her gut. Getting involved with someone would only complicate her already tangled life.

Should she cancel and just tell him 'Thanks but no thanks'?

Ashley chewed her lip, glancing back to where Tyler was across the room, laughing and chatting, invigorating the space.

Damn, he was so handsome.

And he smiled so...*easy*. Bright. Pure. Happy.

What if...

Maybe this was just the distraction Ashley needed from the pressures awaiting her back home.

As the night continued, her table's conversation flowed effortlessly around the auctioneer's loud words, punctuated by laughter and playful banter. Tyler stopped by several times. Each time, doting over her in little ways like brushing her hair back, adjusting a piece of her dress or wiping an invisible something from her cheek.

Each time felt as natural as if he had done it every day for the last ten years.

And while it still caused a shockwave of heat to blast through her, it felt...right.

Fuck.

The unspoken tension and desire between them simmered, threatening to boil over at any moment. Ashley couldn't ignore the way her body thrummed with need whenever Tyler's hand brushed against hers or the way her heart raced when he leaned in close to whisper something in her ear.

Which he did...

A lot.

Now she was transfixed as she watched as Tyler sipped his drink, the condensation from the glass leaving a ring on the table. Her tablemates' laughter echoed in her ears, and Ashley couldn't help but smile at the playful teasing they shared throughout the evening. He had the girls in stitches, and she was starting to worry that they were correct.

The guy was a total sweetie.

Which meant she was fucked.

"Okay, I think I've got it," Tyler announced, setting his drink down and leaning in close. She could feel the warmth radiating off his body, and Ashley inhaled deeply, catching the subtle smell of him again.

Damn, she needed to stop doing that! She wasn't a bloodhound!

"What do you have?" Ashley asked, raising an eyebrow, and feeling her heart pound in her chest. Sometime over the night, they had both settled into a more comfortable banter, one that wasn't quite as overly sexual as it had been when they'd first met at the auction table.

The substitution of water rather than alcohol probably had a lot to do with it.

And her fear that their relationship would develop into something 'more'.

That was a good damper on any sexy banter.

"I have an idea for our date," he replied, his voice low and doubtless. "But I'm not going to tell you what it is. You'll just have to trust me—and show up *where* I tell you, *when* I tell you."

Ashley playfully tapped her fingers on the table. "I thought we already established I don't like taking orders?"

Tyler tipped his head back and laughed, the muscles in his throat and neck bobbing deliciously. "Yes, yes we did. Okay, what about, you just have to follow my *requests* about when and where to show up?"

She dipped her chin. "Acceptable."

"Good," Tyler said, his eyes flickering with mischief. "I promise you, though, it'll be worth the wait and pain of following instructions."

Mmmm. Instructions? Ashley would only entertain the idea of taking instructions from Tyler...in bed.

Ashley tried to rein in her imagination; she couldn't help but picture their bodies writhing together, their breaths mingling as they explored each other with feverish passion.

Focus.

"All right," Ashley said, her voice steady even as her pulse raced. "But if this date doesn't live up to the hype, I reserve the right to demand a do-over."

Woah. Where did that come from?

In fact, there should be no flirting or talks of do-overs at all!

Ashley should be getting the fuck out of Dodge, not finding ways to prolong her stay!

At this point, she was just asking for trouble.

Maybe her brother *was* right.

Was she stupid? Sure seemed like it.

"Fair enough. Do-over permission granted. You did pay enough for it," Tyler agreed with a smile.. His fingertips brushed against the top of her hand, sending a jolt of electricity up her arm. "I have a feeling you won't be disappointed, though."

As the evening wound down, and they reluctantly said their goodbyes, Ashley thought about what lay ahead. And as she lay in bed that night, her thoughts were consumed by the memories of Tyler's touch, his laugh, and the promises he'd made.

One thing was certain: she couldn't wait to see what he had in store for her.

And Ashley hoped it was spectacular enough to give her a lifetime's worth of memories to replay.

And terrible enough that it didn't break her when it was gone.

CHAPTER SIX

September 27, Monday

Ashley

The day after the auction, Ashley sat at her cluttered desk, drowning in a sea of paperwork. It was a never-ending stream of child abuse cases, substance abuse interventions, and families struggling to find shelter from the unforgiving streets. The small office buzzed with activity as the staff around her juggled phone calls, and hastily scribbled notes with brows furrowed in deep concentration.

"Mrs. Hardy, I understand your concern," Ashley said into the phone, trying to calm the irate foster parent on the other end of the line. "We're doing our best to find a solution for Zane's situation."

She bit her lip, brow creasing with worry as she tapped the edge of her pen against the desk, feeling the weight of so many little lives resting on her shoulders. Each case was a new opportunity to make a difference, to pull someone from the darkness and set them on the path towards a better future.

Good thing her donation from last night was going to be cycled right back into the social services programs that she worked for. Maybe it would make a difference. Maybe.

"All right, Mrs. Hardy, I'll see what I can do," Ashley promised before hanging up the phone.

As she exhaled deeply and glanced back at the mountain of files piled high on her desk, she thought about the approaching deadline for her return to Dariqat. The thought of leaving this life behind—to return to Dariqat and fulfill her familial duties—felt like a noose tightening around her neck.

Not to mention the weight of the guilt settling heavily on her shoulders for abandoning her social work families for a title in Dariqat that she didn't even want.

Ashley tried her best to ignore those spiraling thoughts, instead turning her focus to the task at hand. There were still countless people who needed her help, and Ashley refused to let them down—not while she still could.

"Let's see what we can do for you, Zane," she whispered to herself, flipping open the familiar file.

Fuck, if she could take him in, she would.

The door to Ashley's cramped office creaked open, and Babs, her coworker and friend, peeked in with high brows. "Hey, Ash. You've been in here all day. How about we take a break and grab some coffee?"

Ashley looked up from Zane's file. She'd been at it for hours, still hopeful she'd find something—anything—that would be her golden ticket for getting through to the teen.

Time was running out for him as well.

Ashley managed a weak smile. "Thanks, Babs. Coffee sounds great."

As they made their way to the break room, the scent of brewing coffee mingled with Babs' familiar perfume, creating an oasis of comfort in the bustling office.

Once they filled their mugs, Babs leaned against the counter, studying Ashley with evident concern. "You look like you haven't slept in days, hon. What's going on?"

Ashley patted her carefully styled hair and tugged at her shirt to pull out any wrinkles.

Come on, she didn't look *that* bad.

"It's this one case," Ashley admitted, taking a sip, the heat of her piping hot coffee grounding her as she dove into the dirty details. "It's this teenager, Zane. He's having a hard time.. His parents can't stay sober, and he's suffering because of it." Her heart was clouded with frustration and pity.

"Been there," Babs empathized, reaching out to give Ashley's hand a squeeze. "But you know how these situations can be. Sometimes people are able to turn it around."

"I know," Ashley sighed, running her fingers through her hair. "I just wish there was more I could do to help him right now. I hate seeing kids stuck in the crossfire like this."

"Hey, if anyone can make a difference in that boy's life, it's you," Babs said confidently. "You're the most dedicated social worker I've ever seen. Just look at that mountain of files on your desk. Anyone else would have thrown in the towel by now."

Several people already had thrown in the towel—it's how she had gotten her job in the first place.

"Thanks, Babs," Ashley replied, a small smile tugging at her lips. They stood in companionable silence for a moment, drinking their coffee and letting the warmth chase away the shadows of the difficult cases that haunted them daily.

"Speaking of towels," Babs said with a small grin, changing the subject. "How'd the bachelor auction go last night? I heard you snagged yourself one of the Cyclones players. I thought you said you weren't going to bid in that 'sexist and superficial shit.'" Babs bobbed her fingers as she quoted Ashley from last week.

Whoops.

Ashley laughed. "Oh, it was an experience all right," she admitted. "I may have...gotten a little carried away."

Babs watched her incredulously. "Girl, do you want me to repeat what I heard your little 'carried away' cost?"

Ashley winced. She didn't exactly brag about her financial position here at work.

"I know we're salary, but *damn*. I need to ask for a raise." Babs gave her a haughty, questioning look that made Ashley grimace again.

Ashley rubbed at a place behind her ear and wet her lips before answering. "It was an inheritance that my mother left me. It was all I have left of her. Her and my brother are the only reasons that I was allowed to come here and even use my degree...even if it was for such a short time." Ashley shrugged and tried not to show how much her circumstances bothered her—to show how powerless she felt.

As Babs continued to wait her out, Ashley felt her temper spark.

Why was she feeling compelled to explain herself? She was a freaking princess.

No way her father and his advisors would have allowed that liberty if she were back in Dariqat.

Actually, she probably wouldn't be allowed a friend like Babs at all.

The advisors would worry that Ashley would get 'ideas.'

And to allow herself to even be questioned...and judged?

There'd be lashings. Or jail time.

So, if she wanted to spend her last months here in the States in the company of a sweet guy? So what? And it's not like her money was any good for her back home in Dariqat. Where did Babs get off on judging her? It was all consensual and for fun for fuck's sake!

Ashley straightened up and looked at Babs. "I felt compelled to bid on a guy. It was a good cause. I had the money. I did it. So, what?"

Babs' eyebrows shot up and she cocked her chin out, staring Ashley down. "Girl, chill the fuck out. I was just teasing. Your business is your business. Jesus."

Ashley felt her cheeks warm.

Maybe she had overreacted.

Ashely rolled her lips together again and set down her mug before turning to face Babs again. "I'm sorry. I was feeling a little guilty about it already, and—"

"Say no more. You didn't give me shit when I snapped at you last week when I was having a moment. Friends move on. Consider it forgotten. Though," she leveled Ashley with a serious look, "I want to hear *all* the details after your date."

"Goes without saying."

Babs raised her mug in toast. "Damn, remember when that Greek hotel magnate took you out on his private yacht and you—"

"We don't need to discuss that." Ashley pulled the plug on Babs' reminiscing before she was forced to relive one of her more embarrassing experiences. "And, yes, I'll tell you all about my date with Tyler. Though, I have a feeling that there won't be any public indecency charges that he has to pay to have covered up."

Babs sniffed, "Well, that's good, because hockey players aren't known to be billionaires."

"If I wanted billionaires, I'd have stayed in Dariqat."

"Oil country—right. Feel free to drop my name when you get back there."

Ashley shot Babs a grin. "Goes without saying," she promised for the umpteenth time.

They shared a somber smile, both dreading the day in a few months that Ashley inevitably had to leave.

"So, tell me about this guy who stole your heart...or your checkbook."

"Tyler is...well, he's something else. And before you ask, yes, there was alcohol involved. You know how it brings my inner femme fatale out."

"For real. Drunk Ash is a hoe bag. I love it," Babs declared, leaning in closer with an excited gleam in her eyes. "Tell me everything. Is he a total hunk? Over six feet? Built like a Greek God? Thighs like tree trunks?"

"He's absolutely pretty..."

Babs blinked and started worrying at her lip. "Oh..."

Ashley waved Babs' dismay away. "No, I'm serious. He's just...classically pretty. Clean shaven. Bright blue eyes. Short brown hair. He's probably a bit shorter than six feet because I didn't have to look up too much when I was in my heels. But yes to the tree trunks for legs. He's still lean though. And...sweet. So sweet." Ashley paused, smiling as she recalled his initial bravado, then how he'd sobered into a much less intense, but much more fun and flirty guy as the night went on. "And he can't hold his liquor, either. Apparently, we both get a little...loose." Ashley's smile widened.

Damn, he was adorable.

Babs' eyes narrowed, watching Ashley closely. "And...then he wasn't sweet and then took you into the coat closet for a quickie?"

Ashley couldn't lose the smile as she shook her head.

"Okay...so, then he...brought you into his car for a quickie?" Babs asked, fishing for the details.

Ashley kept shaking her head. "There was no quickie, Babs. He wants to take me on a date first." Ashley was outright beaming now.

Babs blinked and pulled back, clearly surprised. "Oh."

Girl, preach.

Ashley still couldn't believe it.

"But there was just something about him," Ashley began, her cheeks flushed. "If he had wanted a quickie...I wouldn't have said no. I think I'd climb that particular tree again. And again. And again." She winked at Babs, who burst into laughter.

"Well, damn. Okay, then. I'm glad you finally landed yourself a good one. Have yourself a nice final, farewell fling and build up enough memories to hold you over when you're trapped back home."

Ashley felt her smile slip. "Yeah, that's what I was toying with as well."

Babs slapped her on the shoulder. "One last hurrah. Make it count and enjoy it for what it is. You won't get another chance."

And with those final words, Babs snagged her coffee from the counter and chased down their boss who had just walked past the open kitchen door. The woman was impossible to track down lately, so Ashley didn't blame Babs for seizing the moment and dashing after her.

With some new thoughts to ponder, Ashley returned to her private office. As she settled back down into her chair, she allowed herself a brief moment to revel in the memory of Tyler's strong arms around her, the electricity of their connection sparking anticipation deep within her.

What if...

What if she chose to embrace the sweetness that was Tyler? What if she allowed herself to feel something real and passionate in the short time she had left? What if, rather than focusing on the clock winding down, she chose to throw her caution to the wind and see if she even had the capacity to feel something real. Did she even know how to open up to someone like that?

But with Babs' words in her ear...Ashley was tempted to try.

With that final thought, she dove back into her work with her heart lighter and filled with anticipation for the passionate connection she and Ty could share, if just given the chance.

Even in the face of a looming deadline.

Chapter Seven

September 28, Tuesday

Ty

The pungent locker room's stench clung to Ty's skin, a thin sheet of sweat already forming in his full practice gear as he hunched over and laced up his skates.

The guys around him were exchanging the latest trade rumors they had heard.

"Someone said Ilya might be gone by the end of the season. Something about picking up his old teammate from college, and dropping him." A teammate murmured to another from the far end of the row of lockers.

Across the room, Ilya's shoulders bunched.

Super hearing, that one.

"Nah, man. He's a lifer. They'll let him retire here. It's gotta be Tommy," the other man replied, the concern evident in his tone.

No fucking way the team would trade Tommy—the man was a machine.

The roster was deep—even if every team thought that of themselves—and Ty just couldn't see why management was in trade talks already when the off-season trades had been so successful.

Ty gritted his teeth and focused on threading the laces through the eyelets, trying to ignore the anxiety gnawing at the pit of his stomach. This was just part of the game, he told himself. Trades happened all the time. But that didn't make it any easier to swallow. The last thing he wanted was to be uprooted again. The trade to the Cyclones was a big enough blindside, he didn't need another.

The locker room door swung open, drawing Ty's gaze. Coach Montgomery strode in, and the room simmered with an anxious hush. Conversations died down, replaced by the sound of sticks being taped and helmets being adjusted. The coach's stride was purposeful, his broad shoulders squared, and his jaw set in determination. His piercing gaze scanned the room before landing on Ty.

"Ty, a word?" Coach Montgomery asked quietly, an unreadable expression on his face.

"Sure, Coach." Ty forced a casual smile and stood up. The familiar sensation of butterflies fluttered in his stomach. With one last tug on his skate laces, he followed the coach to a quieter corner of the locker room, away from curious eyes and prying ears.

"Your performance last night was impressive," Coach Montgomery said, his voice low and cautious. "You've got a real gift for finding those openings."

"Thanks, Coach," Ty replied, trying to gauge the man's intentions behind the compliment; Coach Montgomery's eyes held an air of ambiguity and it left Ty feeling uneasy.

"But something felt off. You weren't your normal self. I haven't had a chance to chat with you due to...circumstances outside my control, but I wanted to make the time now. Anything we need to discuss tonight, before or after, practice?"

Shit.

What was Ty supposed to say? That the trade rumors were messing with his sense of security? That the thought of being uprooted again made his stomach churn? He'd be laughed out of the locker room for showing that kind of vulnerability. The douches on the team would call him a 'pussy' for the rest of the season.

Joke was on those fuckers, though. Ty couldn't think of a stronger body part—it pushed out babies and then bounced back, for Christ's sake. Maybe being called a pussy should be a compliment. Ty took a deep breath and shook his head.

"Nope. Just finding my groove, Coach."

The older man nodded. "Yeah, I think we're all trying to adjust to Bobby's new style of play since his injury and recovery. We'll get there. In the meantime, you know where to find me if you need me." The coach patted Ty on the shoulder and breezed over to another player, before pulling that guy aside for another round of private words.

As Ty watched the coach move among a few select players, he felt a sense of disquiet. He replayed the conversation in his head, searching for hidden meanings and reading between the lines. Was that really just a simple compliment and an offer for open discussion, or was there more to the Coach's words? Coach Montgomery had been around long enough to know how to play the game—both on and off the ice. Was he buttering Ty up? Gauging his commitment? Preparing him for the possibility of being traded?

"Fucking hell," Ty muttered to himself, shaking off his doubts. But as he grabbed his gear and made his way through the halls to the rink, he couldn't help but dwell on the possibility. He'd finally started to settle into life in Springfield, and the thought of leaving behind his teammates, learning new team dynamics, and moving again, filled him with dread.

And it shouldn't even be a factor, but...he was really looking forward to a date with Ashley, and seeing where that went.

There was no denying it: being traded was pretty much his worst fear at this point. Yet, despite the coach's seemingly positive words, Ty couldn't shake the nagging suspicion that something was amiss—that he was being played.

"Everything okay?" Bobby asked. Judging by Bobby's frown, he must have noticed the tense expression on Ty's face as they warmed up together on the ice.

"Fine," Ty lied, forcing a smile. "Just...trying to shed the rink rust from the off-season."

He wished he could believe his own words.

Bobby's forehead wrinkled when his frown deepened, but he let Ty's lie slide.

Good man.

After a quick lecture from their coach and an outline of the practice, the players broke apart and prepared for the upcoming drill. The shrill blast of the whistle echoed throughout the practice facility as Ty and his teammates leapt into action, skating across the ice with practiced precision. Drill after drill passed in a blur. Thank God for muscle memory, because Ty couldn't focus with a fog of discomfort and mistrust clouding his mind. Even with his technical precision during the drills, his movements still felt out of sync with the rest of the Cyclones.

Ty could feel Coach's eyes boring into him, and the sensation sent a tingling down his spine.

The camaraderie and trust he had shared with his previous team and coach were unmatched. His former coach was a grizzled veteran of the game and not known for compliments, but his raw honesty was something Ty missed dearly...especially given his current situation. Coach Bowman had been just as shocked, and pissed, when Boston management had announced Ty's unexpected trade...and he'd let everyone know it.

What he wouldn't give to know exactly where he stood with his coach and teammates.

As he skated alongside his teammates, Ty wondered how long he could maintain this delicate balance before the ice beneath him finally cracked.

Chapter Eight

October 1, Friday

Ty

Ty had spent the rest of the week preparing the most elegant, once-in-a-lifetime dinner date at the Baystate Arena's master box suite.

Sure, it wasn't something fancy like a candlelit dinner at Versailles, but something told him that a woman like Ashley had attended millions of dinners like that.

However, he'd bet that she'd never had a catered meal overlooking the Cyclones' gorgeous, glowing rink.

The ice glistened beneath the overhead lights, its smooth surface a perfect canvas for their date later that evening. The elite suite was decorated in a vomit-inducing amount of twinkle lights and candles. Soft Sinatra played on the speakers. He'd even decorated the direct elevator that led down to the private parking garage below the arena.

The wall phone had just rung, alerting him that she was on her way up, and now he couldn't stop pacing the suite.

Fuck, he hoped she liked it.

Ty stalked back to the floor-to-ceiling window showcasing the ice and chewed on his thumbnail...or what was left of it.

His gaze flicked between the opulent table set for two and the elevator where the light was blinking in ascending floors as it carried Ashley up.

The anticipation made his palms sweat, and he wiped them on his pants.

He wasn't a fucking virgin for Christ's sake. He was no slouch in the sack.

But damn, she wanted a lady-killer.

She wanted an alpha.

And he was...not that.

He was just Ty.

He'd thought all week long about how to play it tonight. Should he channel his inner man-whore again and continue to pretend to have swagger in spades?

But the very thought of putting on such a performance made his stomach churn.

That just wasn't who he was—it felt too much like lying.

Liquid courage had gone a long way in helping him embody that persona last weekend, but that wasn't the real Tyler Daniels. He didn't want to have to rely on getting drunk to bring out his inner Lothario and without it, there was no way he'd be able to maintain that façade all night. No, that just wasn't the way to go—especially not if he truly wanted to get to know Ashley.

So, she'd have to make do with him.

Just Ty.

And even if it was disappointing for her...she deserved to know that.

As he was rolling his shoulders to loosen the tension, the elevator dinged, and the doors slid open.

Ashley sauntered into the climate-controlled room, her eyes going wondrous and wide as she took in all the lights twinkling throughout the room. She moved with an effortless grace, her lustrous hair framing her face like a work of art.

Finally, her eyes met Ty's and he felt his heart skip a beat, and suddenly all his confidence vanished.

There he was. A virgin, reborn.

How did she do that?

"Wow," Ty breathed, his voice barely audible, even to himself. She looked even more enchanting than she had the other night.

As she moved gracefully towards him, the long, flowing dress accentuated her petite yet elegant figure, and the dress' intricate embroidery added to her allure. Her eyes seemed to sparkle in the soft lighting of the room, and her delicate gold-layered chains caught the glimmering candlelight, making her glow like a manifestation of his dreams.

For a moment, Ty was lost in admiration, unable to look away from her. Time stopped and the world faded into the background.

Ashley wasn't just captivating; she was *enchanting*.

What in the hell was someone like her doing with someone like him?

"Hey, Tyler," Ashley called, flashing him a smile as she approached. "This place looks amazing."

He leaned in and pressed a warm kiss to her cheek—the way she presented it to him made it seem like that was a common greeting for her.

"Ty," he corrected, his brain not working properly as he registered the wonderful floral smell of her again.

She blinked and cocked her head. "What?"

"Ty. You keep calling me Tyler. Only my mom calls me Tyler. You can call me Ty."

A gentle smile graced her full lips. "Ty, then."

Ty swallowed and nodded.

"Did you arrange all this? Or did you order a lackey to do this?"

He chuckled and shook his head. "Nope. All me."

"How did you manage that?" Ashley asked, glancing away to admire the setup. "Doesn't the arena have a lot going on with the season starting?"

"I promised my firstborn." When she whipped around to look back at him, he chuckled. "They wanted the first two, but I said, 'That was the deal, take it or leave it.'" He leaned in, "I think they're hoping it's a boy and he comes out wearing skates."

She gave him an uncomfortable smile and moved toward the table that was set for two.

Shit.

He'd fucked it up already.

Son of a bitch.

As he followed her to the table, he stole glances at her, marveling at how the light from the rink seemed to dance across her skin.

He pulled out her chair and she lowered herself into the seat in a fluid, practiced motion.

"The flowers, the candles, the lights. It's all very beautiful. Thank you for the care that you put into this." Ashley said, as she took in the romantic scene.

"At the auction, you had mentioned that you had never been to the arena, so I wanted to give you a taste."

"It's wonderful," Ashley agreed, her eyes twinkling with pleasure. "And here I was thinking you were going to take me to the Five Hole for some beers."

He groaned. "Who told you about that?"

She pursed her lips to combat a smile. "A lady never reveals her sources."

"That's unfair," Ty chuckled. "I had just been drafted and was more broke than a church mouse." He paused for a beat, catching his breath at the twinkle in her eyes. "Besides, the Five Hole's burgers are legendary. It was a first-rate choice for a first date!"

His date had *not* agreed.

Ashley chuckled and placed a cloth napkin on her lap.

"Okay. If you don't believe me, I'll take you to the bar after our evening wraps up and we can grab a couple of beers. You'll see—the Five Hole is no dive bar. And we can do their burgers another night. With how much you spent for some time with me, I think you ponied up enough for *two* dates." He gave her a teasing grin. "*Maybe* three."

Ashley smiled and shook her head. "We'll see. You still have to impress me enough for the rest of this first part."

She was a tough cookie.

And he liked it.

The warm scent of roasted garlic and rosemary filled the air as Ty pulled metal lids off the awaiting plates.

"So, how has your week been since the auction? Bought any more Springfield athletes? Maybe a Spartan or two?"

"Only three. I'm on a diet. They started calling me the Patron Saint of Athletes, so I had to scale back."

He snickered as he spooned some more food onto his plate, following her lead.

"But it was good. Some crappy things at work, but..." she swallowed hard and looked down at the food in front of her.

Oh. Maybe she wasn't quite as unflappable as she seemed.

"Anything you want to talk about?" Ty ventured.

She reached out and took the crystal goblet of ice water, before taking a thoughtful sip. Ashley paused a moment before swallowing and setting the glass back down. "I, uh...I appreciate that, but I can't. There's too many confidentiality factors."

"And that is..."

"I'm in social work."

Oh.

Ty cocked his head, staring at the put-together queen in front of him. "Seriously?"

Hopefully she didn't take offense.

And by her smile and shake of her head, she didn't.

"Seriously," Ashley answered. "I got my degree in Dariqat and then came to the States about three years ago. I primarily work with kids but there are some adults too. It's heartbreaking and rewarding at the same time."

"I was wondering about your accent. I even tried snooping online but nothing came up. Where are you from?"

Almost imperceptibly, she stiffened—her shoulders tightening and her fingers and utensils stalling over her plate.

Had he misstepped?

"Uh…it's a small country. You might not have even heard of it."

"Try me. I was a geography major."

She blinked incredulously at him, but he nodded emphatically. "Seriously. I was. Promise."

Ashley shook her head and answered slowly, the words seemingly ripped from her. "Dariqat?"

Woah. She wasn't kidding about it being small.

Ty knew it was a teeny country in the Middle East. Not one of the more progressive countries.

An oil baron's heaven, though.

And the source of his favorite nonprofit's headache.

"I'm actually pretty involved with the *Global Preservation Alliance for Natural Lands*, and we're knee-deep in a proposal to safeguard some key areas from drilling. We're hitting major roadblocks in the legal system, though. Maybe I'll tap into your insights on our next date to help break through those barriers." He noticed the color begin to drain from her face and Ty caught himself, not wanting to overwhelm her with boring judicial holdups she probably couldn't care less about. "It's cool you're from there. Small world. It's on my travel list for the off-season. Hiking and exploring new terrains is my thing."

Ashley warmed, then, as she leaned forward with a bemused expression at his talk of travel. "Hiking? Do you usually travel a lot for that? Can't you just go to local parks or something?"

Ty finished a bite and wiped roughly at his mouth with his crumpled napkin. "Yeah, I'm a bit of an outdoors nut. I grew up in the great Canadian wilderness and, even though I left and moved to the city, that love of nature never left. So, I've been all over. I love it. Unfortunately, my coaches don't love my choice of hobbies. They're always on me about what would happen if I got hurt.

Haven't been broken by the outdoors though yet. Women? They've broken me. That should be what they warn me about." He gave her a self-deprecating shake of his head. "Not that I'd probably listen."

She leaned forward, her eyes searching. "You don't look brokenhearted."

"Nature healed me."

She sniffed. "I'm not sure it has that kind of magic. It's kind of...dirty."

Ty stilled and then threw back his head, laughter bellowing out of him. He grabbed at his chest when his heart started to hurt.

Fuck. She was adorable.

'Dirty.'

Fucking hell. His cheeks hurt from smiling so huge.

After a few moments, he sobered and tipped his chin back down to look at Ashley to respond to her comment and he paused when he saw her expression.

Wonder was dancing in her eyes.

And so was fear.

Fuck.

What was that about?

He watched as she blinked the look from her eyes, a bland and pleasant expression following it.

Okay, good to know. She could win an Oscar.

"Yes, the outdoors can be dirty." He said it slowly, unable to stop the humor in his voice, or the chuckle that broke through as he said it. "But it's also so freeing. There's a wildness out there. No judgment. No eyes on you. Nothing out there lies or cheats. It's just nature and what you see is what you get."

Ashley watched him for a moment. "Have you met a lot of liars and cheaters, then?"

Shit.

Ty took a moment before answering, letting his eyes break away from hers and survey the room. "A few."

"Do you want to talk about it?" Her tone was soft and sweet. Her accent was barely noticeable.

Ty looked back at her and shrugged. "Nah, can't. Confidentiality clauses, ya know?"

She smirked at the callback to her own earlier deflection and tipped her glass to him.

"Fair enough."

"Maybe someday."

She watched him from across the cozy table, the candles and twinkle lights causing her dark eyes to sparkle. "Yeah," she whispered back. "Maybe someday."

Okay. Topic change, so she didn't go home that night lamenting about how dreary her date was.

"So, give me the dirt. Where are Ashley Winter's bodies buried? You don't have social media—what's up with that?"

As they revealed more and more about themselves, Ty couldn't help but feel that something magical was happening between them. He'd been on plenty of dates before but none had ever felt quite like this. There was a spark in the air, an undeniable connection that made his heart race and his palms sweat.

Apparently the fake-confident and overly sexual persona he had put on at the auction had nothing to do with their chemistry.

Because being here, right now, as nothing more than himself, seemed like it *was* enough.

The way she leaned forward when he spoke or kept touching his forearm whenever he made her laugh. The way her eyes caressed him when she thought he wasn't looking...and even when she knew he was.

She *liked* him.

Even when he was just Ty.

Who would have thought?

She was in the middle of sharing a funny story about her coworker when he stopped her.

"Okay, hold up. I'm sorry, but I really have no idea what a social worker is besides someone who can put kids into homes when they need it. So, what do you guys do exactly?"

She laughed and lowered her fork. "You're not alone. Consider yourself lucky that you don't know all the details. It means you probably never needed one." She wiped daintily at her mouth with the corner of her napkin.

Her manners were impeccable. Actually, everything about her was always so refined. Were her parents sticklers for etiquette?

He had so many questions for her...and he hoped he had a chance to ask them all.

Because the more she revealed...the more he wanted to know.

"I work with children and families, helping them navigate through challenging situations. I connect them with the support and resources that they need. It's a rewarding, though sometimes demanding field, but I'm passionate about making a positive impact on people's lives." She took another sip of water. Ashley chuckled, her eyes alight with amusement. "So anyway, Babs once tried to organize an office potluck. She's this whirlwind of energy, always buzzing around with a bossy smile. She had this grand idea to have everyone bring a dish that represented their heritage. It started off great until one of our colleagues, Phil, who's notoriously terrible in the kitchen, showed up with what he claimed was his 'authentic Japanese sushi.' Turns out, it was a hodgepodge of rice, weirdly cut vegetables, and a ton of soy sauce poured over everything."

She giggled, remembering the fiasco. "We spent the rest of the day trying to discern what it was and whether it was edible. We're still not sure whether Phil was trying to be funny or if that was his genuine attempt at making sushi."

Ty laughed at the mental image. "So, you guys just rolled with the sushi debacle?"

Ashley nodded, a grin playing on her lips. "Oh, we had to. You should've seen the effort to keep a straight face while eating it. Babs was the MVP that day, trying to keep the potluck from turning into a disaster. But hey, that's what it's all about, right?"

"The good days, to balance out the bad," he agreed.

Ashley sobered. "Lately, it's been feeling all bad. Must be the time of year. I don't know." She took a deep breath, causing her dress to shimmer and shift. "I just have a couple specific families that are just...falling apart. I can't get the parents sober. Or to show up to court. I can't keep some siblings together in placements, or one kid is just repeatedly acting out. That sort of thing. I just want to help them. I *need* to help them." She stilled and stared at her almost-empty plate; her eyes glazed with deep thought. After a moment, she looked up and met Ty's gaze. "I'm leaving. I have to return to Dariqat."

Oh.

Ty moved to scoot his chair back, but she snapped her hand out and rested it on his arm.

"No. Not right now. Just...in three months, I have to return to Dariqat. My specialty visa is expiring. And if the situation waiting for me is anything like what I think it is..." She looked up at the ceiling, resting her head back in her chair. She let out a whoosh of a sigh. "I don't think I'll be coming back."

Her soft hand was still on his forearm, so he twisted his arm slightly, so her hand was clasped in his.

Holy fuck, she had tiny hands. He rubbed his thumb over her knuckles as he watched her, unsure what to say.

Did she want him to listen, or did she want his advice—that was a lesson his mother had taught him very early on.

He figured he'd stay silent until he knew for sure what she needed from him.

"I don't want to go, but I have to. And even though I want to come back, I also know I can't. I'm stuck. I have three months to try to do as much as possible for these families before...I abandon them. Just like everyone in their lives has abandoned them."

Okay—listening. Not advising.

He hummed in acknowledgment and continued to rub her silky knuckles comfortingly.

Who would have thought the high-and-mighty sex kitten from the bachelor auction would have such a sweetness there under all that spice.

He was digging it.

So was his dick—but that wasn't the head in charge right then.

"It breaks my heart to promise that I'll be there for them, only to know that I'll be breaking it soon. You know?"

Fuck, did he ever.

Ty nodded and hitched the side of his lips in a small, sad smile.

Now that the cork had been pulled, it was like she couldn't stop. She just let it all out.

She spoke about the cases under her care: the kids, the families, the adults, the elderly. All of the people that she helped on a daily or weekly basis. The trips to deliver groceries, the buying of Christmas presents and clothes, the car rides to and from job interviews.

The woman was superhuman. *Holy fuck.*

"What the hell do you do for fun? Do you even have *time* for fun?"

She blinked like the concept was foreign to her.

"What do you mean? I help these people..."

"Yeah, but what do you do for you?"

She cocked her head and started nibbling at her plump lower lip again.

Fuck, he wanted to bite it, too. Ty shifted in his seat.

"I guess, I don't really. I mean, I go to charity events..."

"And spend money for those people in need. Therefore, still helping them."

"And animals."

He gave a chuff of laughter but kept pushing. This felt too important. "Ash, Princess. What do you do for *you*?"

Ashley looked at him, her eyes wide and vulnerable, like he'd just told her that he dove down to the Titanic and retrieved the fictional gemstone just for her.

It was a look of astonishment.

And *fuck*. It was the most beautiful thing he had ever seen.

"I knew I had a deadline. I had to squeeze a lifetime's worth of helping people into a short window. I didn't have time to fuck around." She pursed her lips together and looked back out over the ice. Ty watched as her expression looked pained and then emptied, evidence that she was shutting down her emotions. Again. "But I guess that's your answer. I fucked around. A lot. I could help other people during the day while I helped *me* at night." She shrugged, unashamed. "Is that a problem?"

He leveled her with a sardonic look. "I'm a professional hockey player. Do you think that bothers me?"

She let out a soft laugh. "Different girl in every port?"

"Doesn't hurt as bad that way."

"Preach," she agreed, with a tip of an imaginary hat.

He sat frozen, captivated by the way her eyes sparkled, a mix of excitement and curiosity dancing within them.

The night was young, but their attraction felt like it had been brewing for an eternity.

"Going back to this nonexistent free time of yours. What's your favorite part about your job? Not the sad parts—we're trying to stay positive tonight." He leaned forward and tacked on, in a staged whisper, "If I make you sad, you'll never agree to a second date."

She tucked a long curl of dark hair behind her ear and his eyes snagged on the delicate row of golden hoops. Everything about this woman was gold.

Made sense. She deserved nothing less. Not just because she was gorgeous, but because her heart was pure. He'd never met anyone who was so determined to save the world, but who held no hope for their own future.

"Definitely my developmental projects and outreach. Working with women and young girls has always been something I'm deeply passionate about," she explained, her voice filled with conviction. "I believe in empowering them to reach their full potential, and that starts by creating safe spaces where they can learn, grow, and thrive. They should be afforded the same opportunities as men. Not just as token pieces to parade around, but in reality. It's a rebellion against my upbringing, I guess." Something about that made her embarrassed, shy, or angry. Maybe all three. The emotions flashed too fast across her face for Ty to catch them before she once again reset and readjusted her mask.

"It's inspiring," Ty said, genuinely impressed by her dedication. "It must be incredibly rewarding to know you're making a difference like that. Even long after you've moved home."

Ashley's cheeks flushed at the compliment, but her smile remained bright. "It is. I've been fortunate enough to work with some amazing organizations like *UN Women* and *Lean In*. It's been a truly humbling experience."

Ty raised an eyebrow, "And hey, who knows? You don't think you'll be able to come back, but maybe you will."

He was trying to be supportive, but it must've been the wrong thing to say judging by how she paused in raising her glass to her lips.

Shit. Offside—he was crossing the line before the puck.

He tried to backtrack. "Then again, I have no idea what your situation is. But I'm a hopeful sort, so I tend to hope for the best. I know personally, I hope you come back." He shot her a saucy wink in an attempt to bring a smile back to her face.

"Thank you," she replied, graciously accepting his offering. "I'm fairly confident that...politics...will not afford me the opportunity to come back. But like you said, it's good to have hope. Hell, I remind our clients to have hope all the time. Maybe I should take my own advice and hope for a miracle."

"Hope for the best, plan for the worst?"

"Exactly. But even if I never make it back, I have no regrets. I made my time count. There are so many moments that have touched my heart. And what matters most is knowing that I'm helping others find their voices and regain control of their lives."

As their conversation continued to flow, Ty found himself opening up to Ashley in ways he hadn't with anyone else before, sharing stories about his family, his teammates, as well as the many trials and triumphs of his hockey career. He even dipped his toe into sharing about his concerns about the roster rumors and the unshakeable feeling of an impending roster shakeup. Ty couldn't help but feel grateful for the stupid bachelor auction...not if it led to this chance encounter with Ashley. Not only was she stunningly beautiful, but her apparent wit, humor, and heart made her truly interesting.

Ashley, for her part, seemed just as drawn to him. And apparently dropping his Lothario act didn't bother her in the least. In fact, she seemed to grow even more comfortable with him now that he wasn't pretending to be some alpha hole. She laughed at his jokes, offered thoughtful insights, and listened intently to his every word, her dark eyes never leaving his face. He couldn't help but marvel at the wonderful woman sitting across from him; and even though she was all doom and gloom about her chances of staying in the States...he had strings he could pull. Contacts. He wasn't lying when he said he was an optimistic sort. If they hit it off, he would find a way.

As they finished their dessert, Ty raised his glass in a toast. "To new beginnings," he said, his voice filled with warm affection.

"New beginnings," Ashley echoed, clinking her glass against his.

And as they sat there, basking in the glow of their newfound connection, Ty couldn't help but think that he'd finally met someone truly special. For the first time in ages, he felt a genuine connection—one that went beyond mere physical attraction—and he couldn't wait to see where it would lead.

Chapter Nine

October 1, Friday

Ty

"Hey," Ty said, catching Ashley's attention with a playful grin. "I hope you're not too full. At the time, I thought I was clever for planning this surprise, but I realize now that I should have prepared you so you could have dressed more...appropriately. But, I have a rink guy on standby and I thought we could head down to the ice and skate for a bit."

Ashley's eyes widened, and she hesitated for a moment before admitting, "I don't actually know how to skate...but I'm willing to give it a try if you're up for teaching me."

The idea of this empowered woman not knowing how to do anything surprised him, though he used every ounce of willpower not to let that show. He had a feeling she wouldn't have appreciated that.

Proud people don't like their weaknesses poked.

"Of course. I'd love to teach you. Trust me, it's not as hard as it looks."

A mixture of anticipation and nervousness flickered across Ashley's face, but she nodded, determination shining in her eyes. Ty took her hand. "All right, let's do this."

They made their way down to the rink, where Ty helped Ashley pick out a pair of skates. He nabbed a pair of extra socks from one of the cardboard boxes sitting off to the side next to the bench. As he knelt to help her lace her skates, he noticed the way her ankles tapered, and how defined her small calves were under her flowing skirt.

She even had gold anklets on.

Fuck, he wanted to run his tongue along every golden chain on her body.

She was an empress to be worshiped.

While he worked on lacing up one skate, she copied his movements on the other.

"You know, for someone who's never skated before, you're doing a great job at pretending you know what you're doing."

Ashley laughed, rolling her eyes. "Well, fake it 'til you make it, right?"

"Exactly," Ty agreed, grinning as he stood up and offered her a hand. "Now, let's get you on the ice."

With Ty's steady presence by her side, Ashley stepped out onto the ice, wobbling slightly as she found her balance. Ty could see the uncertainty in her posture, and he was quick to offer reassurance. "It's okay, just relax. I've got you."

“Is it always this chilly on the ice? For some reason, I was expecting the air to be...warmer?”

Ty grinned and shrugged off his thin coat, again chastising himself for not planning ahead and letting her know to dress a bit more comfortably for the skating part of their evening.

“You warm up pretty fast when you’re zipping around on it during practice or a game. But when you’re just coasting along...or learning,” he gave her a small grin, “it can get chilly.” He plopped his jacket over her shoulders and gave her an apologetic look. “Sorry again for not giving you a heads up that we might be doing this so you could wear something that would allow you to move a bit easier.”

“Nah, it would have ruined the surprise. So, no worries. And trust me, there’s not much I *can’t* do in a dress. I just maybe could have chosen a slightly warmer one.” Ashley then shifted and slid her arms into his sleeves.

Something about the movement was so...confident...and comfortable.

It was sexy as hell.

“But I’m warm now. So...I’m all yours.” Ashley grinned gamely up at him and held out her hand.

The petite woman was completely drowning in his jacket.

And it was fucking adorable.

And again...sexy.

Taking her hand, Ty began to guide her around the rink, offering gentle encouragement and the occasional tip as they went. The sight of her growing confidence filled him with a warmth that radiated from his chest.

"See?" he said, beaming at her as they glided along the ice. Showing off just a bit, he turned around so that he was skating backwards while in front of her, holding steady to her hands. "You're getting the hang of it already."

"This is ‘getting the hang of it?’” Ashley laughed. “I feel like a toddler learning to walk.” She barked out a smaller chuckle. "Though, I am enjoying it. I’ve been in the States for years and it never even occurred to me to try ice skating. I’m kicking myself for not trying it sooner, it’s so...peaceful out here.”

“Not during a game,” Ty promised. “The arena is *very* different during games. Peaceful is the last thing that would be used to describe it.”

Ashley grinned at him before darting her attention back to her feet, absently twisting her lips to the side as she focused on keeping her balance.

“I’ll get you tickets to a game sometime. You can see us in action.”

“Sure, sure. You just want to show off your ice-skating skills some more.”

He swiveled back next to her and carefully nudged her side with his own. “Shh. Pretend you can’t see through my ‘moves.’ This is my best stuff and it’s totally emasculating me.”

Ashley quickly turned to look into his face and her look of worry quickly slipped away at the wide grin he was giving her. She tried her own shoulder bump into him and lost her balance. Ty wrapped an arm around her quickly before she took them both down.

"Liar." Ashley's lips tipped up as she looked down at the ice. "'Emasculating. Ha! You dork."

Ty tried to stop the wide smile from taking over his face as they bantered back and forth, but her mix of spice and sweet was addicting. He couldn't stop teasing her, trying to guess her reaction.

And he couldn't stop the surge of affection that bloomed every time she surprised him with an unexpected one.

The woman was as confusing as all hell.

And he liked it.

Ty liked learning her various nuances, mostly because, it felt like she was learning them too.

How a woman could be so independent and confident, but also so...vulnerable and fragile...

Ashley was a master at putting on a brave and unflappable front, but every time she made a comment that could be interpreted as a barb, she would freeze the smallest amount and peek up at him, waiting for his reaction.

It gave him an idea of the type of men she spent her time with.

Men that weren't like him.

Ty wasn't going to look for offense in her comments when clearly none was meant.

And, if she gave him a chance, he'd love nothing more to wipe those small looks of insecurities from her face and teach her that not everything she said needed to be carefully modulated and considered before exiting her pretty mouth.

Eventually, Ashley pulled her hand away, trying to navigate the ice on her own. It didn't take her long before she was trying to pick up speed.

The woman was a force of nature.

She was the kind of woman who knew exactly where she was going and wasn't about to let anything or anyone stand in her way.

And that included, mastering a skill she had just learned not even an hour before.

It was weird to feel pride for a woman he practically just met, yet here he was, admiring her determination to excel at a new ability.

By the smile on her face, it was clear she loved the challenge and newness of it all. There was something really cool about the fact that he'd given her one of her last 'firsts' while she was here in the States.

Ashley's laughter echoed through the arena as Ty attempted to teach her a simple spin on the ice. Her eyes sparkled with mischief as she leaned into him, trusting his steady grip on her waist.

"Okay, let's try this one more time," Ty said, his voice warm with encouragement. "Just follow my lead."

"All right—but if I fall, it's on you," she teased, her breath visible in the chilly air. Her dress hampered their movements, but luckily it was flowy enough at the bottom to allow her enough independent movement for her legs.

The spin ended in disaster but both of them were laughing too hard to care.

As they continued to skate together, their movements became more fluid, and Ty found himself sharing stories about his childhood in Canada and the countless hours he'd spent on frozen ponds learning to skate. Ashley listened intently, nodding along as she shared her own anecdotes about growing up in Dariqat and the challenges of adapting to life in the United States.

At one point, Ashley stumbled slightly, and Ty instinctively wrapped his arm around her waist to steady her. He felt the heat of her body through their layers of clothing, and for a moment, he was acutely aware of just how close they were. The intensity of their connection sent a shiver down his spine, and he couldn't shake the feeling of power that came with seeing her wrapped in his winter coat gazing up at him in wonder.

"Thank you," Ashley murmured, her face flushed from the cold and exertion. "You're an excellent teacher."

"Only because I have an amazing student," Ty replied, grinning at her. Their eyes met, and for a heartbeat, time stalled and all that mattered was the sparkle of Ashley's smiling eyes.

As they made their way back to the entrance of the ice rink, Ty hesitated before helping her remove her skates. He didn't want this night to end, not when it had been one of the most memorable experiences of his life.

She rolled her ankles gingerly once the skates came off and he winced. He should have thought about her newbie-ankles and called it a night sooner so she wasn't in pain. *Shit.* With the way she was beaming, though...maybe she didn't mind.

"Tonight was incredible," he said, struggling to find the right words to convey just how much their time together meant to him. "I'm really glad I got to share this with you."

"Me too," she replied softly, her eyes filled with warmth and gratitude. "Thank you, Ty. I'll never forget this."

As they stood facing each other, Ty took a gamble. It wasn't a big gamble—as they had been having a good time all night, so he figured she'd return the sentiment—but going for a kiss was always a gamble.

Some gambles just had naturally better odds.

Their kiss started out soft and gentle, but as their lips melded together, it grew more passionate and teasing. A perfect mirror of how their date had gone. When they finally broke apart, both were breathless, their gazes locked with unspoken desires.

"Hi," Ty whispered, his heart pounding in his chest.

"Hi," she murmured back, a surprised smile tugging at the corners of her lips.

"I, uh...not to seem too forward...though, that is my position..." he cleared his throat, fighting the sudden onset of nerves, "Do you want to get together again sometime? I mean, you did pay a king's...or maybe in your case, a queen's ransom for me."

Something about that caused her to wince and he instantly regretted asking, but then she shook it off and flashed a million-dollar smile up at him. “Am I Richard Gere in our little, forbidden prostitution?”

“Most expensive hooker you’ll ever have, Princess.” He punctuated with a wink.

Ashley’s smile grew. “Yeah. I think another date sounds perfect. Even if it’s just beers and burgers at the Five Hole.”

Ty rolled his eyes. Well, he sure as fuck couldn’t do that now!

After he walked her to her car and she drove away, Ty had to fight off the urge to whoop excitedly at the top of his lungs. The parking garage was quiet and empty besides a few random cars, but even then, it felt too eerily quiet to do something like that. Still, he was vibrating with excitement.

He felt like he'd met someone truly special. He wanted to see her again, to explore this connection further and discover everything there was to know about the enigmatic woman who had captured his heart. As he replayed the events of the evening in his mind, he couldn't help but think that maybe, just maybe, fate had brought them together for a reason.

CHAPTER TEN

October 4, Monday

Ty

"Okay, but seriously. How soon can I ask her on another date? We had a great time. She likes me. But she's classy. Refined. What does Miss Manners say about proper date timing?" Ty stickhandled the puck quickly, enjoying the rip of his skates against the rink. He dug his feet a little harder into the ice, feeling it scrape and pull under his feet and his blades cut into it.

Fuck, he always loved that sensation.

His buddy and teammate, Bobby Davidson, looked up from under the barely-there plexiglass shield on his helmet. "Dude, don't look at me. I don't 'do' elegant. I'm more drawn to 'down-to-earth and relatable.' Or they exist on paper..." Bobby grinned unashamed about his book obsession. "I wouldn't know what to do with—what did you call her?—an Egyptian Goddess?"

"A Goddess from another world? Or a lost princess? I go back and forth," Ty supplied with a chuckle, while transitioning to shuffle his feet back and forth and bound the puck off his skates and back to his stick.

He heard shouting from across the ice and looked up to see Ilya, their captain, ripping shots on their new goalie, Teemu.

"Okay, so you're fucking useless." Ty shot a loose puck at Bobby. Ty promptly had to spin out of the way of a returning flick of Bobby's own puck.

"Jackass." Bobby laughed as he scooped up a free puck and charged toward the opposite end of the rink, maneuvering the puck expertly with his winger speed and skill.

"Bookworm!" Ty fired back.

A single gloved finger rose to give him a response.

Tommy Kolbeck, the second line's center, skated over and iced Ty's skates. "Did you put out?"

Ty sighed. He was never going to hear the end of this.

"We had a great date. She seems awesome and I want to see her again." Ty braced for the unavoidable onslaught of teasing.

"She sure as fuck put out enough cash. Jesus Christ. The least you could do is sleep with her. It's not like she's hard on the eyes."

Yup, there it was.

"Yeah, she shelled out some big cash for a charity *date*. I think the alcohol had something to do with it. But she didn't fucking pay for sex—so don't be a douche about it."

Tommy grinned wickedly and opened his mouth to say something else when Jason Miller coasted over, his stick up on his shoulder. "Stop harassing Ty. He got lucky and had a knockout of a lady bid on him. Better than being won by some grandma. So, stop giving him shit. He heard enough of it in the locker room earlier."

Jason wasn't wrong. Ty's cheeks still felt stiff from all the fake smiling at some of his teammate's tasteless comments.

Tommy's expression still had a teasing glint to it though. Despite his shitty jokes, Tommy really was a good guy. Just a bit...immature at times.

Apparently, Jason wasn't putting up with any of that. He continued in a low voice, his eyes flicking over to where Ilya was standing with another teammate, "If you're so interested in discussing the auction, maybe we can talk about your winning bid and what the fuck that was all about."

Tommy stilled.

Even Ty froze in his stretches.

Fuck. Jason went *there*.

Ilya was their team captain, and Ilya's little sister, Kira, was as out of bounds as they came.

And she bid on Tommy. And won.

Fuck.

Ty looked up from under his small mask and watched as Tommy's face paled. Tommy shot a glance over to where Ilya was and then back to Jason. A short, silent nod and Tommy was gone, doing his own warm-up sprints down the ice.

"Thanks, man." Ty said, dropping to the ice to stretch his inner thighs.

Jason peered down at him and said simply, "Don't fuck it up."

"I'm trying not to."

"Then don't. Like Yoda says, 'there's no 'try' about it.'"

Ty leaned a little harder into his stretch, feeling the pull of muscles in his legs. "Fine. Then what do you suggest I do? How soon should I ask her out on a second date and not scare her off?"

Jason leaned against the boards and crossed his arms, a thoughtful expression on his face. "First, be real with her. Don't try to impress her with some false persona or pretend to be someone you're not. You'll never be able to keep that up. And from what you said, Ashley seems like the type of girl who appreciates authenticity."

Ty nodded. He had come to the same conclusion before their first date. He had always tried too hard to please others, molding himself into what he thought they wanted him to be.

"Second," Jason continued, "don't be afraid to take some chances. Relationships require vulnerability, and that means putting yourself out there. Taking risks, being open to new experiences. From what I saw at the auction, Ashley seems like she's not afraid to live life to the fullest—so embrace that energy and let it fuel your own actions."

Ugh. Yeah, *that* was the problem.

Typically, when Ty took a chance with a woman, he was burned. Again and again.

He'd been down that road before.

And they were so inherently different. Who was to say they wouldn't self-destruct too?

She called the outdoors 'dirty' for Christ's sake.

Sure, it was absolutely adorable, but still. He lived for spending his free time outdoors and she didn't seem to be into that.

Would they even mesh well? Was it worth the risk?

Then again, she had never tried ice skating before, and she handled that with grace and determination.

And totally kicked ass at it.

Maybe she wouldn't be so opposed to his interests...

"And lastly," Jason added, with a mischievous glimmer in his eyes, "don't forget about passion. I don't just mean in the bedroom, although that's important too. I'm talking about finding something that ignites a fire within you and pursuing it with all your heart. Ashley seems like she knows how to live passionately, and you should too."

Ty chuckled, the image of Ashley's fiery spirit coming to mind.

Yeah, he could probably find a way or two to teach her to enjoy the outdoors...if she gave him a chance.

He blinked.

Well. There was his answer.

That was certainly a way for them to bridge their two interests.

Well...he'd at least put it out there and see what she did with it.

Ty couldn't stop his smile as he looked down and adjusted his shin pads.

Their coaches called out for them to assemble, and Ty copied his teammates as they made their way to the center of the ice to listen to their coaches' outline for practice and the expectations leading up to the season opener in two weeks.

Even though he needed to focus, Ty was already impatient for practice to be over. Then, he could call Ashley to schedule their next date.

If his intuition was correct, she'd say yes.

And then he'd know if he was the only one feeling like there was something there, or if she felt it too.

And if they did have the potential for something real, he just hoped he didn't fuck it up.

Chapter Eleven

October 8, Friday

Ashley

Ashley's breath caught as she hopped down from Ty's truck and gazed up at the towering pines of the nature reserve. Ty had called earlier that week to ask her out on a second date once the Cyclones got back to Springfield from their last preseason game in Dallas. Since his initial phone call, there had been a constant flow of texts, funny videos, and cat memes.

He was sweet as fucking sin and Ashley was in deep trouble.

Proven by the fact that when Friday rolled around, she was *giddy* with excitement. All for a freaking hike!

She, Ashley Wazir, was excited for a *hike.*

She could still hear her brother's shocked laughter from last night when she mentioned it on the phone.

To be fair, it's not like she was excited to go out into the *decaying* autumn wilderness.

And it wasn't the rush of orchestrating another covert adventure far from any possible paparazzi that had her body buzzing all week.

It was *Ty*.

The promise of spending more time listening to him talk and share stories about his life...it had consumed every free minute of her thoughts this week. His voice, his body language, his easy smile...it was all just so...uncomplicated and honest.

And didn't that just scare the living shit out of her.

All this excitement over a second date with a guy she just met. It was ridiculous. Juvenile.

Even so, she couldn't stop her smile.

The crisp mountain air filled her lungs, and she closed her eyes, soaking in the earthy scents of pine and soil.

Who knew nature could smell so...good.

Actually, it reminded her of Ty.

He smelled exactly like this.

Like *perfection.*

Ty came around the truck, a wide grin on his handsome face. "Ready for an adventure?" he asked, blue eyes twinkling. Ashley smiled back, tentative exhilaration thrumming through her. "Absolutely. Lead the way."

They started up the trail with Ty setting a brisk pace. She matched his long strides, stealing glances at his athletic form as they hiked. His enthusiasm was infectious, and she found herself getting swept up in it.

Oh! Look at this cool plant!

Oh! Look at that funky rock!

Oh! Check out that salamander!

Being in the wilderness wasn't exactly her 'cup of tea,' but all of Ty's fan-boying made it easy to forget the fact that her fresh manicure was getting destroyed with every new excitement that Ty just insisted she had to 'touch' or 'feel.'

At this point, with his skin glistening with a faint sweat and his pine smell wafting to her as they walked, the only thing she wanted to 'touch' or 'feel' was his body against hers. Not that he seemed to notice.

She had a healthy sexual appetite—so, what?

She kept waiting for him to bring them to a secluded cove where they could learn about the birds and the bees....

Yet, he just kept on hiking.

She was starting to think that "let's go hiking" wasn't an innuendo.

Hmmm. That was new.

As the trail grew steeper, Ty interrupted Ashley's fixation on his ass by turning to extend a hand to help her onto the rocky outcropping. His strong grip ignited a spark in her as he pulled her up.

"My hero," she said playfully, flashing him a flirtatious smile. He laughed, the sound warm and rich.

"Anytime, Princess."

The nickname made her pulse quicken. She knew he meant it casually because he was unaware of her true royal status, but the word thrilled her coming from his lips. She gazed into his bright eyes, tempted to close the distance between them. But she held back, savoring the tantalizing tension.

There would be time for that later.

Probably.

Maybe.

If he ever made a freaking move!

Ashley tore her eyes away from Ty's handsome face, focusing on navigating the rocky trail. She could feel his gaze lingering on her as they hiked, sending delicious shivers down her spine.

"So, what's been your favorite outdoor adventure?" she asked, glancing back at him.

Ty's eyes lit up and his lips hitched to the side. "Definitely heli-skiing in Alaska. We got dropped on top of a glacier and just carved fresh lines all day. It was unreal."

"Unsubscribe!" Ashley said with a laugh. "Your coaches allowed that?"

His face froze and he paused mid-step before turning to face her. "Let's just say, they aren't entirely aware of that particular excursion. We can blame Jason on that one, he was playing in Boston with me at the time."

She let out a laugh and shoved at his firm biceps. "And there you were, calling *me* naughty!"

The smallest blush kissed his cheeks and she was hit with a wave of desire so strong that she actually caught herself leaning towards him.

She loved his passion for daring activities and exploring new places. It reminded her of her own restless spirit. His idea of exploration was apparently a little more...clothed, though.

"How about you? Any crazy adventures in your past?" Ty asked.

Ashley hesitated. Her upbringing meant activities were often restricted for security reasons. But she did have a few rebellious stories to share.

"Well, once my brother and I snuck out of the pal—uh, our house—and went night swimming in the nearby lake," she said, catching herself just in time. "It was thrilling breaking the rules like that."

Ty grinned. "I'm sure it wasn't the first, or last time, you broke the rules."

His approval sent a rush of excitement through her. With Ty, she could let her passionate, adventurous side loose.

Their conversation flowed as easily as the trail that led them higher into the hills. Ashley was struck by how much they had in common despite their vastly different upbringings. She had never felt such an instant connection with someone before. Especially with someone who was very clearly an outdoorsy introvert.

What the hell was he doing with someone like her?

"Did I tell you about the latest development with the protected lands dispute in Dariqat? We got the update this morning. Apparently someone was detained and the embassy had to step in."

Ashley bit her cheek at that. She could have his problem solved in three seconds if she wanted to. Unfortunately, that would require bringing attention to herself and she preferred to be out of sight out of mind for her father. Then he wouldn't be tempted to bring her home early as he had threatened to do on multiple occasions.

Being here with Ty only solidified Ashely's preference to stay under the radar as long as possible.

When they finally reached the summit, Ashley gasped. The sweeping valley below was breathtaking; but Ty's eyes were fixed only on her.

"Beautiful, isn't it?" he said softly.

"Yes," she whispered, meeting his warm gaze. "Truly beautiful."

The air crackled between them. Slowly, Ty reached out and tucked a loose strand of hair behind her ear, his fingers trailing down her neck. Ashley shivered at his touch, her heart pounding.

Finally!

They drew closer, lips just inches apart...

Ashley's breath caught in her throat as Ty's lips met hers in a tender kiss. At first it was soft, almost hesitant, as Ty was testing the loose boundaries between them.

Fine, she'd take charge if he wouldn't.

She tipped onto her toes, deepening the kiss. Ty elicited a deep groan as he took her cue.

Soon, their passion ignited like a forest catching fire.

Ashley ran her hands up Ty's muscular back, pulling him closer until their bodies were puzzled together. She could feel his heart beating rapidly in sync with her own. Ty's hands caressed her hips before moving lower to grasp her backside. A soft moan escaped Ashley as desire coursed through her.

Yes!

Eventually, they broke apart, both breathing heavily. Ty's eyes blazed with want.

"Hi," he murmured.

"Hi back," Ashley replied, smiling up at him. She traced a finger along his clean-shaven jaw. "I've been waiting for you to do that all day."

Ty gave a soft chuckle. "Got sick of waiting?"

She chewed on her lip. The motion drew his eyes to her mouth, which was unintentional, but she'd take it by the way his gaze darkened. "I was turning gray."

He leaned forward and rested his forehead against hers. “Sorry about that. Just still trying to figure out our dynamic and what’s protocol.”

Ugh, protocol.

She fucking hated that word.

Ashley shrugged. “We’ll figure it out. No worries. Also, just as an FYI, I don’t really do the whole ‘protocol’ thing. Just do what feels right. That’s how I live my life.” Here in the States at least. “And don’t worry, eventually if you dragged your feet long enough, I would have taken charge.”

He smiled down at her, a soft, awed look on his face. “Yeah, I definitely believe you would have taken charge eventually.”

“All day, every day,” she confirmed with a haughty look.

He chuckled. “Hate to say it, Ash, but you’re in for an exhausting ride with me. I’m not exactly a ‘throw you up against the wall-type.”

Hearing her name on his lips sent a thrill through her. No one here knew her as Princess *Ashira*.

With Ty she could simply be who she was.

Just Ashley.

It was glorious.

“What about against a tree?”

Ty chuffed out a laugh and shook his head.

"What do you say we find a more private spot to continue this?" Ty suggested, his voice low and tempting.

Ashley grinned, taking his hand. "Lead the way."

As they descended back down the mountain, Ashley was practically drooling at the thought of getting her mouth on him.

Fuck, she was already drenched, and it was only a kiss that they’d shared.

She was ready to throw caution to the wind and see where this adventure with Ty might lead. Even if it only amounted to a flash in the pan.

Ty led Ashley off the main trail, ducking under a canopy of trees.

Oh, *this* had potential.

Her heart sped up.

This would do nicely.

It was no coat closet, but it still had an air of forbidden, public naughtiness that she'd discovered was her favorite kink.

Once she got back to Dariqat, the ability to explore that kink would be put out faster than a fire in space.

Ashley looked around at the small clearing, checking if they could see the trail from their small alcove.

Would he take off her shirt? Expose her to the woods...and anyone in it?

Would he pull down her pants just enough to pump himself inside her?

Would he pick her up and push her roughly back against the biting bark of a tree?

Would he—

Ashley paused her fantasies as she watched Ty pull a blanket out of his backpack and spread it out on the ground.

To her somewhat-horror, he was now pulling out various containers, creating a cozy picnic spot for just the two of them.

A picnic!?

He wasn't going to ravage her in the woods!?

Where was the open-air fucking? The public, risky rendezvous? The thrill of potential discovery by passersby?

"I hope you're hungry after all that hiking," he said, opening the containers to reveal an assortment of snacks—fresh fruits, cheese, crackers, and a bottle of wine.

He looked so freaking proud that her heart squeezed.

She was being an asshole.

Here she was...just wanting him for his dick, and here he was, just trying to give her some thoughtful attention.

Fucking hell.

Why did she suck so much?

Ty was way too good for her.

"This is perfect," Ashley said, swallowing past the thick lump in her throat. She gingerly sat down next to him. "What have we got?" She surveyed the goods and popped a grape into her mouth, savoring the sweet juice.

She wished it was a different type of ball that was in her mouth, but alas. Ty was not a wham, bam, thank you ma'am, kind of guy. Funny how things worked out.

As they ate, Ty regaled her with stories from his travels. He told her about the time he got chased by an angry moose in the Canadian wilderness, and how he once got stranded overnight in a tiny rural airport during a blizzard.

Ashley listened, enraptured. She loved this adventurous, daring side of him. It wasn't *sexually* daring, but it was a type of bravery and risk-taking that was similar all the same. The way his eyes lit up when he told the tales made her heart flutter. He had such a thirst for adventure.

Maybe they weren't so different after all?

"They all sound like self-imposed disasters," she said with a laugh. "Like, they were all totally preventable."

"Maybe. Or maybe fate knew I'd need a good story to impress a girl someday," Ty countered with a grin. "Who knows. Maybe I'm making all this up just to sound adventurous." He took her hand, his thumb grazing over her knuckles. "We could go on an adventure together sometime. See what disaster chooses to strike. I'd love to show you the great, untamable wilderness and how breathtaking it can be."

Ashley's pulse quickened at the promise in his words.

Oh, how she wished to throw caution aside and run away with this wonderful man.

But the weight of her responsibilities remained ever-present in her mind.

Ty noticed her sudden shift in mood. "Everything okay?"

"Yes, sorry," Ashley said, forcing a smile. "Just thinking about...things back home. You're right though, a trip together would be amazing. Exploring with you might even be worth the dirt under my nails."

She didn't want to ruin the moment with talk of the future.

Right now, all that mattered was being here with Ty.

She leaned over and kissed him, taking charge. Enough talk.

Ty responded eagerly, his strong arms encircling her as their mutual desire picked up where it left off earlier. Ashley shifted closer, hands roaming over his muscular chest.

She needed him, wanted to get lost in passion and forget everything else, if only for a little while.

Sick of waiting for him to defile her, she leaned backwards and pulled him atop her on the blanket, so his body covered hers.

She felt his momentary pause and could almost hear him thinking as he processed what she was doing. She also felt the moment that he thought 'fuck it'—it coincided with her rubbing her hips roughly against the front of his jeans.

The October chill disappeared as they kissed. Ashley's breath caught as Ty's hands slid under her shirt, caressing her skin. His touch burnt away any lingering doubts or worries. She fumbled with the buttons of his shirt, desperate to feel him against her.

Ty kissed a heated trail down her neck, nipping at her collarbone. Ashley moaned softly, and arched into him, her fingers pulling him closer.

"This okay?" Ty murmured, his voice rough with need.

"More than okay," she gasped as his thumbs brushed over her nipples.

"Let me know when you want to stop."

The only thing she wanted him to stop was *talking*! She grabbed the back of his head and pulled him back down into another hungry kiss.

She could feel his lips turn up in a smile.

Fuck, this man could kiss.

She ground against him again, her hands now boldly winding around to his front and down into the front of his pants.

A pure, possessive growl ripped from him as she held him. Stroked him.

Gone was the cinnamon roll who wanted to make sure she was respected and treated like a lady. This man...

She shivered as he plucked at her nipple again, slightly harder this time.

"Yes." She moaned, arching into him.

Clumsily, she undid his pants, all too aware that he didn't seem to suffer from the same clumsiness. It was like he flicked his wrist and boom—her pants just slipped down.

For a man who wasn't an alpha hole, he still clearly knew what he was doing.

He was just...smooth about it. Polite. Respectful. Considerate.

Fuck, maybe that was his strategy. He foreplayed all the women to death and it forced them to jump him or die.

What a way to go.

Ty claimed her mouth again, kissing her deeply while their hands explored, and clothes were shed piece by piece. Finally, skin met skin in a fervent heat. After playing with her for an extra minute, dragging sweet moans from her, he rolled on a condom and slipped inside.

Ashley moaned low as Ty entered her, wrapping her legs around his waist to draw him in deeper. They found their rhythm, losing themselves in each other over and over again.

He was smooth, slick, and long.

Fucking hell, how did it feel so good?

She'd had her share of cocks, but wow. Why did Ty's cause her breath to leave her body?

Then he started to move, and she had to take back her earlier compliments. If she thought it was good *before*...

Yup. Okay.

She should have been dating hockey players all these years because those hip movements...

She moaned hard and loud into his mouth as he fed more delicious kisses to her.

"Fuck, Ty."

He rolled his hips in another impossible way that caused her fingers to dig into his back.

She distantly heard him hiss in response, but she was all too aware of how he was hitting *that* spot just right, and how he had brought his hand in between them in the most glorious way.

Normally, she'd be on top by now, giving her a better view, but *fuck*. She couldn't do anything but lie there and relish it.

It was fucking glorious.

Who knew her sweet, charming, considerate man had the skills of a fucking porn star?

He rested on his opposite elbow, but the hand wasn't lazy. It was playing as well, cocked at just the right angle to play at her breast as he pumped into her. And his lips. *Fuck*. His lips were now leaving searing kisses on her neck, his back arched impressively as he bent low to nibble at her skin, all while unleashing devastating pumps inside of her.

The complexity of the sensations were becoming too much.

Her toes curled. Her knees bent. Her back arched. And she gave a mini shout as her orgasm hit her hard and fast.

He didn't let up his pursuits, though. He rode her through her release until she was a quivering mess under him, and then, a few jerky movements later, and he was spent as well.

Slowly, he lowered his body to align with hers, gently sliding himself in and out. In and out.

It felt so good.

Ashley slowly opened her eyes.

He was smiling down at her, a gentle, wonderful look on his handsome face.

Fuck, he was so pretty.

She didn't deserve a soul like his.

"You okay?"

"I can't feel my face." She breathed, staring up at him.

Somewhere along the way, he had pulled an extra, soft, thin quilt up and over them.

A contented smile curved her lips. This was the most marvelous—

"I know it wasn't a coat closet..."

She bit back her laugh.

Ashley rocked him a bit with her arms, enjoying the warmth of having him still in her. "A coat closet has its merits. But this was better than any coat closet. Ever."

He gave her a wry smile. "It wasn't supposed to happen today—"

She put a finger over his lips. "That was fucking perfection and if I hear you say a single thing about regretting it—"

Ty mimicked her actions and silenced her with a salty finger pressed to her lips.

His eyes darkened when she reached out with her tongue and gently licked it. "Naughty minx." He laughed. "Anyways, what I was going to say—before I was rudely interrupted—was that we were supposed to be sprawled out on a king-sized bed with a box of condoms at the ready for our first...and subsequent...times. Not on a bumpy forest floor. This part was supposed to come *after* the hiking date...not that I was presuming or anything."

"Am I complaining?"

He peered down at her. "Not yet. Tomorrow I might hear nothing but bellyaching about how sore your back is from me ravaging you on the hard ground..."

Ashley shoved him again. "Troll."

He zipped in to steal a quick kiss. "No, you're not complaining yet. But I only have one condom in my wallet, and I have a feeling I know exactly what your response will be to that."

"You should have packed more," she chastised imperially.

His eyes sparkled. “I heard you say it in my head that exact way, my demanding princess. Then again, this wasn’t supposed to happen *here*.” He said in a mock-stern voice. “It was supposed to be with wine and roses. Soft music. Silk sheets. Something fit for someone like you. Not...” he looked around. “A wilderness claiming.”

Ashley looked around with a chuckle. “I’m digging the caveman vibe.”

He leaned his forehead against hers. “I argue your point. If anyone’s the sexual caveman here...it’s you. I was at least *trying* to be good.”

Ashley smiled up at him. Her goody-two shoes.

Fuck, he was adorable.

She leaned up slightly and caught his lips in a wet and sloppy kiss, giggling as he finally slipped out.

“Time to clean up?”

He closed his eyes and leaned forward, rubbing his nose against hers. “Yeah, I guess. Before the state rangers come out here to find who was killing one of the local bears.” He rolled off her but not before she landed a swat on his arm.

“I wasn’t that loud!”

He grinned at her as he pulled up his pants. “I’ve heard quieter dying moose. But that’s okay. Now I just know to make it my mission to see just how loud I can get you. That was nothing compared to what I can do in a bed with time and space.”

Oh?

Okay, yup.

They needed another go. Stat.

Ty leaned in and pressed a gentle kiss to Ashley's forehead as he dressed.

"I don't want this day to end," Ashley murmured, tilting her face up to the warm autumn sun.

Ty brushed a strand of hair from her eyes. "Me neither. But it doesn't have to, not yet at least."

A smile curved Ashley's lip. "What did you have in mind?"

"Dinner tonight?" Ty traced his thumb along her jawline. "I know this great little Italian place downtown. We could share a bottle of wine, a delicious meal, have sex again—"

She didn't even give him a chance to continue. "I'm there." Ashley propped herself up on one elbow.

A grin split Ty's face. "Your appetite is impressive."

"You treat me like I'm made of glass. I'm not."

He looked at her and narrowed his eyes as he inspected her. "No, you certainly are not."

What did that mean?

Ashley opened her mouth to ask when he looked up at the sky and sighed. "You...confuse me. You're so polite, refined, and proper. But you have this wildness about you. And I can't tell if it's because you are truly a wild one...or if you're just so desperate to cram in your last tastes of freedom before going home..."

Ashley blinked.

Well, fuck.

"Maybe both, I guess. I don't know." Ty answered for her. Was he even talking to her now? "Something to bring up with a therapist on a rainy day." Ashley again opened her mouth to say something but then he looked up and a smile broke out on his face. He eagerly pointed and crouched down, his finger pointing at something beyond some nearby pines. "Do you see the bald eagle? I've never seen one here before."

Ashley craned her neck to try to see the bird through the treetops and gasped as it swirled lazily into sight. "No way." Her voice was quiet, like she'd scare the bird away if he heard her.

The thing was a freaking mile in the sky, there was no way it heard her.

But still, there was something magical about seeing it.

America's bird.

They watched it for a moment before the angle of their neighboring trees caused it to disappear.

As she sat up to pull on her clothes, she watched Ty clean up the snacks and blanket. Thoughtfully, she chewed at her bottom lip.

She *liked* him.

So much.

And she was going to lose him.

Fuck, it was going to hurt.

Might even hurt him, too.

Was it worth it? Should they call it quits now?

Just then he looked up, caught her staring, and gave her an adoring grin.

Yeah. He was fucking perfect.

And she was going to hurt him.

But for now, he was hers.

It would have to do.

CHAPTER TWELVE

October 11, Monday

Ashley

"Mr. Baylor, I appreciate your willingness to engage in this discussion," Ashley said in a measured voice. "It's essential to convey that my role here isn't to cause harm to you or Connell. Rather, I aim to present available options and assist both you and Connell in securing a safe and stable life."

Garrett Baylor's eyes held a weary intensity as they focused on Ashley across the table. Seated beside her, Babs observed with a disapproving expression. Ashley signaled subtly to Babs, urging a more neutral demeanor, and the judgmental look softened.

Addressing Garrett, Ashley continued. "Following court proceedings, it has been determined that Connell will remain with the Jenkins until our next court date. We acknowledge your efforts toward sobriety and stabilizing your employment, but Connell has been in the Jenkins' care for the past two years during your transitions between programs and periods of incarceration. And while Connell's mother has relinquished her parental rights, leaving you as the primary custodian, the Jenkins have expressed an interest in a foster-to-adopt arrangement for Connell. Legal counsel advised me to discuss this option with you for your consideration."

"You're suggesting I give up my son," Garrett interrupted sharply, his hands visibly tensing on the table.

Given that said son had found his dad passed out with needles in his arms more times than he could count, Ashley was certainly hoping Garrett would relinquish his son to a family life where he didn't have to worry about fentanyl overdose simply from accidentally touching something on the ground. That was no life for a six-year-old.

"Of course not," Ashley responded calmly. "I'm only presenting this as one of several possibilities available to you. I'm here solely to provide you with comprehensive information and options, ensuring you're equipped to make informed decisions."

Garrett's eyes flickered with an unsettling mix of rage and despair, the raw emotion pricking at Ashley's heart. The room was silent for a moment as he began to process what she had said, his gaze darting between her and the documents spread across the table.

"But I want him," he croaked out, his voice breaking with a desperation that sent chills down Ashley's spine. His hands moved restlessly as if he was struggling to keep them from shaking. Absently, his fingers wandered to his arm, scratching at it incessantly. His belligerence crumbled into vulnerability right before their eyes, the primal fear of losing his son radiating off him in waves.

Ashley watched him pick at an old scab on his forearm. She noticed a fresh needle mark discreetly hidden beneath a crudely drawn tattoo of Connell's name. Her heart ached for the man; it was clear that Garrett loved his son in his own tortured way. Yet love alone couldn't erase the past or guarantee a healthier future.

Babs visibly stiffened beside Ashley, discomfort etching deep lines onto her stern face. They had seen this deterioration too many times: the itching, the erratic behavior, the defeated look in a parent's eyes.

Ashley murmured gently, "We understand that, Mr. Baylor. Nobody is questioning your love for Connell." She adjusted her glasses and met his gaze head-on. "This isn't about wanting him or not. It's about what's best, and safest, for him. And sometimes, what's best for a child...might hurt us as parents."

Garrett's face turned a mottled red, and his palm slammed down on the table, rattling the paper cups of coffee they'd drank earlier. "Don't tell me what's best for my son," he spat, venomously.

Ashley startled but quickly recovered and kept her composure. They'd done this song and dance before.

Babs shifted uncomfortably beside her, her hand instinctively but discreetly ghosting over the panic button under the table.

Garrett seemed to sense the rising tension and took a shaky breath, visibly trying to control his temper. With effort, he lowered his voice, but the frustration remained. "You don't know anything about us."

His accusation hung in the air. Ashley sighed quietly, a sound of resignation rather than rebuttal. "You're right," she conceded, softening her tone even more. "I don't know everything about you or Connell."

Her admission seemed to pacify Garrett slightly, his taut shoulders slightly relaxing. Ashley continued, her gaze never leaving his. "But I've seen the love you have for your son. We all have. And sometimes, love means making the toughest decisions for their well-being...even if it breaks our hearts. Connell has been doing incredible at school this year. He's making friends. He has fewer outbursts. Fewer nightmares at night. He's adjusting and growing. The therapist agrees that there's been a marked change in his demeanor as well. He's more trusting of adults and is smiling easier."

The room fell into a tense silence, save for the hum of the fluorescent bulbs overhead and the distant bustle of activity beyond their closed office doors. Garrett's eyes welled up with unshed tears, brimming with a potent mixture of frustration, remorse, and fear. An unspoken battle was being fought within him—between his addiction, the raw love for his child, and a bone-deep fear of failure.

With his eyes fixed on Ashley, he murmured almost inaudibly, "I'd die for that boy..."

"And we know that," Ashley replied. "Connell knows that too. But what Connell needs now isn't a father willing to die for him; he needs one who will fight to live for him—live soberly and stably."

Garrett flinched as though physically struck, his head bowing low as he wrestled with the truth of her words. Babs gave a small nod next to her.

Aching at the sight of Garrett's suffering, Ashley slid a pamphlet across the table. "Get sober. Stay sober. We can go from there. But...Connell has a loving family willing to take him in. I'd...it'd be a shame if he lost that opportunity. We both know how fucked up the system can be at times. How the courts could move him in a heartbeat. The next family...he might not..."

Shit. She needed to stop talking.

This wasn't exactly an approved conversation in the context of her job.

She'd crossed lines before, but...somehow doing it now, at the end of her time there, when she wouldn't be around for the next court visit...

It felt wrong.

"I'm leaving, Mr. Baylor, and I won't be coming back. Babs will do her best to keep the pulse on you. But there will be no more late-night calls and pickups. No more requests for me to get groceries or a winter jacket for Connell. I won't be here. So, just...consider it? Please?"

Garrett stared at her with dead eyes, unmoving in his chair except for random finger flexes. "He's the only person I have left." His voice was barely audible, and Ashley's heart ached.

"I know."

And she was trying like hell to make it so Garrett wasn't the only person left for Connell as well.

Garrett took the offered papers and folded them up tight. He then slipped them in the sealable plastic gallon bag that Ashley had supplied. It helped some of her clients keep their documents dry after they left the office.

Garrett slid the documents inside and slowly stood, staring at Ashley and Babs.

"He's all I have left."

Without another word, the man limped from the meeting room, his worn boots making soft thumps on the floor as he made his way out the door.

Shit.

Chapter Thirteen

October 13, Wednesday

Ashley

Days later, Ty fulfilled his promise to show Ashley the gloriousness of The Five Hole. The hockey bar that the team favored was a total dive...and it was perfect.

Despite the homey appearance, the owner made sure that the patrons were well-vetted and that they weren't going to harass any of the athletes that had found their way inside for a burger or drink. The atmosphere was friendly, private, and welcoming...as long as you didn't overstep and make things weird for the professional athletes inside. The bouncer at the door looked bored as hell, but it was worth it, if it meant the team had a place to retreat to that wasn't full of photographers, journalists, or tabloid writers.

Ty's date from years ago was *totally wrong* for hating on him for taking her to the Boston branch of The Five Hole because this place was freaking *amazing*.

Laughter bubbled up in Ashley's chest as Ty shared a story about his rookie season in the NHL. His animated expressions and spot-on impersonations of his gruff coach had her clutching, gasping for air at their high-top table for two in a back corner.

"I swear, the man had it out for me that first season. Probably didn't help that I accidentally checked him into the boards during our first practice." Ty's eyes crinkled at the corners, a self-deprecating grin tugging at his lips.

Ashley shook her head, still chuckling. "I can only imagine the look on his face."

"Priceless." Ty leaned forward, his knee brushing against hers under the table. A spark of heat shot through her at the contact, her cheeks flushing. "But in all seriousness, Bowman may have ridden me hard that first season but if it wasn't for his mentorship, I wouldn't be the player I am today."

Hmm, speaking of riding someone hard...she needed another round with Ty. They hadn't hooked up since this last weekend and she felt like she was experiencing the longest drought—and foreplay—of her life.

Their sex was incomparable.

Like she'd been with amateurs this whole time and finally got brought up to the big leagues.

How Ty could have those...skills...while still being such a wholesome, unassuming, and *humble* man, was an absolute mystery.

He had to have been a porn star in another life.

There was just no other explanation.

The things he could do to her...the noises he could drag from her...

"I miss playing for him sometimes actually. I love the guys here, and though Coach Montgomery can be tough, he's still a great guy. He understands that we have outside factors that can fuck with us. Sometimes I worry he gives too many allowances for that shit. Sometimes it's nice to be treated as if hockey is the only thing in our lives. It makes it easier to shut it off—like it's an excuse to block it all out." Ty shook his head. "I guess I miss Bowman's hardass-ness sometimes." He paused, a slight frown causing a small wrinkle to form between his eyes. "He certainly wouldn't have let us slack off during practice. There'd be no 'we'll get it next time' bullshit. There have been rumors of Montgomery already talking with management about some early season roster moves...not that he's talked to us about it though. So we don't even know who's potentially on the chopping block." Ty sighed. "At least Bowman was *honest*—sometimes brutally so—but that's what you need. Even if it's tough to hear, it's better than being blindsided later."

Ashley reached out and patted his forearm in consolation. "I get that. But don't you think it can be hard for some people to be that straightforward? Maybe they're afraid of the fallout. Montgomery is still trying to cement his place as a coach—I'm sure there are a lot of pressures on him from different directions. He's just trying to find the best way to get the team to succeed."

Ty shrugged. "Yeah, I get that. But I'd rather deal with the truth head-on than live in some sugar-coated lie. At least then, you can make real decisions and improvements. There's not much worse than going along with your life and then being destroyed by a hit you didn't see coming. Do you know how many players don't get any heads-up when they're about to be traded? It's ridiculous. How can you build a worthwhile life in a new city when you don't know if you're building on sand or bedrock?"

Ashley flexed her toes in her shoes to relieve some of the tension building in her. "I guess that's true, but try not to be too harsh on him. We're all fighting battles that others know nothing about."

Ty looked at her intently and then sighed, his strong shoulders lowering slightly. "You're right. I need to stop complaining and judging him. He's mostly transparent with us. I'm just a little unnerved by some of the rumors I've been hearing."

Ashley's heart pounded in her chest. "I'm sure you're fine. They wouldn't have traded for you last year if they didn't want you. I'm sure you're fine."

Right?

Oh, jeeze. What if they traded Ty away before she was set to go home? Her already short time with him would be cut even shorter!

Ty smiled weakly before taking a quick drink of his water.

Be peppy, be confident, be a rock.

"Good," she said, uncrossing her arms and beaming at him. "I'd hate to see you become bitter and suspicious because of silly rumors. You're better than that. They don't call you 'Ty "Thoughtful" Daniels' for nothing."

A hint of a smile teased at his mouth as he looked at her, unimpressed. “No one calls me that.”

“No. But they should.”

He rolled his eyes again.

He was too adorable.

She beamed at him and uncrossed her arms before leaning forward.

“Maybe I’ll get Lexie to put it on a sign for Saturday’s game. You never know. Maybe it will catch on.”

“God. Spare me that *thoughtful* gesture. I’m fine with just being Ty.”

“Psh. You’re hardly ‘just Ty.’ From my research on last season, you have the record for assists. And if the preseason games I watched are any indication, you might just break your own record this year. So hey, the name might just stick.”

The way Ty froze at her comment had her own heart racing.

Ashley had told him from the beginning that she wasn’t a sports girl.

And yet...

The look of awe and happiness on his face was worth every minute she spent reading past articles and watching old games.

Ty rubbed at the back of his neck, still staring at her in joyful shock. "You...watched my old games?"

Dangerous territory here. He was too happy...and she was too happy *giving him* that happiness.

Fuck.

"It was on at the gym." Ashley lifted a shoulder, feigning nonchalance. "Besides, I figure a girl has to keep up with her favorite player, doesn't she?"

"Favorite, huh?" Ty seared her with his gaze, causing the hair on her arms to raise. “Does that mean you’re rocking my jersey this season?”

"Don't get cocky." Heat flooded Ashley's body under the intensity of his stare. "You still have a lot to prove before you reach jersey-wearing status. That's a bit of a commitment."

One that might bring dangerous attention to him if it were to get back to her father.

"Prove? Like what?" Ty leaned across the table, getting so close she could see the various shades of blue rippling through his bright eyes. "Is that a challenge?"

Ashley's lips curved. "Maybe."

She wasn't prepared for the sultry heat in his eyes, or the husky quality of his voice. She squeezed her legs together in response.

"Careful, Princess. I never back down from a challenge."

Ashley tilted her chin up. "Good. I'd hate for you to disappoint me."

Ty's gaze dropped to her mouth. "Haven't yet and I don't plan on it. Not you. *Never* you."

Man, he was so *fucking sweet.*

His banter, his smile, his laugh, his adventurous attitude, his energy.

Everything about him was just so fun.

Freeing.

When she was with him, she could *breathe.*

She wasn't second-guessing how he was going to interpret her comments. He wasn't looking for a hidden agenda or a way to turn her words around on her. He just...read her intent, and even if the words themselves weren't right, or her tone was reserved...he still *knew.* He *knew* her.

Ty saw her.

In more than one way.

Especially now, with that darkened, hungry expression.

Whenever Ty thought about sex with her, he would get this intense look on his handsome face, and...Holy fuck.

Normally, he *was* 'just Ty.'

Sweet, considerate, trusting.

But when it came time to *play*...he was the king of toe-curling-confidence and sex-god-goodness.

Man, she was fucked.

He was perfect, and he still hadn't noticed that he was way too good for her.

Ashley was hoping she could get another two months out of him before he caught on and ran for the hills, leaving her with a lifetime of fond memories and precious smiles.

With Ty's knee pressed against hers and his eyes dark with promise, Ashley's breath caught in her chest. Her heart wasn't supposed to pound this fast over a man she had just met weeks ago.

And yet, one look from those blue eyes had her pulse racing.

She was falling and falling hard.

Thank God the restaurant didn't allow any sort of media presence that might notice them and snap a pic. With the way they were staring at each other right now, it wouldn't have been fit to print in the papers. Maybe a porn magazine though.

A flush crept up Ashley's neck as Ty's gaze dipped to her mouth again. She ran her tongue over her lower lip and watched in fascination as his pupils dilated. The air between them seemed to crackle with electricity. She could almost taste his desire, feel the heat of his touch through the thin barrier of clothing separating them.

Her heart thudded wildly, desire pooling low in her belly. She wanted to drown in the depths of his eyes, explore the hard planes of his body, rediscover all the ways they fit together.

No one had ever provoked such a visceral reaction in her before. But one look from Ty, one whispered word in that husky tone, and she came unglued.

How soon could they get the check paid? She needed to touch him. Now. And imprint the feeling of his skin and worshiping touch to memory. She needed to get a lifetime of memories. Now!

He leaned in imperceptibly, his voice deep and raspy. "You're busy trying to remember where the closest closet is, aren't you?"

Ashley's eyes fluttered shut as she struggled to form a coherent thought. "A girl can dream."

And she *would* dream. For the rest of her life, she'd remember—and dream—of this too-incredible man who was ripped away from her by fate and circumstance.

What she wouldn't give to have the courage to spit in the face of her family and abandon her duties.

"Then I won't tell you about the empty apartment he keeps upstairs for players who need a place to retreat to." At her dramatic moan, Ty reached out and gave a soft caress of her cheek. "Breathe, princess." He dragged his finger down her cheek, neck, shoulder, and arm, before twining their fingers together in a tight grip. "There's plenty of time. We'll get to that after. But for now, just...talk with me."

Ashley opened her mouth but what was she supposed to say? That she was barely holding onto her panic at the thought of losing him—a man she basically just met? That he could take his 'breathe' and shove it because they had memories to make?

He was going to be busy all week as the team prepared for their season opener. This was one of their last chances for a sex marathon before his season began and stole him from her. Their risqué texts were incredible and that she loved that he didn't make her feel foolish for starting them. Not only that, but in typical Ty fashion, he dove right in and upped the ante on their spicy messages. They also had a couple late-night calls where they would listen to each other get off but even that hadn't *remotely* taken the edge off. Ashley was starving for more of him; however she could have him, but if he expected to be able to look at her like that and not send her mind to a place of handcuffs, toys, lingerie, silk sheets, and blindfolds, then he wasn't paying attention.

And Ty was always paying attention.

Even now, he stroked the back of her hand with his thumb, watching her with a soft look on his face as she struggled with jumping him right then and there and sprinting to the bathroom so she could take the edge off herself.

Masturbating in a bar bathroom...that would be a new one for her.

Judging by his sweet, yet hungry, expression, he knew it too.

The bastard.

He knew exactly what kind of havoc he was wreaking on her.

Ty winked and growled across the table, "If you behave yourself and don't run to the bathroom to do what I know you want to do...I'll reward you with something special later."

Ugh, God!

Ashley crossed her legs and almost moaned at the friction it caused in her damp undies.

Yeah, her Ty was *always* paying attention.

She wanted to *choke* him.

After she rode him, that is.

Or, he rode her. Whatever. She was flexible.

She gave him a pouty look.

Ty grinned, reached out and tugged her lower lip out from between her teeth. "Don't give me ideas. I don't need to see those pretty lips all wet, plump, and swollen from your adorable nibbles. You deserve to be wined and dined. I'm trying to be a gentleman, here. Even if it is at a low-key bar."

How many times could she tell him that she didn't need to be wooed?

Though, it was pretty wonderful...when she wasn't at risk for combusting in spontaneous orgasm fire!

"Try less," she fired back with a scowl. Ashley tried to pull her hand out of his grip so she could properly pout but he didn't let go and just continued his soft strokes.

The secret-sex-God only chuckled and then leveled her with a steady, and surprisingly somber, look.

The expression had her heart stuttering.

Oh, God. What was wrong...

"If I invited you to my place for dinner and beers, you'd jump me as soon as we were in the front door." At Ashley's 'yeah, so?' expression, a smile flitted over Ty's lips. "We'd never get around to actually having dinner. We wouldn't have any conversation. And I wouldn't get to hear more stories about your dreaded nursemaid, Pria, or your hilarious riding instructor." He reached out and laced his fingers with hers, ignoring her petulant expression. "I like *you.* I like hearing you talk. Your accent is faint, but beautiful. I love watching you lose yourself so much with me that you forget to filter your words or expressions. And the more time we spend together, the less often you peek up at me out of the corner of your pretty eyes to see how I've taken your words. You're trusting me and I'm *into* that. And, I'll be honest, it's a nice ego trip that you're so ready for another night of debauchery, but I know once we get naked, everything else is off the table. So," he gestured indicatively at the dim bar, "bear with me and suffer through a few nice dates and getting-to-know-you-talking. Then I'll give you all the orgasms you can handle, okay?"

Yes, *Daddy*. Ashley shifted in her seat and felt another twinge shoot straight to her core. "So, you're saying we can never have any quickies in a coat closet?" she whined for good measure, twirling his fingers between her own.

Ty laughed. "What *is* it with you and coat closets?" He shook his head. "Tell you what, if I hit my goal targets—or assist targets apparently—this year, I'll buy you your own portable coat closet and we can fuck in there *whenever* you want. Yeah?"

Ty said it with a smile, but it fell when he took in her expression. "Oh...right."

Ashley pursed her lips and looked around the dimly lit room, fighting back the sudden burn in her sinuses.

Fuck. Where did the fucking tears come from?

"I, uh...forgot you were leaving for a sec. I didn't..." Ty swallowed and his face was full of regret. "I didn't mean to..."

Shit.

She swallowed and looked back at him before giving a tight smile and a shrug. "It's okay. I know it's happening. It's hard to remember to *not* make plans, you know? There's so much I would love to do with you—with everyone—but..." Ashley stared at the place setting in front of her, trying to not ruin the thoughtful evening he had planned for them.

Ashley needed to get her shit together and lock down her emotions.

She had enough years practicing, it should only be a matter of seconds.

And yet....she couldn't.

Fuck.

She was usually much better at it than this. She sniffed and didn't even have enough headspace to be embarrassed by the gross, wet sound.

A low groan rumbled in Ty's chest. "Ash." His fingers grazed the inside of her wrist, sending a jolt of electricity up her arm. "I...keep forgetting. Plus, part of me is still hoping that something will change, and you'll decide to stay."

Her to his, her pulse skittering. "It's not a matter of *deciding*, Ty. I have no choice."

Ty gave her a sad but still hopeful look. "I have contacts. My contacts have contacts. A guy on my team, David, his wife wasn't American either but he—"

No. She needed to douse his hope.

It sucked, but it wouldn't benefit anyone for him to hold onto that particular flame.

"Ty, baby. It's complicated and *none* of your contacts will be able to fix this. My family needs me. I *have* to go back. There is no way out of this."

"And why can't you come back after you've got them all sorted out?"

She chewed on her lower lip again.

Why indeed.

She couldn't tell him.

Everything about their dynamic would change and she didn't want that.

"My dad's controlling. My brothers are his robotic minions. They said that they need me in Dariqat, so I'm needed in Dariqat. If I fought it, even if I could get my specialty visa extended—which I probably couldn't because it took some serious favors to get in the first place—I'd be manipulated and coerced every which way till Sunday and I'd never stand a chance. My family needs me home and that's all there is to it."

And if her father thought for one minute that Ty was preventing that return...Ty would find himself in the trunk of a nondescript black sedan quicker than he would have dreamed possible.

He watched her with an incredulous and frustrated expression. "You've said that before—that they need you and that's that -, but you're not a fucking prisoner, Ash. You're allowed a choice."

"Not in Dariqat."

"Well, then, don't go back. The US wouldn't send you back to an abusive situation."

Ashley scoffed before she could stop herself. "If my visa is up, my visa is up, Ty. Have you seen what happens to illegal immigrants here?"

"Then we can get married."

Her heart skipped a beat, but the desperation in his voice forced her to not allow that fantasy to grow...in either of their minds.

"That wouldn't be...safe." Ashley wet her lips and tried to figure out how much to tell him. "My family has...contacts that could make life very...messy for you—or me—if we were to derail their expectations."

"And by messy you mean..." Ashley let out a harsh breath that had him looking at her in horror. "You can't be serious."

"Dariqat laws are different. And diplomatic immunity for the people my father knows...well...let's just say my family can...get things done through a variety of channels."

Ty just continued staring, disgust etched in every line on his face. "Jesus. He sounds like a real fucking winner."

Ashley shrugged but otherwise couldn't argue.

"And that's what you grew up with." His expression was more contemplative now, like he was working something out.

Ashley nodded.

"And that's what you're going home to."

She gave him a sad, mockery of a smile. "Yay."

Ty took a big sip of his water and stared at her, his gears turning.

Ashley blinked, trying to maintain her composure.

"They're family. My father is...my father. But I have brothers. Sisters. Some whom I actually like, believe it or not. And, by going back, maybe I can do something for them...help them somehow. I at least got a chance to *live*, Ty. I was given a chance to experience *life*. My mother and older brother *moved mountains* for me to have the chance to come here. My siblings—and countless other people back in Dariqat—will *never* have that chance. But maybe they could...if I went back. *When* I go back."

Ty frowned. "Sure, but—"

"Family is family, Ty. I always knew my stay here in the States would be a temporary one. Just because..."

"Just because, what?"

Well, shit. Okay then.

"Just because I found *you*, it doesn't change the reality of the situation. I need to go back. This was just a...vacation of sorts."

Well, this was a heavy conversation to have after knowing each other for only a few weeks. But with all things Ty, it felt so much longer.

Ty stared at her, emotions flitting across his face so fast that Ashley couldn't pin down what they were. For once, he didn't have what he was thinking written right there for the entire world to see.

Unfortunately, he must have been taking notes from her.

She took a quick sip of water before continuing. "I *like* you. I *really* like you. I like spending time with you. I want to spend more time with you. But...it doesn't change the fact that there's an end date. Our story has an ending. It might be bittersweet...but at least we had the 'sweet'. Right?"

Ty's face was somber, his jaw was clenched tight.

"I met a girl after my sophomore year in college," he started. "We worked at the same internship that summer and I had never been more in love. At the end of the summer, I thought we'd make the long-distance thing work as we went back to school. She needed to be convinced." He paused. "That should have been the one and only red flag I needed." He looked at a couple at a nearby table, the candlelight flickering across his sharp features. "I surprised her at her dorm one weekend. Turns out she was fucking a guy down the hall. He didn't know about me. I didn't know about him. When we all found out and he took off...she chased after him."

Oh, Ty.

Ashley wanted to reach out and touch him, but he was too far away.

"After I was drafted by the Bruins, I met someone who worked in the Garden. An HR specialist. She was incredible. Smart, sweet, gentle. I thought it was the real thing. Until I asked her to bring me some relationship disclosure forms so she could move in with me."

Ashley's heart squeezed.

"Turns out, I wasn't worth the risk of losing her job. She'd been explicitly told that they weren't allowed to date any players."

"Ty—"

"Then another girl, two years later, who was at least happy enough to tell the world we were dating. Even fucking partially moved in with me. Started talking about kids. The whole nine yards. I was ecstatic." Ty's jaw was clenched, fingers tight around his glass.

"Ty—"

"She was married. To a Marine. Found that one out when we were grabbing a bite to eat at an outdoor café, and he walked right in. Home from the Middle East. Still in his fucking military garb." Ty tossed her a sour look. "They'd been trying for kids for years. Turns out, she never stopped taking The Pill. I was just a 'good time' while he was gone." Ty shook his head, dragging a hand through his hair.

God, what a fucking disaster.

"Ty. If you'd just let me—"

"I know what it feels like to be a passing fancy, Ash. I've had practice. That's not even counting the puck bunnies who just want a taste of a hockey player." He waved a hand between them, "*This* isn't *that*. Don't try to tell me it is. I know it isn't. I feel it. You feel it. It's not just some stupid, passing fancy." He stared at her, his beautiful lashes emphasizing the vulnerable blue in his eyes, a fragile hope glimmered there.

Ashley felt tears pool in her eyes. "No, Ty. This isn't that. It's...real."

Which was completely fucking insane given that they hadn't even known each other a month but yet, here they were.

They were as real as it got.

Ty cleared his throat, glancing away. "So, maybe there's hope. Maybe something changes. And we'll just...take it day by day."

"Ty...I wish things were...different. I wish I could tell you that I believe there's a chance...but my circumstances aren't likely to change. Trust me. I've been hoping for almost three years to get a phone call from my brother telling me that things were different—that I was free to stay and live my life. We're in the final lap and there's still no status change...so no, Ty, I don't have hope. But I'll give you my days. *Every* day you want—it's yours." Ashley swallowed hard and stared through her tears at his watery figure. "I will live each of my remaining days here with you, and treat it as if we had forever, because in my heart, that's how I want to remember it as."

She ignored the unpleasant twisting in her belly.

It would only cause even more heartbreak when the time came for her to leave. But breaking things off with him now felt like it was going to shatter her.

It was so easy in theory to just say, 'Hey, I'm a princess. I have to go home and get married to form an alliance between our families and I'm expected to pump out a zillion kids, none of which they will let me raise myself, and I'll just need to be okay with being a trophy piece—silent and unseen—for the rest of my life. My degrees will be for nothing as I won't be allowed to work. Oh, and my husband may choose to have many wives, and in that case, I will just be yet another vessel to carry his children.'

In theory, it was simple. Honesty was always the best policy, right?

Ha!

Anyone who believed that all misunderstandings could be solved with a simple conversation was a hypocrite who had never been put in a situation where sharing the truth would cause them to lose the only person who had ever truly *seen* them. Or maybe that person was just better than her, because Ashley just couldn't do it. She couldn't lose him yet.

Ty reached out and took her hand again, giving it a small squeeze. "We'll figure this out. Day by day. Hell, maybe I could come visit while you get shit worked out."

Ah, fuck.

It was on the tip of her tongue to shut that down when one of the informal waiters approached the table with a glass pitcher and started refilling their glasses.

They stared silently at each other until the server moved on and dropped off some burgers and fries at a table a few yards away.

"Ty–"

"I mean, it makes sense," he interrupted her. "The guard you have up at all times. If that's what you're dealing with at home--or whatever that prison is to you. It makes sense now. Why you don't want to talk about them. Why you refuse to give them headspace. Why you think it's impossible to find a way to stay here. I would love it if you shared more with me...at some point," he added quickly at the look on her face. "But for now, I think we're at a good place. They exist. They suck. And we aren't going to give them any more of our evening. Especially if you think they're going to take the rest of our lives."

Oh, Ty.

Ashley's body sagged as a wave of premature grief washed over her.

Ty raised his glass. "So, for now, here's to tonight, and the *many* more we *will* have. And I recognize that you think this is doomed to fail, but I'll reserve my judgment of when it's over when I see you flying away on that plane...and even then, who knows, maybe I'll chase after you."

"Tyler!"

He chuckled and leaned forward, knocking his drink against the one she never raised in matching request. "Here's to us."

Ashley heaved out a breath that had her shoulders nearly touching her ears.

Damn.

Ty watched her as he sipped at his drink, his eyes narrowed on her face.

"It's not that simple, you know," she said one final time, a firm resolve settling over her features. "And you absolutely cannot come to Dariqat, Ty. Ever. You need to trust me on this." Ashley swallowed hard and used a word that had not been taught to the royal children of Dariqat, "Please."

"I know. But for the rest of the night, we're pretending. You do what you need to do to compartmentalize. I'll do what I need to do to keep you here with me." When she opened her mouth to argue, he rushed to add, "Or, at least, I'll do what I need to do in order to *pretend* that there's actually *something* I can do to keep you." He let out his own harsh breath. "I know the score, Princess. I'm not placing any bets. But...a guy can hope. Right?"

Another corner of her frozen heart chipped away and brought with it a searing pain.

Oh, fuck.

Ashley quickly looked up and away, gulping in a steadying breath so she didn't start sobbing.

"So, can we put that behind us and enjoy the rest of our dinner?"

Ashley brought her attention back to his blurry form and blinked quickly, trying to erase the sadness from her face. "Of course, Ty."

"Good girl."

A little flurry of butterflies broke out on her skin, and she shot him a small grin at his attempt at breaking the somber mood.

"There she is. My tough-as-nails, badass, girlfriend."

Ashley blinked in surprise at the g-word. Was she his girlfriend?

The thought forced a true smile onto her lips. Yeah...

She *really* liked the sound of that.

Fortunately for Ashley, Ty was far from finished. He launched into a lively stream of conversation, weaving one amusing tale after another into their evening. Over the next hour, Ty regaled her with the highlights of his most memorable exploits: his mischievous escapades as a kid, the fender bender that marked his first car accident, and the sweet awkwardness of his first kiss. Every sweet story had the ice melting a little more from Ashley's hardened heart. She went her whole life thinking her heart was made of solid rock.

Turns out it was just ice.

And here it was...starting to thaw.

She hated Ty a little bit for giving her that realization.

But not as much as she thought she might love him. Or at least might be starting to...

When the server finally came back and asked them if they wanted dessert, the sad mood from earlier was a distant memory.

Ty gave her a heated look across the table and a delicious shiver ran down Ashley's spine at the hunger in his gaze. She wet her lips, desire unfurling low in her belly.

Ty's eyes flickered down to her cleavage before giving a distracted dismissal to the server. "I think I have desserts at home."

She bet he did.

"We'll just take the check."

As the man bustled away, Ashley extended her leg and ran her foot up the inside of his leg. All the while, toying with her ridiculously low v-cutout by her breasts. Ashley cocked her head at Ty and bit her lip. "Ahh, no dessert? You said this place had the best chocolate cake and I'm still hungry."

Ty looked at her for one point two seconds before digging in his wallet, throwing down a couple of hundreds, and thrusting his tall seat back from the table.

Holding his hand out, Ashley delicately grasped it as she slid off her own seat, taking her sweet time in making a show of it.

Clearly, her man was on a mission.

And she'd never been known to be easy...in *that* way.

It was good to make him wait for it. To want it like she did.

As they left the restaurant and made it to his truck, Ty closed the distance between them. He pinned Ashley against the passenger's side door, claiming her lips in a heated kiss.

Ashley sighed into his mouth, sparks of pleasure igniting under her skin. She'd never felt desire like this, as if she might combust from the passion burning between them.

Hell, she would miss this.

When they finally broke apart, chests heaving, Ashley could only stare up at him with fondness.

Ty brushed a stray curl behind her ear, his touch reverent. "Dessert?"

Ashley laughed, the sound breathless. "Yes, please."

The grin that lit Ty's face made her heart skip a beat.

"Good girl." He pressed another swift kiss to her lips. "Manners maketh man." He patted her ass with a firm smack as he opened her door and then shut the door firmly behind her.

She was in *way* over her head.

And she couldn't tell whether drowning was painful or freeing.

Chapter Fourteen

October 13, Wednesday

Ty

Being with Ashley felt right in a way Ty couldn't explain.

Both of them had been broken and bent, misused and tossed around; but when they were together, the jagged, worn corners of their puzzle pieces matched up perfectly.

The scars of past betrayals still ached, but when he was with her, the pain lessened.

He wanted to know all of her—every quirk, every smile, every secret she held close to her heart.

And there seemed to be a lot of secrets. But despite the secrets and unknowns that still lingered between them, they shared a sense of humor, passion, and thirst for life that only further flamed their pre-existing sexual spark.

As he drove them back to his place, Ty cautiously allowed himself to imagine what the future might hold for them.

He didn't dare hope for forever, not yet, especially with how unconvinced Ashley seemed that she wouldn't be able to stay—but he was still eager to nurture the clear connection they had. Ty may have been a small-town boy turned professional hockey player, and Ashley a wealthy daughter from Dariqat, but when they were together, none of that mattered.

Ty made a mental note to reach out to some of his contacts about what it would take to get her green card either extended or renewed. Whatever it took to keep her here.

And maybe, just maybe, he could open himself up to love again and not get burned by someone who was just looking for a fling.

As they walked up to his upscale apartment, Ashley's fingers stroked his skin under his shirt and down his pants as they walked, all while her lips were at his chin, his neck, his mouth. By the time he got his door unlocked, Ashley had successfully claimed about 90% of his brain cells. They stumbled through his front door, lips fused, hands roaming. Ashley walked him backward until his shoulders hit the wall. Then she was sliding down his body, her fingers working at his belt.

"Easy, tiger," Ty said with a soft laugh, pulling her up for a slow, deep kiss. "We've got all night. No need to rush."

"But I want you now," Ashley protested, eyes gleaming with desire. She traced the bulge in his jeans, grinning at his sharp inhale. "Don't tell me you really do have desserts you want to eat first." She almost sounded like she expected that to be the case.

Good, he was keeping her on her toes.

Heat simmered in Ty's veins as he gazed down at her. She was temptation incarnated, a forbidden fruit he couldn't resist.

Cupping the back of her head, he brought her mouth to his for a scorching kiss that left them both breathless. "Patience, Princess. I'm going to take my time with you."

Ashley huffed, though her lips twitched. "If you insist.'

"I do." Ty scooped her up into his arms, carrying her toward the bedroom. "Now, let's get you out of those clothes and see if eating you will satisfy my craving for sweets."

Ashley's laughter followed them down the hall. It was music to his ears. By the end of the night, he fully intended to have her singing his name.

Ty kicked the bedroom door closed behind them and lowered Ashley to her feet. His fingers slid into her hair, tilting her head back as he took her mouth in a deep, drugging kiss. Ashley melted against him, her hands grabbing at his chest and shoulders.

He wanted to re-explore every inch of her, relearn all the ways to make her gasp and moan.

He then trailed his lips along her jaw and down the graceful arch of her neck. Ashley shuddered, fingers tightening on his shirt. "Ty..."

The needy plea in her voice had him groaning. He slid his hands down to grip her waist, walking her backward until her calves hit the edge of the bed. "Patience," he reminded her, even as his own control began to fray.

Ashley huffed out an impatient breath. "I don't like being told what to do."

Ty chuckled, nudging her to sit on the edge of the bed. "Oh, Princess, you love it when I tell you what to do."

He slid his hands under the hem of her shirt, slowly pushing the material up. Ashley lifted her arms, allowing him to strip the shirt off and toss it aside. His gaze roamed hungrily over her lace-covered breasts that had tempted him all throughout dinner.

"Gorgeous," he rasped, brushing his knuckles over the swells of her breasts.

Ashley shivered, reaching for the button of his jeans. "Your turn," she said breathlessly. "I want to see you, too."

Ty captured her hands, pinning them above her head. "Patience," he repeated, dropping a kiss to the corner of her mouth. "I want to take my time unwrapping you."

Ashley stared up at him, eyes dark with desire. "Then what are you waiting for?" she challenged.

A wicked grin curved Ty's lips.

Tonight, he was going to absolutely *wreck* her. And by the end, she'd be begging for more.

And maybe she'd even be begging to stay here...with him.

Her dark eyes seemed to bore into his soul, and his heart quickened in response.

Ty's traitorous brain chose that moment to remember the secrets she kept hidden from him, and he forced the reminder from his mind. He wanted nothing more than for her to open up and trust him completely. But right now, she was looking at him with an intensity that made his blood run hot.

Without a word, Ty pulled Ashley into his arms, his fingers pressed firmly into her skin as their lips met in a searing kiss. Their mouths moved together hungrily, fighting for dominance. As they kissed, Ty's hands wildly roamed over Ashley's body, savoring the feel of her soft skin beneath his fingertips and imprinting it into his memory.

Ashley let out a soft moan and the hungry sound sent a shiver down his spine.

Ty growled in response, the noise low and thick with lust.

The room filled with the sound of their ragged breaths and their hands exploring, their movements fueled by a primal need. With every squeeze, pinch, and bite, the fire burned hotter.

"Tell me what you want, Princess," Ty whispered into her ear, his fingers deftly tracing patterns on her skin that caused a hitch in her panting. "Tell me how to make you feel *good,"* he whispered against her ear, nipping gently at the lobe.

Ashley arched into him, her body rubbing against his in her pleasure. "I want you," she murmured, her voice thick with desire. "And I want you to take control, to show me all the ways you can make me lose myself in you."

With a low growl, Ty pulled her close, his strong hands roaming over every inch of her body as he sought out her most sensitive places.

He reveled in each gasp and moan that escaped her lips, using them as a guide to explore her further. He made his way down her body, taking his time to tease and torment her.

"God, you're beautiful," Ty murmured between her thighs, his fingers pulling her open with a boldness that forced a small, needy whimper.

Ashley responded by spreading her legs wider and tilting her hips up into his face.

"*Show* me how much you want me," she whispered.

"Ty, oh God," Ashley whispered, her voice trembling, "I'm so close."

Ty let out a deep growl and increased the speed over his ministrations.

"Oh God, Ty," Ashley whispered, her voice trembling, "I'm so close."

He was sucking hard at her clit when her back arched and her knees clamped hard at his ears. Ashley's body writhed away from him and he looked up into her face, her wetness on his lips, cheeks, and chin. Her eyes were closed, her back arched, and a strangled cry tore past her parted lips as she reached her peak, waves of pleasure washing over her. Ashley's fingernails were digging into the hand that Ty had moved up to her nipple, leaving crescent marks behind as she rode out the orgasm.

Fuck, she was glorious.

Regal.

Majestic.

He leaned back in and started slow, long licks—each one causing an instinctive jerk from her newly sensitive body.

Her moans were a mixture of pain and pleasure as she pushed into it, even as her body tried to pull her away.

"Ty," Ashley whimpered, reaching for him, her eyes pleading for more. "Please, I need you inside me. Now."

He smiled devilishly at her eagerness.

"Your wish is my command," Ty replied, his voice husky with arousal. He moved, and positioned himself at her entrance, pausing briefly to revel in her heat before pushing forward, claiming her completely.

The sensation was electric, their connection deepening with every thrust and caress. They moved together in a dance of desire and ecstasy, each seeking to bring the other to the heights of pleasure. Ashley clung to him, her nails digging into his shoulders as if to anchor herself to reality, while Ty held her possessively, determined not to let her slip away.

"God, Ashley," Ty panted, sweat beading on his forehead as their bodies strained against one another. "You feel..."

"Ty..." Ashley moaned, her voice barely audible over the pounding of their flesh and combined ragged breaths.

The knowledge that they were both so near the edge of oblivion driving him to push harder, faster. He could feel the tension in her body, and knew that she was teetering on the brink again. He pulled back and slid a hand between their bodies, plucking at her nipples before diving down and giving her clit a delicious little pinch. Ashley groaned hard at both touches and he felt her squeeze his dick tight.

Fuck, yeah, she was close.

He did another swirl and flick of her clit and she erupted.

With a groan that seemed to echo through Ty's very soul, Ashley surrendered completely to her orgasm, her body shuddering beneath him as wave after wave of ecstasy washed over her.

Ty kept his pace of firm thrusts but removed his fingers to let her ride it out. As soon as her orgasm faded, Ashley's eyes popped open and locked on his with an intensity that threatened to consume him. Her dark gaze held a vulnerability that only seemed to heighten the passionate fire within her, and it stirred something fierce and protective in him.

"More," she gasped out, her legs and hips shifting as she locked him tight against her again, her hips thrusting against his in an almost violent manner. "Rougher, Ty," she panted, her words strained through clenched teeth. "I can take it. I *want* it."

He grinned, appreciating her honesty and the heat that coursed through him at her request. With a firm grip on her hips, he flipped her onto her stomach, holding her in place as he positioned himself behind her.

"Are you sure? You want to take a second to stop pulsing before we start from this angle?" Ty asked, his voice strained with effort, barely able to hold back any longer.

"Nope. I'm ready. I'm *very* ready," she breathed out in a hungry voice, her body pulsing with anticipation as she arched her back and displayed herself even more openly for him. His balls tightened at the tempting sight.

Fucking hell.

Would she want him to take that hole too? Ty pushed himself into her and leaned over her, covering her body with his own. Hungrily, he started pumping into her and began a round of dirty talk that would make a pornstar blush. All the while, asking her how much she wanted his cock and how good she tasted. When he asked her about her ass and if it was off-limits, Ashley stilled for only a moment, before thrusting back hard onto his dick and turning her head to catch his mouth in a savage kiss.

Fuck, yeah, she wanted him to take her ass.

"Feel me, Ash," Ty growled, his voice low and primal, as he continued to drive into her, each thrust more powerful than the last. "This is us, together. This is what you do to me."

As Ty took control, finding her boundaries and testing their limits, the room filled with the symphony of their moans and whispers. Their bodies moved in perfect harmony, each thrust and caress driving them closer to the pinnacle of pleasure. And as Ashley's cries grew louder, more desperate, Ty could feel his own climax approaching.

"God, you're amazing," he groaned, his fingers digging into her hips as he struggled to maintain control. Ty leaned forward and dove a hand into the heat of her, searching for her clit again. He wanted her orgasm to leave her *weak*. As he played, stroked, pinched, and pumped, her noises got higher and higher in pitch. Eventually, Ashley let out a ragged moan, her body arching beneath him as she cried out her climax.

Fine with settling for a hat-trick for now, Ty let himself join her. He'd eat her again when she was ready and see if he couldn't rip a few more orgasms out of her. She always enjoyed the second and third rounds later in the night...especially when she got to play a little longer while they waited for his own body to recover

As they lay tangled in each other's arms, their breathing slowly returning to normal, Ty marveled at the woman beside him.

She was so...complex.

Confusing.

Seductive.

Fierce but still vulnerable.

How could one person be all of that?

Ty traced his fingers along the curve of her waist, thinking how perfectly she fit into his embrace.

Ty tightened his hold on her, his determination flaring within him. He would do whatever it took to keep Ashley in his life, but the nagging thought still lingered in the back of his mind—he couldn't do it alone—she needed to fight for them as well.

"Hey, Ash?" Ty ventured cautiously, not wanting to disrupt the tranquility of the moment but needing to voice his thoughts.

"Yes?"

"Whatever is going on back home, whatever big drama that you're dealing with...I just need you to know that I'm here for you, no matter what. Say the word and I'll do anything I can to make sure that you're not pressured into something that you don't want."

A soft, sad smile played on Ashley's lips as she looked into his eyes, moisture collecting in them. "Thank you, baby."

He pressed a gentle kiss to her forehead, his chest warm with affection for the incredible woman in his arms.

In return, she snuggled closer to him as if trying to merge their bodies into one.

He wanted to assure her that he would always be there for her, regardless of the secrets she held close to her heart. But he knew actions spoke louder than words, and so he simply held her tighter.

As they lay there, basking in the afterglow of their lovemaking, Ashley traced her fingers along Ty's strong jawline.

Ty could feel the weight of Ashley's thoughts, her lingering touches speaking volumes about her fears and desires. And as they drifted off to sleep, wrapped in each other's embrace, their bodies entwined like vines reaching for the same sunlight, Ty breathed in the sweet scent of roses that clung to Ashley's skin and prayed that their love would be enough to weather whatever storms may come.

Chapter Fifteen

October 16, Saturday

Ty

The arena rumbled with the crowd's thunderous roar as the Cyclones fought for a foothold in a quickly deteriorating game.

Ty skated hard, but the sound of his blades slicing through the frozen surface was barely audible over the away crowd's enthusiasm. The puck passed quickly between his linemates, Bobby and Ian, as Ty sprinted toward the opposing goal.

As they approached the blue line, Ty took a hard hit from an opposing defenseman. The force caused him to spin into the boards but, luckily, he was able to stay on his feet. He glanced up and saw Ian swooping toward the back of the net with the puck still on his stick. With a glance, he spotted Bobby crashing the net and Ty hustled to get into position. After a series of quick passes, Ty slipped a pass to Ian who fired a shot at the net—only to have the goalie snag it.

"Damn it."

His breaths burned in his lungs and throat and he felt the weight of the game's pressure bearing down on him. How many more chances were they going to get before this period was up? Not many probably.

What a shitty start to their season.

Hopefully, Ashley wasn't watching it back home.

"Ty! Get your head in the game!" Ian barked, frustration lacing his voice. Ty nodded, clenching his jaw.

Shit.

Nothing like a teammate noticing your distraction...

Fucking hell. He was as good as traded if Ian was casing him, too.

As the players crowded the face-off circle, every muscle in his body tensed, ready to spring into action as soon as Ian won the face-off...hopefully.

The linesperson dropped the puck Ian lost the face-off, and away the players scattered as they transitioned into defensive mode *again*—for the millionth time that night.

They were spending ninety percent of the game on their fucking back foot. They were lucky that Teemu was having an insanely good night in goal, or else they would have been sitting at nine to zero already.

The ice seemed to splinter under Ty's furious strides as he raced back, trying to cover the open man. Bobby, still not fully recovered from his injury last season, struggled to keep pace with the opposing players as they counterattacked.

"Watch—" Ty shouted, but it was too late.

A quick, one-time slap shot later...and the puck rocketed past their goalie, increasing their deficit to three.

Ty could almost feel the vibrations on the ice from the collective roar from the away team fans celebrating and jeering at them.

Fuck.

Ty knocked his stick against the boards as he skated to the bench for a line change.

Once the second line was on the ice and ready for the fresh puck drop after the goal, Ty squeezed a cold jet of water from his bottle into his mouth before wiping his face with a sweat towel.

Fucking hell.

Carolina won the face-off again and started pummeling Teemu with shot after shot. The rebounds from his pads and the ringing of the shots that bounced off the crossbars and posts, echoed in the goal-hungry arena.

The intermission buzzer rang out like a death knell, signaling an end to their disastrous second period. Sweat dripped off every square inch of the team as they trudged back to the guest locker room, their expressions grim and unyielding. Ty glanced at Bobby, noting the pain etched across his face despite his best efforts to hide it.

"Hey, you okay?" Ty asked, concern lacing his voice.

"Yeah, just... achy...and slow," Bobby admitted, forcing a weak smile. "But we're down, not out, right?"

Ty grimaced.

As the team settled into the locker room, Ty let his thoughts wander to what this poor performance meant for their team—the trade rumors clawing at the back of his mind like a persistent itch. What if they *completely* fell apart in this final period? What if he was the one who was on the chopping block because he was trying to cover for Bobby's slow start to the season? Bobby would never forgive himself.

Ty shook his head to dispel the buzz of anxiety that hummed in his bones.

His eyes met Bobby's for a moment, and Bobby gave him an apologetic wince.

Shit.

After everything Bobby had done for this team, and his teammates, over the years...

Ty should be working harder. There was no excuse.

He needed to get his focus straightened out and get his edge back. He owed it to his friend.

He owed it to his team.

He owed it to himself.

No more distractions or worrying about drama.

What would happen...would happen.

He couldn't control that. Ty *could* control his actions, behaviors, and attitude though.

It was time to step up.

The air was thick with tension as the men spread about the room and waited for Coach Montgomery to outline the new plan.

"Listen up, boys," Coach Montgomery began, his voice—calm but urgent—cut through the heavy air. "We need to tighten our defensive play and make quicker transitions. Stay focused and *keep your heads in the game.*"

Ty tried to keep his expression neutral as he started to unlace his skates. He was one of *those* guys who needed clean, fresh, and dry gear before each new period...that included socks.

Just as their coach was about to delve deeper into the new strategy, the locker room door swung open with a harsh clang. Blaine, one of the long-time assistant GMs, stormed in, his face a thunderous mask of displeasure.

Why the hell was *he* at an away game? He *never* came to away games.

"Montgomery, a word," he barked. His tone left no room for argument.

Ty exchanged glances with his teammates as Coach Montgomery followed Blaine into the hallway, his expression completely neutral. Even the assistant coaches looked confused.

The teeming silence in the locker room was shattered by Tommy's mischievous grin as he edged toward the door, propping it open just enough to eavesdrop on the conversation in the hall between the two men.

Ty looked toward the other coaches, expecting a reprimand, but found them staring at the door, visibly straining to hear what was said. As if that gave them all permission, almost as one, all of the players quieted their movements and breathing and let the loud, self-important voice of Blaine fill the room.

"Change the strategy," Blaine's voice seeped through the crack in the door, his impatience palpable. "Play more defensively. You're not using that new guys that I grabbed in the off-season. Do you realize what we had to do to *get* some of them? And you put them down on the third and fourth lines like...*some sort of grinding rookies? Do you know how easy it would be to replace you? Easier than replacing some of those players, honestly."*

The assistant general manager then continued to berate and belittle the performance of every player, including Teemu, who was the only reason the score wasn't more embarrassing.

Ty's jaw clenched at the criticism, anger bubbling up within him even as helplessness gnawed at his insides.

When Blaine started bringing up potential upcoming roster moves in his rant, the players got so quiet it was like they stopped breathing entirely. This wasn't just about the game anymore—their careers, their futures were on the line. And they all knew it.

"Blaine doesn't know what he's talking about," Tommy muttered under his breath, but there was no conviction in his voice. Only frustration. "It's still the start of the season for fuck's sake. We're doing our best out there."

"Are we, though?" Jason countered, his own disappointment evident. "Maybe he's right. Maybe we need to change something if we want to try to salvage this with any sort of dignity."

After a few more minutes of critique and threats, Montgomery finally put a stop to the onslaught and interrupted Blaine mid-rant. Tommy let the door slide shut and bustled across the room on his skates to his locker stall, his face taking on an innocent expression that was sure to fool absolutely no one.

As Coach Montgomery re-entered the room and resumed his earlier position in the center of the floor, everyone went back to their normal intermission rituals, pretending like they hadn't just heard the assistant GM demand that their coach change up their lines or risk being fired.

Ty's eyes narrowed as he stared at the floor, his fingers drumming restlessly against his hockey stick. He could feel his teammates' apprehension, their collective unease, a palpable force that threatened to crush them all.

"Sorry about that, gentleman. But listen up," Coach Montgomery called out, his voice strained.

Ty *would* be worried about Blaine's savage demands of using new line combos, but thankfully Coach Montgomery was no idiot, and would know exactly how stupid it would be to try outrageous combos that had never even been practiced—

"We're switching things up. Pavel is moving up to the first line with Ty and Ian."

Holy fuck.

The room fell silent, the sudden hush echoing like a thunderclap in the confined space.

Ty's heart sank as he looked over at Bobby, whose quiet strength had been a constant source of support for him on and off the ice. Bobby tried to put on a brave face, but Ty could see the disappointment flicker through his eyes before he quickly masked it with a determined nod.

"Coach, we haven't practiced with Pavel on the first line," Ty was unable to keep frustration from seeping into his voice.

He knew they needed to make changes, but this was *management* interfering where it didn't belong.

"Management's call," Coach Montgomery replied tersely. "We need to adapt and make it work." He then continued to outline the changes and how each line would change up their approach for the final period. After the coaches left the room, the players gave voice to their concerns.

Ty clenched his jaw, forcing down the bitter words that threatened to spill out. He knew arguing wouldn't change anything, but that didn't make it any easier to accept. Glancing around the room, he saw similar expressions reflected on his teammates' faces—a mix of uncertainty, determination, and the underlying fear that they were being manipulated by forces beyond their control.

"Let's give it a try," Ian chimed in, his tone bordering on cocky. His self-assurance would normally have been a welcome boost, but now it felt grating.

Bobby's eyes met Ty's, the quiet guilt and shame shining through the pain.

Fuck.

Ilya cleared his throat and channeled his inner 'captain.' The tall man clapped his hands together and drew the attention of the team. "Our original plan wasn't working. might as well give this a shot," he said.

Ever the dutiful alternate, Bobby, chimed in. "Damn right. What can it hurt? It's not like I'm doing much good out there."

The atmosphere remained heavy, though bumping Bobby from his spot on the first line felt like...being told that their mom was divorcing their dad and marrying her yoga instructor.

It felt *wrong*.

Like a betrayal.

And they all knew whose side they wanted to take in the divorce.

Unfortunately, their *dad* was being *typical Dad,* and publicly saying he was supporting the divorce and was even going so far as to get officiated so he could host the fucking ceremony for the wife's new wedding.

Fucking hell, Bobby!

Ty glared at him.

As if sensing Ty's frustration, Bobby turned to look at Ty and cringed before looking away.

Ty caught Tommy and Jason exchanging dark glances. Tommy even muttered under his breath. "This is just another sign that management is walking all over our coach. Trades are coming, mark my words."

The locker room echoed with the new somber mood, each player trying to figure out what this new development—and management interference—meant for them.

Ty's anxiety spiked as the minutes passed and they finished their intermission routines in silence. Trying to distract himself, he thought of Ashley and her bold confidence. She would have called Coach Montgomery out and asked who was the coach of the team: he...or the executive team. Ashley would have held no prisoners as she demanded the truth about what the hell was going on. He envied that ability to not shy away from conflict. He admired *everything* about her. She was incredible...even with the star-crossed fate she had already assigned to their future.

Hell, with how things were looking, maybe she wasn't quite wrong. Perhaps he'd be traded and gone before her visa was even up.

The irony of him being the one to leave her...it was almost enough to make him crack a smile.

Before they headed back out to the ice, the team huddled together, sharing terse nods and muttered encouragement as Ilya *tried* to pump them back up for the forthcoming, unprecedented period.

The speech fell flat and judging by the worried frowns on the coaches' faces...they agreed.

Once on the ice, the chilly air hit Ty's flushed skin like a slap, and the familiar sharp contrast triggered the adrenaline that Ilya's speech failed to create.

Ty needed to step it up. Big time. He had come to that conclusion earlier.

But if he did...what would that mean for Bobby? If Ty managed to turn things around...would it look like adding Pavel to the line was the reason? Would that add unintended fuel to Blaine's fire?

They took their spots on the ice, and Pavel taking Bobby's usual spot beside him felt alien.

Ty would have felt bad for the resentment that was going to fall on the young kid's shoulders...if Pavel himself didn't look so devastated for being the one chosen to bump Bobby from the line. Pavel had been chosen to be the sacrificial, yoga teacher in the affair...but the problem was that Pavel *idolized* their Bobby.

Being the reason that Bobby was bumped down to the fourth line? Well, it looked like it broke the kid's heart.

Bobby didn't deserve that shit, it was an overreaction to a poor performance. And Pavel didn't deserve the hate that was coming his way for being forced into a situation that he simply wasn't ready for.

So, fine. At the risk of making Blaine feel like the hero, Ty would step up, just as he intended anyways. But he wasn't going to be fucking happy about how this all went down. And he wasn't giving up until Bobby was back where he belonged: on first line.

Chapter Sixteen

October 17, Sunday

Ashley

The paintball gear was heavy and stiff, limiting her range of motion as Ashley made some practice movements. The mask had a faint disinfectant smell and restricted her vision and had an annoying bridge over her nose. As it slipped a little, she reached back and adjusted the strap of her mask, tightening it, heart pounding in anticipation.

Across from her, Ty double-checked the seal on his own mask, eyes glinting with challenge through the polycarbonate lens. "Remember, stay low. Use cover. Don't get overconfident – it can still hurt when you get hit with a shot." His tone was somewhat worried—apparently he didn't think she could handle this.

She'd show him soon enough.

As he stepped forward and held out his gun one more time, going over the different pieces, *again*, Ashley bristled. She wasn't an idiot, she'd heard him the first time.

"I know how to handle a gun, thank you very much."

Idris had made sure his sister was well-versed in self-defense.

Not that she told Ty that.

At his narrowing eyes, Ashley broke the tension by grinning. And though he couldn't actually see the grin, he could see her eyes crinkle. "Maybe you're the one who should be worried."

Ty barked out a muffled laugh and shook his head. "We'll see about that, Princess."

The nickname made her chest tighten. When was she supposed to share the truth?

Ashley didn't want their dynamic to change by telling Ty that she was a foreign princess who's future husband would help ensure the safe future of her entire nation—which was why she couldn't afford to scorn him by bailing on their arranged marriage for the possible chance of love with some random hockey player in the States whom she had just met...

Yeah, that would change things. A lot.

Once again, Ashley felt grateful that Ty had arranged yet another private outing—not that he was doing it on purpose. While she doubted anyone was actively searching for one of the Princesses of Dariqat here in Springfield, Massachusetts, it never hurt to be discreet. So far, all of their dates had been surprisingly private affairs. Ashley couldn't help but wonder when her luck would run out and she'd need to employ some fancy footwork to avoid a publicized event.

With a buzz, the heavy metal door slid open, revealing the giant indoor paintball course.

Without giving Ty a chance for anymore 'instructions,' Ashley darted behind the nearest bunker, running through the maze to get a feel for the obstacles. Maneuvering to the right, she spotted a flash of movement and fired off a shot. A splat of orange paint burst against the barrier shielding Ty.

"Nice try!" His voice echoed through the space.

Ty had rented out the entire indoor paintball warehouse just for them. They had it for a two-hour block and because it was just for fun, there were no staff refereeing their game.

Ashley edged along a wall; senses strained to the max. The gear made her movements awkward, but she stayed light on her feet. When Ty peeked around the corner, she unleashed a flurry of shots, grinning as he yelped and ducked away.

Her heart was pounding in her ears. The damn mask was obscuring her vision. Luckily, so far it wasn't fogging up, but with how hard she was breathing and how hard she was concentrating...it was only a matter of time.

She freaking loved this—the thrill of the hunt, the competition.

She thought of how Ty had looked at her in the locker room, a smoldering heat in his gaze as she'd tugged on the gear over her tight spandex. The memory made her shiver despite the stifling mask and heavy chest padding.

Another shot splattered against her barrier and Ashley refocused, peering around the edge to fire back. She glimpsed Ty in the instant before he scrambled away, paint dripping down his arm, and desire flickered low in her belly as she watched his toned ass move in his snug suit.

This was turning out to be an interesting game indeed.

Ashley darted away from her corner, ducking behind a barrier as paintballs whizzed past. She fired off a few shots in Ty's general direction before sliding behind another wall for cover.

Her heart raced, equal parts excitement and arousal. Her mind went back to the way Ty had looked at her, his heated stare promising all sorts of wicked delights; it made her ache with need. She wanted to pin him against a wall and devour his mouth, feel his hands roaming her body as she ground against him.

Something about him...it was like heroin to her libido.

She wanted him. All the freaking time.

A shot splattered nearby, and Ashley shook off the fantasy, refocusing on their game. She peered around the edge of the wall, catching a flicker of movement from down the way. As Ty emerged from behind a barrier, she unleashed a succession of shots, grinning when he laughed and took cover.

"You're going to pay for that!" Ty shouted.

Warmth flooded Ashley's veins and she laughed, too. "You'll have to catch me first!"

She sprinted to the next partition for cover, firing over her shoulder. A shot burst against her arm and Ashley winced, the sting lessened by the padding—but it still bit. When she slid into place behind a barrier, she assessed the splotch of blue paint and chuckled. Apparently, he was done warming her up.

Ashley peered around her cover, searching for any sign of Ty. She caught movement behind a wall to her left and pivoted, firing with a triumphant shout.

Ty made a taunting sound from the completely opposite direction from where she had fired, and Ashley's grin widened. Two could play that game.

Chapter Seventeen

October 17, Sunday

Ty

Ty darted between barriers, staying low. His hamstrings were screaming from last night's game, but it was worth it to give Ashley another once-in-a-lifetime experience.

Especially if she was still so convinced that she wasn't going to be able to stay.

He tossed another paint grenade over his shoulder in the opposite direction and heard Ashley fire off some quick shots in the direction where the grenade landed.

Ty smiled to himself and kept moving in his attempt to flank her and catch her by surprise. His heart pounded, blood rushing through his veins as he shuffled along.

When the shots ceased, Ty peered around the edge of the wall. A flicker of movement caught his eye and he fired, clipping Ashley's shoulder. She whipped around, eyes flashing behind her mask, and unleashed a barrage of shots in his direction.

Ty laughed and ducked away, the ache in his groin intensifying. The tension simmering between them was palpable, charging the very air. He wanted nothing more than to pin Ashley against the nearest wall and devour her. But not yet. The anticipation was almost as delicious as the act itself.

They'd have time *after* their date.

After they had made another fun, non-sexual fueled memory.

He grinned as he thought about how often Ashley teased him for always insisting on 'dates' first. She had no idea the reason.

If she really did have to leave, then she had countless random nights with random men that she could look back on. But, dates? Fun, exciting, get-to-know-you dates?

If there *was* a deadline – one that he was going to work to erase – and they couldn't get it fixed somehow...he wanted her to look back on her time with him and see it differently. He didn't want to be just like all the other guys.

He was just Ty.

But, in her heart, after she went home, he wanted it to be 'Only Ty.'

He waited until her shots slowed, then darted behind a stack of barriers, circling around to flank her again. When he emerged behind her, Ty wrapped an arm around Ashley's waist and yanked her tight against him. She squealed in surprise, the sound morphing into a throaty laugh.

"Got you," Ty growled through his mask and up against her covered ear.

Ashley shuddered, her ass pressing against his groin. "Looks like you did." She twisted in his arms, paint-splattered suit rasping against his. "What's your policy with POWs?"

The smoldering look she shot him made his cock twitch. "I have a few ideas."

She pulled up her mask, somehow managing to keep her hair from going everywhere, and looked up at him. Ashley dropped her gun and then reached forward, using both hands to pull up Ty's mask.

Ty crushed his mouth to hers, swallowing her moan. Her hands fisted in his hair and she arched against him, deepening the kiss. The heady taste of Ashley flooded his senses, drowning out everything but the feel of her in his arms.

When oxygen became necessary, they broke apart with a pant. Ashley's eyes were dark and hungry, her chest heaving against his. "I think you have the right idea."

"The night's still young," Ty murmured. He nipped at her jaw, relishing her shudder. "And your country isn't cooperating with our negotiators. Someone has to pay."

Ashley laughed, the sound husky and full of promise. "I volunteer. I'm patriotic like that."

Ty scooped her into his arms and carried her toward the nearest bunker, a small house with no windows that he'd learned years ago to *never* hide in.

There was no way to see if anyone was waiting for you once you opened the door.

That kind of blindsiding onslaught could knock the wind right the fuck out of you.

He preferred to know what was coming.

Ty kicked open the door of the small house, tumbling inside with Ashley in his arms. Laughter bubbled up as they crashed to the floor in a tangle of limbs, Ashley landing on top, straddling his waist.

"Well, well," she purred, eyes gleaming wickedly. "Look at the position you've gotten yourself into. The captor has become the captive."

"If this is the position I'm in, I don't want out." Ty's hands slid up her thighs to grip her hips. "In fact, I'd like to get into a different position altogether."

"Is that so?" Ashley rocked against his erection and heat speared through him. "I'm open to...negotiating. I'm a magnanimous dictator."

More like dick-*taster*. Ashley loved sucking him off.

The way she drew out the word sent lust spiraling through him. "Negotiate away."

Ashley's fingers walked up his chest, leaving trails of fire in their wake. He had foregone the padding that he had forced her to wear. "I'm thinking...you on your knees. Preferably with your head between my legs."

Ty groaned, clutching at her hips. "I can work with that."

"Can you, now?" Her nails raked over his nipples and he hissed in pleasure. "Prove it."

He hesitated. *What*? "When we get home?"

"Oh, no. No, my little war general. I want it right here. Right now. It's the only thing that will save your people." She gave him a look that said she would accept nothing less.

Well, *fuck*.

His entire blood volume sprinted into his dick, making the decision for him.

Ty glanced around to check if there were cameras inside the bunker, but Ashley caught his chin and put her face in his.

"Is something the matter, Private?"

Private? Had he been demoted? She had called him General earlier. Ty smiled up at her. "No, ma'am."

"Good boy." The haughty look on her face had his dick pulsing.

Fuck, how could she do this to him so easily?

She gave him an imperial look. "Do I have to ask a second time? At some point, I'm going to start lopping off body parts."

She did *not* have to ask him twice. Ty surged up and flipped them, pressing Ashley onto her back. Her delighted laugh cut off on a moan as he latched onto her neck, sucking a mark into her skin.

"Ty, yes," she gasped, arching against him. Her hands fisted in his sweaty hair, holding him in place, and heat raced south.

He kissed a path down her chest, paint smearing against his lips, and unzipped the front of her suit. With some fast movements, he pulled the padded chest protector off of her and rolled the onesie suit down to her hips. Ashley sprawled out in front of him, her bottom half in the onesie's pants, her top half in nothing but her pink, front-zippered spandex bra.

She was breathing hard as he leaned forward and grabbed her bra's zipper with his teeth. Ty dragged it down, causing her breasts to spill free, the dusky peaks tight and begging for his mouth.

"Fuck," Ty rasped. He palmed one breast, kneading the soft flesh, and closed his lips around the other nipple.

Ashley moaned, back bowing off the floor. Her hands tightened almost painfully in his hair and Ty groaned, flicking his tongue over the sensitive bud. He lavished the same attention on her other breast until Ashley was writhing beneath him, soft cries flowing from her sweet lips.

"Please," she whimpered, rocking against the erection straining against his suit. "Ty, I need—"

"I know exactly what you need." Ty kissed down the flat plane of her stomach, nipping at her hips, dragging the suit down under her ass as he went. "Just relax, Princess. I'm going to take care of you."

He eased the entire suit off her body, tossing the material aside. His mouth went dry at the sight of her, almost naked before him. He ripped her spandex pants down her legs and found she was commando.

Perfect.

"You're so fucking beautiful," he rasped, eyes devouring every inch of her.

Ashley flushed, equal parts pleasure and embarrassment in her eyes. "Less talking," she said breathlessly. "More action."

Ty grinned, sliding down until he was eye level with her clean-shaven pussy. "As the lady commands."

He hooked her legs over his shoulders and buried his face between her thighs.

Ashley cried out as Ty's tongue started playing, swirling around her clit before thrusting inside her. Her hands fisted in his hair, holding him in place as her hips undulated. Ty groaned against her.

Fuck, she always tasted so sweet.

"Yes, yes, just like that," Ashley panted, thighs clamping down around his head.

Ty redoubled his efforts, lapping at her like a man starved. His cock throbbed almost painfully in his suit, straining for release, but Ty ignored it.

There'd be time for that later.

Ty worked her harder, increasing the intensity until she was writhing restless under him. When he felt her get close, he slid two fingers into her, crooking them just so, and Ashley shattered around him with a cry. Her inner walls clenched in her release, and Ty gentled his strokes, letting her ride it out easily.

He pressed a soft kiss to his princess's inner thigh. He could worship her like this all-freaking day.

"Holy fuck," Ashley panted, body going lax against the floor.

Ty eased his fingers from her body and sat back on his heels, wiping his mouth with the back of his hand. The sight of Ashley splayed out before him, thoroughly corrupted, sent another surge of heat to his groin.

"Feel better?" he asked, voice rough.

Ashley cracked an eye open, gaze heated. "Not yet. Get up here."

He surged up her body and captured her lips in a blazing kiss, letting her taste herself on his tongue. Ashley moaned, nails scraping down his back to grip his ass, grinding his erection through his suit against the apex of her thighs.

"Fuck me," she demanded, nipping at his lower lip. "Now, Ty."

Ty cursed under his breath, "Ash, hun..." She was *not* going to like this next part. "I, uh, don't have a condom..."

She stared at him, her eyes wide and her mouth hanging open. "Dude! You rented out the whole freaking warehouse, no staff on site, and we haven't seen each other in days. Did you *not* think I was going to seize the opportunity? We're basically in a warehouse full of tiny coat closets! This is my jam!"

Ty gave her a wry smile, shaking his head. "Ash. I mean, I have one in my truck."

Her head jerked. “What are you going to do, run out to the truck, grab something from the glove compartment, and sprint back in?” Her voice went high at the end.

Yeah, that was a pretty sucky idea.

Ty just shook his head and leaned in for a kiss. “I’ll bring one next time. I promise.”

She returned his gentle kiss, a tiny crinkle of annoyance still present between her eyebrows.

Then she stilled and looked down his body, a contemplative look taking over her expression.

Oh, hell.

“I’ve got an idea.”

Chapter Eighteen

October 17, Sunday

Ashley

Ashley sat up and gently pulled at his zipper, each downward tug causing her heart to hitch in excitement.

"You got to eat. Now it's my turn."

Ty froze and grabbed at her hands, halting her progress.

Sex-personified, with want humming through her veins, Ashley peeked up from under her eyelashes, making eye contact. "Don't worry. I won't make a mess."

Frozen, Ty watched as she rallied from his grip and continued her undressing of him.

When she pulled his cock out of his pants, her palms closed around him and he let out a soft grunt.

Yes.

Fuck, he was so warm and smooth.

Without taking her eyes from his cock, she murmured, "Do you want to be standing up or laying down for this. I'll also accept kneeling." Ashley rubbed her thumb over his tip and he groaned again.

"Laying down."

"Good choice," she hummed in agreement, her fingers still playing.

As soon as he laid back, she pounced over him, putting her lips on him.

She licked, nipped, sucked, bit, breathed. Ashley pulled out every tool in her arsenal, prepared to make this the best experience of his life. Anytime she sensed he was getting close, she'd back off.

The most exquisite torture.

While she played, his hands started to roam as well. "Can we do this at the same time? I'm hungry again, too," he asks.

Around his cock, she moaned, "No."

This was just for him.

Maybe he'd remember her when she was gone.

Arousal coursed through Ashley's veins like molten lava, heat pooling low in her belly as she kneeled between his legs. She could feel the evidence of her desire, past and present, coating her inner thighs as she stroked and sucked Ty's cock, reveling in the weight of him on her tongue. His musky scent surrounded her, filling her senses until all she could focus on was giving him pleasure.

Ty's hands tangled in her hair, tugging in a way that sent sparks of desire straight to her clit. She moaned around his length, the vibrations drawing a strangled groan from his throat.

"Ash, I need—" His hips bucked, shoving his cock deeper into her mouth. "Fuck, I can't—we have to—"

She pulled back with an obscene pop, meeting his lust-blown gaze. "This is for you, baby," she rasped, fisting his cock in a firm grip. "Just enjoy."

Without waiting for a response, she dove back down, hollowing her cheeks as she took him as deep as she could. His hands tightened in her hair and she moaned encouragement, the slight pain heightening her own arousal.

On and on she worked him, breaking out all her finest techniques; edging him until he was practically whimpering by the time she finally let him come.

Ty had a spectacular climax, groaning harsh, as he pumped up into her mouth. Ashley made sure to catch every single drop, reveling in his salty flavor.

Not every guy tasted the same, some were downright gross.

But Ty?

He must have the diet of a God because he fucking tasted like forbidden fruit.

Divine.

Proud and satisfied, Ashley sat up and stared down at her man.

Ty's hand rested on his chest like he was checking his heartbeat and he stared up at her in awe.

Still feeling the wet between her legs, Ashley coyly wiped at the corner of her mouth and leaned forward, pushing her breasts into his chest. "The next time I say bring a condom, I mean it," she purred. "Or you're taking me bareback. Consequences be damned."

Ty groaned, his soft cock twitching against her hip. "Is that a promise or a threat?"

"A little of both," Ashley chuckled, nipping at his earlobe.

This was dangerous territory, she knew. But with Ty, she found she didn't really care.

"Holy fuck, Ash." Ty panted, dragging a hand through his hair. "That was..." Ashley sat up, watching him struggle to find words.

A surge of feminine pride flowed through her at the utterly rocked look on Ty's face.

She had done that.

Reduced him to a quivering mess with just her mouth.

"Exhausting?" she said, smirking.

Ty huffed out a laugh. "Fucking, yes." His eyes darkened as he met her gaze. "But now I know my game plan for tonight back at your place. Payback. Glorious payback."

Heat coiled low in Ashley's stomach at the promise in his words. She leaned in close again, scraping her nipples against his chest and licking at his lips. He opened up quickly to kiss her back but Ashley pulled away with a satisfied hum, standing to get dressed. Ty watched her with hooded eyes, his attention glued to her glistening upper thighs. Absently, he licked his lips and looked like he was going to go for round two before she quickly pulled up her spandex pants and zipped up the paint-splattered suit the rest of the way.

"Suit up, chuck. We only have a little bit of time left."

Ty groaned, head falling back. "You're evil. I need time to recover. I can't feel my legs."

She smiled at him.

See? He wasn't the only one with porn star skills. She could hang.

"All's fair in love and war, darling," Ashley chuckled and nudged him with her foot. "Now get dressed. We've still got a game to finish."

With that, she darted out of the small house they'd taken refuge in, chuckling. The thrill of victory and power coursed through her veins. She felt wild, unrestrained in a way she never had before.

A few minutes later, she heard him jogging about the warehouse, looking for her.

Ashley relished the buzz of poaching for each other. The hunter and the hunted.

Each narrow miss of her paintballs had her pulse racing, body buzzing with energy and life.

After fifteen minutes of stalking each other, laughter on both sides, the buzzer signaled the end of their time. Ashley emerged from her hiding spot, paint-splattered and breathless.

Ty was waiting for her by the entrance, a mix of exhaustion and arousal on his face. "Rematch next week?" he asked as she approached.

Oh, Daddy wanted to play again?

Yes, please. Maybe she could sneak in a toy or two.

"You're on," Ashley said, eyes glinting with mischief.

Ty wrapped his arm around Ashley's shoulders as they walked out of the paintball arena, laughter mingling with the thrill of their adventure. The chill of the night air did nothing to dampen the heat lingering between them. The memory of their encounter – and promise of future ones – left Ashley's skin tingling with anticipation.

Her time in the US was meant to be one last taste of freedom before returning to fulfill her duty. But, she didn't want to give this up.

She didn't want to give *Ty* up.

Duty or desire?

Ashley sighed, glancing at Ty as he unlocked the Explorer and opened the door for her. If only the choice were that simple.

Her life had *never* been her own.

As Ty slid into the driver's seat beside her to bring her back to her place, Ashley wondered.

Was it possible to have both duty and desire?

As Ashley stared at Ty's beautiful profile, she couldn't stop the thought from taking root.

Duty be damned.

Chapter Nineteen

October 18, Monday

Ty

Ty took a seat next to his teammates, their tense banter filling the locker room as they prepared for an afternoon skate. They were all pretending as if they hadn't heard Blaine strong-arm their coach, and based on Coach Montgomery's attitude since, the assistant coaches hadn't felt like cluing him in.

But even with the drama circulating on the team, at least his relationship with Ashley was going well. As he laced up, he couldn't help but grin as he thought about paintball with Ashley.

As if reading his mind, Tommy asked, "So, how did the date date go? You've been uncharacteristically silent today. Even for you." Tommy reached out and rat-tailed him with a spare towel.

"Dick," Ty laughed, blocking the snap mostly with his arm. "It was awesome. She's insanely competitive—which I knew—but I wasn't quite expecting her to be such a deadly shot."

"Did wittle Tyler get a boo boo from a wittle paintball?" Jason chuckled and tossed a roll of tape at him. "Oops, sorry, did that hurt you?"

Ty chucked another roll back at him, knocking Jason in the chest. "No, but only because she took mercy on me. I swear, her aim was dead on. I'm not entirely convinced she's not an Olympic shooter or something because it was like she placed them exactly...all while acting like it was a new experience for her."

"So, she's a liar?" Bobby remarked, barely looking up from lacing up his skates.

"No, she's not a liar." Ty sighed and shook his head. Of course, Bobby would go there. The guy was even more sensitive than Ty was. "She was just..." How could he explain it? "I don't know. She's...hiding something." Real clever use of words, Ty. He shook his head at the brilliance of his own description.

Ilya nabbed one of the tape rolls from the floor and examined it before tossing it back to Ty. "Hiding what?"

"The fuck if I know." Ty shrugged. "Dude, I have no idea. She's cagey about her home life and why she needs to go back. She makes her family sound like the fucking Mafia."

"She in a cult?"

Ty looked at Tommy and cocked his head.

That didn't sound so far-fetched with how she described her father...

Tommy shot him a wink, "She's crazy, man. Stay away from cults, trust me. Don't fuck with that."

Ilya gave a grunt from across the room where he was finishing up a wax job on his stick's tape.

Ty raised his eyebrows at Ilya, but the captain simply shook his head.

Okay...that would be a story he'd need to ask about another time.

"So, she's definitely hiding *something*. Maybe a cult. Or *probably* something else." Jason shot a heavy look over to Tommy for jumping to that conclusion. "Have you actually tried just...asking her why they need *her* home specifically?"

Shit.

"Well..."

His teammates laughed and Ty felt his cheeks pinken. "It's not like that. I try to ask. Like...all the time. I try to get her to open up about her home life and shit, but she totally freezes me out. I want to know more. I want to know if there's a way I can help. She doesn't act like she's being abused or anything, but you can't always tell. I just wish...fuck, I just wish she'd talk to me about it. I'd..." Ty swallowed hard and looked around at the guys who had quieted down and were watching him, "I'd fucking do anything to help her stay, if that was what she wanted."

"Would you go with her if *that* was what she wanted?" Bobby asked, now completely geared up and lounging on the bench, looking at Ty with a sober expression.

Fuck.

Ty thought for a moment about Ashley's challenging smile, her thirst for life, the way she leaned in and stared at him when he spoke—like each word was infinitely important. Or how sometimes he would catch her looking at him like he was some mythic creature, and she couldn't understand what he was doing with her.

The same look he found himself giving to her, time and time again.

"Yeah, I'd find a way to go with her," Ty admitted softly, eyes on his skates. Hell, if he had a few more practices and games of witnessing the GM and AGMs frowning down at him from the mezzanine, maybe Cyclones' management would *pay* for his airfare to leave and never come back.

Plus, it's not like her family would *really* kill him for being with her. This wasn't the fucking Stone Ages. The country was known for being patriarchal but revolution was sweeping through the cities and towns. It sounded like Ashley's family was a part of that 'old guard,' but again, it's not like hiring hitmen was cheap...he assumed.

If he had to find work over in Dariqat, maybe the *GPANL* would let him help with their various land projects. Ty could work to get the green light for the land protection project that was getting stonewalled left and right. It wasn't as ideal as staying here with Ashley and playing hockey but...if that's what it took, then he would do it.

"If she's leaving soon, then you better find out if she feels the same way. Otherwise...you're the one left with the broken heart, my brother." Tommy slapped him on the shoulder and walked past him, his skates adding a couple of inches to his already over six-foot frame.

Fuck.

"For once, Tommy might be right. Gotta get down to the bottom of that shit or it will eat you up. If you think she's hiding something...then she probably is. And you don't want to be raked over the coals if you find out later on that it's something...unpleasant." Jason gave him a quick nod and pushed up, clomping along after Tommy and most of the other men as they filed out of the locker room.

Ilya stared down at him. On skates, the guy was damn near seven feet tall. With Ty being seated on the bench, it made the height difference even more apparent. And awkward. Ilya just gave him a heavy look and simply said, "That's not even considering what sort of shit she's hiding and how it could affect the team once it gets out. She might not be hiding anything," he rushed to add when he saw Ty open his mouth to protest. "But you've been bitten before, kid. You know how this goes. If it looks like shit, and smells like shit..." He trailed off. "Just, be careful, yeah?"

Ty gave a small nod and Ilya ambled off after the others.

Bobby was the only one left in the locker room, still studying Ty from his own seated position.

"Just say it," Ty said on a sigh.

Bobby shook his head and stood, double-checking his socks and tape job. "You already know what you feel. You already know you feel uncomfortable with how she's acting. You're either going to ask her and get answers, or you're not. I've known you since college and I've seen the women you choose. It doesn't give me a lot of hope."

Ty frowned. "Dude."

Bobby shrugged. "I don't know. Maybe he feels that way about you too. Maybe she could love you back, but she just can't do shit about it, and you're destined to fail either way. Regardless, you gotta decide where your line is. And you gotta decide if you're going to want someone to love you with the same fierceness that you love them. Because all I'm hearing is that you're doing a whole lot of giving—or at least are trying to—and she's...well, she's not making one single fucking concession. So, you gotta ask yourself, what's that say about her level of commitment to you?"

Fuck.

Without waiting for an answer, Bobby exited the locker room, leaving Ty alone with the staleness of the soured air.

It had only been a few weeks. Asking Ashley for 'concessions' or to 'prove' her feelings was stupid.

And fast.

And...stupid.

Shit, he already thought that.

And yet...here he was, already there.

He was falling for her and it had only been a few weeks. Maybe she felt the same.

Weirder and shorter romances had happened for people.

But just because it happened fast for him, didn't mean that Ashley felt the same. So even though he was dying to understand her and to figure out what was happening behind the scenes, maybe she wasn't ready to share that yet—even if she planned to, eventually.

Because, at the end of the day, 'they' weren't even a month old, even though it felt like it had been longer than that.

Fuck.

He heard the buzzer from the rink blare and he swore as he bustled out of the room.

As they started their drills, Ty's thoughts stayed on Ashley. What was so important that they needed her home?

Money?

Doubtful given the wad she dropped at the auction.

Help around the house? In the family business?

He tried to think of what he knew of Dariqat...not much. He'd have to jump on the computer and do some more searches for popular family work, traditions, customs, and the like. Maybe that would clue him in a little more.

Ty found himself daydreaming about the future. He pictured walking hand-in-hand with Ashley along a sandy beach at sunset, both laughing together without a care in the world. Or cozied up by a fireplace on a snowy winter's day, sipping hot chocolate and sharing funny stories.

He could envision road trips across the country, with the wind in their hair and nothing but endless possibilities ahead. Hiking through forests filled with towering pines, the fresh mountain air rejuvenating their spirits. Trying new cuisines at hole-in-the-wall restaurants in cities near and far, making new discoveries at every turn.

The more he imagined, the more Ty realized just how much he wanted to experience with Ashley. He was drawn to her kind heart, captivated by her beauty, and longed to truly know the woman beneath the surface.

She was unlike anyone he had ever met.

During a brief pause in their training, Ty took a deep breath and allowed himself to acknowledge his uncertainties. Yes, he had his doubts about Ashley, but he also recognized the unique connection they shared.

And maybe that was enough to give this relationship a real chance.

With renewed resolve, Ty poured his energy into each drill, his body moving in tandem with his teammates. The sound of their skates slicing through the ice and the crisp slap of pucks against their sticks filled the air.

Despite his uncertainties, Ty couldn't deny the excitement that bubbled up inside him every time he thought about a prospective future with Ashley—a future filled with laughter, adventure, and unbridled passion.

With a smile playing at the corners of his lips, he vowed to face the next two months with an open mind and an unwavering determination to make things work, no matter what obstacles they might encounter along the way.

He was all in; he just hoped she was too.

Because even though he was *just Ty*, he felt like somehow, that could be enough for her.

Chapter Twenty

October 20, Wednesday

Ashley

Ashley's heart raced with anticipation as she prepared for a romantic dinner date with Ty at Versailles, the stunning, famous rooftop terrace restaurant in Springfield. She carefully selected a beautiful gold and red dress that accentuated her figure, giving her an air of confidence and allure. The silky fabric felt luxurious against her skin, reminding her of the roses that perfumed her mother's gardens in Dariqat.

She twirled in front of the mirror, admiring how the dress hugged her curves.

Ty was going to be the one demanding a coat closet tonight.

The very thought sent a shiver down her spine.

And Versailles was known for being discreet. A place where secrets were kept.

So even though it was fancy as hell, she might just get her coat closet rendezvous tonight.

And there was no risk in getting outed for it.

The thought filled her with a wicked glee.

A coat closet with Ty?

"Finally..." she whispered, even though she wasn't entirely convinced he'd go for it.

She added a spritz of her favorite perfume and slipped on a pair of gold heels before heading down the hall, heart fluttering with excitement.

A knock on the door made Ashley's heart leap into her throat.

Jeeze, it's not like she was a freaking virgin. And yet...Ty made her feel exactly like that.

In the best way possible.

Cherished, but not untouchable.

Desired, but not trashy.

Seen, but also heard.

How he managed to do all that when every man, including everyone in her family, up until then had failed...

Taking a deep breath to steady her nerves, she opened the door to reveal Ty looking absolutely dashing in a tailored suit. His bright blue eyes sparkled, and his warm smile sent a jolt through her body.

"Wow, Ash," Ty's eyes were taking in every detail of her outfit. "You look incredible." He took her hand and pressed a soft kiss to her knuckles. Ashley's cheeks heated.

"Thank you," she replied, fighting an outright smile. "You look pretty amazing yourself."

"Shall we?" he asked, extending his arm to her.

"Absolutely." Ashley slid her hand into the crook of Ty's elbow, their fingers brushing against each other, igniting the familiar flame of desire between them. His scent was reminiscent of fresh pine, and it reminded her of their dates to the local parks.

As they walked out to Ty's Explorer, Ashley stole glances at him. He was truly captivating, with his clean-shaven face, strong jawline, and those expressive eyes that seemed to see right through her. And that smile of his—it could melt the heart of even the most stoic woman.

Even her.

"Excited for tonight?" Ty asked, breaking the silence. "I'm finally giving you the fancy-schmancy date that all the schmucks take you on."

She'd have been insulted if he hadn't been wearing such a huge grin.

"Definitely," she replied, her voice barely above a whisper. "I've been looking forward to this all week."

"Me too," Ty said, his eyes softening when he looked at her.

As they drove through the city, they caught up on their work weeks, Ashley sharing what she could of her latest case and Ty informing her about a team rotation shake-up.

She had to savor these moments with Ty, as her time in the United States was dwindling. The thought of returning to Dariqat and fulfilling her duties weighed heavily on her heart. But for now, she pushed those thoughts aside, focusing on the man beside her and the evening ahead.

The sun sank below the horizon, bathing the skyline in a warm orange glow, as Ty and Ashley arrived at the restaurant.

"Versailles awaits, my lady," Ty said, grinning as he parked the truck. Their eyes met, and Ashley felt a surge of something powerful pass between them. It was more than attraction; it was a connection forged by trust and vulnerability.

Fuck, it was going to hurt to lose this.

Ashley leaned in for a tender kiss.

And as they stepped out of the truck and made their way into the building's lobby with its exquisite indoor, direct elevator, Ashley knew that whatever the future held, this time with Ty would forever be etched in her memory.

Almost immediately upon their arrival to the restaurant lobby, they were escorted to their waiting table. The dome above them protected them from the biting autumn weather, and the string lights and glowing fires bathed the rooftop terrace in a warm, beautiful glow.

"The view always takes my breath away," Ashley sighed, taking in the sights below them.

Ty smiled, his blue eyes fixed on her. "Not as incredible as my view right now."

“Cliché,” she laughed, raising her glass of ice water in a toast.

He gave her a saucy wink, which caused Ashley to duck her head with a grin, a pleasurable warmth spreading through her.

As they perused the menu, the conversation flowed effortlessly between them, punctuated by laughter and knowing glances.

Their conversation took a somber turn when Ashley shared about her issues with Garrett Baylor.

"He loves his son so fucking much it hurts. It's so painful to watch him succumb again and again."

"You've worked with this guy a lot?"

So far she hadn't mentioned his name, just the situation, but with how comfortable she was getting with Ty, she wouldn't be surprised if it slipped out in pillow talk one night.

"He was one of my first cases, actually. So, it's been a few long years. He has my cell and email and frequently directs mail to my apartment. I'd be worried about that except the only time he calls is to get something for his son. I think he would let himself starve before letting me actually help him."

"And the kid?"

"Is the sweetest damn thing on the entire planet. He's had a really hard time adjusting to the changes in his life. It went from an unstable life with mom, to an unstable life with dad, to a dangerous life with mom, to...Well, you get the picture. The kid needs stability. He needs safety. He needs a roof over his head, food in his belly, and clothes that fit. He shouldn't have to dumpster dive for food and have to bring it back to their place in their tent city." Ashley swallowed hard and looked away, blinking quickly to dispel the rising tears. Her rant got a little emotional at the end and this wasn't the time or the place.

Plus, what guy actually wanted to hear about that on a date?

After taking another second to compose herself, using all of the skills her education provided her, she wiped her feelings from her face and turned to Ty.

Only to freeze.

From the soft look on his face, she realized…

He wanted to hear it.

From the look on his face, Ty wanted to hear *all* of it.

Fuck, he was so *good*. So pure.

He was a Goddamn angel.

Ashley pushed back the lump in her throat and wiped quickly at her eye, careful not to smear her mascara. "Nope, we're not going there. Tonight is about my fancy-schmancy dinner. There shouldn't be crying on dates."

Ty cocked his head to the side and stared at her, his expression still soft. "Ash, if you've never cried on a date, you've been dating the wrong men." He gave her a small grin. "Then again, I think we already know that."

Ashley laughed and rolled her eyes. "You consider it a success to make your dates cry?"

She felt like it had to be asked.

Ty smiled back, his teeth radiant in the dim room. "No, but the fact that you trust me enough to open up to me that much, to let emotion take hold? That's a win, Princess. It means I'm getting somewhere. It means that whatever walls you have spent years fortifying," he leaned forward like he was imparting a secret, "I'm behind them. No turning back now, Ash. You're mine."

Fuck.

Ashley took a sharp inhale.

He really was.

He was in *there*.

And she had no idea how to get him out.

Or if she even wanted to evict him.

Double fuck.

"So, now that we already opened the emotional floodgates, tell me something about your family. Anything you want: which one is your favorite brother, a story about your mom, your father's worst trait. You pick."

Shoot. Okay. She could do this.

"Um, my favorite brother is Idris, despite him being my dad's show pony."

There. That wasn't too much.

"Show pony?" Ty laughed.

"Yes, show pony. My father says 'Jump' and Idris asks, 'How high?'"

"And this is who you chose for your favorite?" His dark blonde eyebrows were arched, causing adorable wrinkles in his forehead. It made the small scar above his right brow ripple.

Adorable.

"Yes. He's still my favorite, even though he's bossy and high-handed." Ashley sighed happily. "Because even though he's as desperate for our father's approval as any of us, he still openly adores me, and always puts me first. Always. He's the whole reason I was allowed to come to the States in the first place."

Ty's expression turned eager, and she was all too aware of how much she was sharing.

And yet...

She couldn't seem to stop.

"I don't know what deal he struck or what he promised our father, but he got me my Visa and here I am. He's also the reason I have a college degree—something that I probably would have never been afforded otherwise."

Ashley didn't need to go into details about why broodmares don't need college degrees.

"So, he made some sort of deal, and here you are. Having a chance to live life on your terms, even if it has a deadline."

"Yeah." The word fell from her lips.

Damn, she really owed her brother a hug.

And now she felt even worse that she had chewed him out on the phone earlier that day for not taking her side when she was lamenting about the Garett Baylor situation.

"Do you talk to him often?"

Ashley flushed, somehow embarrassed at her answer, though she knew Ty wouldn't tease her for it. "Yeah, we talk at least once a week. Sometimes more, sometimes less."

"About?"

"Anything. Everything. Usually about my tough cases at work." She leaned forward, imparting her own secret. "Don't tell my boss, but I use names when talking to him about the cases. I figured a random dude in a random Middle Eastern country was probably never going to have cause to run into any of the clients from my caseload."

Ty gasped and grabbed at his chest. "Ms. Winters! That is a serious breach of confidentiality!"

Ashley shook her head, kicking his shin lightly, under the table. "Yeah, yeah. They can fire me soon enough." She fought back the damn burn in her eyes again. "I'll be gone anyways."

Ty reached out and held her hand, his calloused fingers interlaced between her own.

"You mentioned earlier that your father puts a lot of pressure on you. What does he do?"

Ashley hesitated for a moment, her gaze flickering at the tablecloth before she met Ty's eyes again. "He's...an influential figure back home. My whole family is, really. They have certain expectations of me, and while I understand where they're coming from, sometimes it feels like I'm being smothered."

"Do you ever talk to them about how you feel?"

"God, no," she admitted. "They aren't that type of family, but even so, I don't want to disappoint them. If they can all handle the expectations then so can I. But at the same time, I want to follow my own path and make my own choices. It's a constant struggle."

"For what it's worth, I think you're incredibly brave for standing up for yourself and pursuing your dreams, even if it does feel like a short stop on a long ride."

"I wish it was longer," Ashley grumbled.

"Life is full of surprises," Ty said, his eyes locked on hers. "A lot can happen in two months."

The electric chemistry they shared seemed to vibrate in the air around them, making it difficult for her to focus on anything else but his optimistic, bright smile.

Day by day.

She needed to remember to live day by day.

With him.

With her Ty.

Ashley shook off the melancholy and grabbed her glass. "Cheers," Ashley agreed, clinking her drink against his.

As the night unfolded, she found herself wishing that she had the guts to stand up to her father and fight for her shot with the sweet man across from her.

If Ashley wasn't so convinced that her father might have him killed for messing up their family's plans, then maybe she would have.

After dinner, they headed back to Ty's luxury apartment building. The entire building was owned by Cyclones' management, and they renovated the entirety to be condos fit for royalty. She would know. But even so, each tenant was able to design and decorate the apartment as they would their own home. Looking around at Ty's apartment, Ashley once again marveled at the warmth and coziness of the space. It didn't feel like just a stowaway spot for players on the team who might not know how long they would last in the city.

It felt like a...*home*.

Ty's home.

The walls were adorned with hockey memorabilia and framed pictures of Ty with his friends and family. It was intimate and inviting, reflective of the man who stood beside her.

She never failed to appreciate just how *pure* it was.

How *Ty* it was.

"I'll get us something to drink?" Ty asked, motioning towards his well-stocked bar. He didn't wait for her to answer.

"Actually," Ashley said, "I wanted to ask you something that I kept forgetting at dinner."

"Hmm?" He looked up from pouring the after-dinner drinks.

By now he knew what she wanted to drink without even asking—why did that give her such warm fuzzies?

Ashley leaned against the kitchen counter, putting on her best puppy dog look as she took the offered drink. "Ty, I know it's a lot to ask, especially during the season, but would you be willing to do a small event for the kiddos I work with? These kids have been through so much, and I think meeting a real-life hockey star would absolutely make their day. Maybe even year."

"Buttering me up?"

"Always." Ashley tossed him a wink, but then turned somber. "I'm serious. It would mean the world to these kids. I can think of at least three who have mentioned that they want to be hockey players when they grow up. It would be...amazing."

Ty slid into one of the stools at the butcher block island, giving her an intense gaze as he processed her request.

"All right," he agreed. "I'm in. Tell me when and where...though, do me a favor and check the team calendar first, yeah?"

Ashley luxuriated in the warmth that spread through her chest when Ty flashed her a dazzling smile. But once again, Ashley had to question why fate would give her such a kind man, only to rip him away.

Chapter Twenty-One

October 27, Wednesday

Ty

Ty's body ached as he leaned over his thighs and rested his stick across his knees. He sucked in a burning breath and blinked the stinging sweat from his eyes. Across from Ty on the other side of the face-off circle, Bobby's leg seemed to be holding up well as he smoothly skated and assumed a pose similar to Ty's.

Thank God Bobby was back on Ty's line tonight—they needed his gritty style. With his rapid turnaround in performance, their forward line was in sync and dominating. The Cyclones' defense? Not so much.

There was no way to miss the strained expression on Ilya's face. The usually laser-focused captain appeared distracted, his gaze distant and movements slower than usual. Ty frowned, concerned for his teammate but unable to do anything about it right then.

"Daniels," sneered Andrews, a player from the opposing team. He leaned in close enough for Ty to feel his hot breath on his neck. "Saw someone from your exec team strolling around with one of our guys earlier this afternoon before the game, talking all about *you*. They must really want you gone if they're personally begging other teams to take your ass. Talk about overpaying and underdelivering."

Asshole.

Ty clenched his teeth, trying not to let Andrews' taunt derail him...and failing.

With a silent vow to make that smug bastard eat his words, Ty focused intently on Ian's hands in the face-off circle.

Ian won the puck and shoveled it over to Ty. A sudden surge of adrenaline propelled him into action. He danced around the opposing players, weaving through them with rage lending him strength. With one last burst of speed, Ty snapped off a quick wrist shot that sent the puck sailing past the flailing goalie and into the net. The bench erupted in cheers, and Ty raised his fist triumphantly as he skated back toward his teammates.

Ty would have loved to give the opposing bench a single-finger salute but didn't want to send a bad message to the kids in the crowd.

He'd have to make sure to chirp something back to Andrews the next time they were on the ice together.

Ty couldn't help but let a grin stretch across his face. He felt electric, alive—this was what he lived for. But as he settled onto the bench, his gaze caught something that made his stomach twist—Blaine, their assistant GM, leaning over the back divider, whispering something in Coach Montgomery's ear.

Why the hell was he at another away game?

He hadn't flown out with the team...

"Great shot out there," Bobby said, clapping him on the shoulder as they slid down the bench in unison.

Ty barely registered the praise as he watched their head coach's expression darken, frustration and agitation etched into the lines of his face.

"Thanks, Bobby," Ty murmured distractedly.

What could Blaine be telling Coach Montgomery that would cause such a reaction? His mind raced, attempting to piece together the puzzle. Ty looked down the bench to see if anyone else had noticed, but all the men were focused on the game...as *he* should have been...and yet...

As the game progressed Coach Montgomery began implementing some of the more *unusual* line changes they'd practiced earlier that week, and Ty's concern grew.

What the hell was going on?

Whenever he was on the bench, Ty kept stealing glances at the coach, whose body posture remained tense, as if straining against invisible restraints.

After yet another goal was pushed past Teemu and the Cyclones lost their lead, the men on the bench started voicing their complaints.

"Damn it," Jason growled, his eyes narrowed. "What's he thinking?"

"Who knows?" Tommy grumbled, equally frustrated. Neither of them seemed to have noticed Blaine's presence earlier.

Ty bit his lip, wondering if he should mention what he saw. But before he could decide, the opposing team scored again, tying up the game. The groans from their bench were painful.

Damn, that was quick.

The game wore on, and the Cyclones lost all hint of their earlier dominance—their once-fluid movements disjointed and chaotic.

Ty did his best to keep his cool, but when one of their other rookies from the fourth line was substituted for Bobby, Ty started to feel the hold on his *usually* nonexistent temper fray.

As if sensing the mounting pressure, Coach Montgomery looked increasingly agitated, his shoulders hunched, and jaw set as he watched the game deteriorate.

Then, as if things couldn't get any more confusing, another assistant GM—who *also* did not come on the team's jet—approached the area behind the bench and summoned Coach Montgomery over to him.

What in the actual fuck was going on!?

Out of the corner of his eye, Ty watched his coach's face grow even more strained as he nodded and started to whisper furiously back to the AGM. The assistant coaches gathered around him to somewhat hide the interchange but otherwise gave them curious looks. Clearly, they didn't know exactly what was going on either.

Coach Montgomery's frown deepened as he listened to the AGM, his shoulders tensing. Ty could see the veins in his neck visibly throbbing with frustration. Whatever news was relayed to the coach, it was clear that it wasn't good.

"Line one, get ready," one of the assistant coaches snapped. Ty stood, preparing to swing over the small wall as soon as the current line was signaled to make their way to the bench.

"Hold up." Coach Montgomery pulled away from the retreating AGM and looked down the line at the confused faces of the men on the team. "Derrick, Pavel, go back to the rotations we had at the start of the game. Bobby, back on one. Jason, back on two. Tommy, swing back to center." As he continued barking out the original line-ups, Ty could almost feel his teammates sag in relief.

Thank *fuck*.

Feeling a prickle on his neck, Ty turned, looking around curiously. Seeing nothing that could have prompted such a feeling, he started to turn back to the ice when he noticed Blaine sitting a few rows back. The man was scowling at Coach Montgomery, his face dark, and his arms crossed. The man stood, his movements jerky and sharp, drawing the attention of a few neighboring fans. Without dropping his scowl, the AGM took out his phone, tapped the screen, put it to his ear, pivoted, and stormed up the stairs.

A shiver crept down Ty's spine.

"Now, line one, you're up."

Ty whipped around and placed his hip on the short wall, scanning the ice and waiting for his chance to leap out there. Within seconds he was skating furiously across the ice, trying to anticipate the next pass. But as he played, his thoughts raced. The two different AGMs at an away game, both summoning and saying something to their coach, and demanding that he coach the team 'their' way. What the fuck? This wasn't how things were done! It was...insane! Was it even legal? Why was Montgomery even allowing it?

An unexpected turnover across the ice led to Andrews getting the puck and barreling down the rink. With a deep breath, Ty clenched his abs and launched himself at the opposing player, catapulting them into the boards. The crowd roared and pounded at the glass above them as he pushed back to his feet. As Ty continued to dance back and forth on defense, a brief thought struck him—would this be his last game for the Cyclones?

He banished the thought and stretched his stick out to intercept a weak pass. The puck caught on his stick and Ty lunged forward trying to slow the game that had spiraled so quickly out of control. He felt the impending hit breathing down his back, so he shot the puck forward to ice it...then was promptly flattened by an open ice hit that left him nearly seeing stars.

Fucking hell *that hurt.*

Chapter Twenty-Two

November 1, Monday

Ty

Days later, Ty walked inside the small event hall, and the excited chatter of children filled the air. The meet and greet was held at a local community center, its walls adorned with colorful posters of the Cyclones and inspirational quotes. Ashley looked radiant in a simple get-up of jeans and a t-shirt—a stark contrast to her usually elegant attire.

Ty was the man of the hour—a small, quaint gathering of Ashley's caseload as a way to build a bit more community and happiness for her families. He was more than willing to offer up some one-on-one time with the people that she worked so hard to help. Pictures, stories, and tossing a ball, or hitting a street hockey ball, were nothing compared to what Ashley did for these people.

Plus, if the latest round of rumors were true, he'd be traded soon, so it was good that Ashley slipped this on the calendar so quickly...she wasn't the only one operating under an assumed deadline now.

"Ty!" shouted a young boy who recognized him. A group of excited kids swarmed around Ty, their eyes wide with admiration. As he squatted down to greet them eye to eye, he had to hide a wince at the movement.

His body had taken a beating over the last week since their dinner at Versailles.

A game in Buffalo, the next one at home, then back-to-back games with the Panthers and Hurricanes, both away, and then a game at home last night.

His body was fucking spent.

"Can we get a picture with you?" a little girl asked, while another tugged on his sleeve.

"Sure thing, kiddo," Ty replied, feeling his face wrinkle with how big he smiled at her.

Fuck, she was adorable with her missing front teeth.

He spread his smile at all the kids, even the big ones who hung back, trying to be cool.

Without getting a chance to even take off his jacket, he was swept up in their eagerness as they rambled on about their favorite games and how they dreamed of playing hockey one day.

After fifteen minutes of being talked at, Ashley finally swooped in to save him, ushering the children away so he could take a breath.

Stretching his back as Ashley redirected the various children, Ty noticed some men hanging out in the corner of the room, shooting the shit, and all still wearing their coats. One man a little further down was still wearing his coat, beanie, and gloves, like it was freaking minus ten degrees inside. Meanwhile, some of the women over on the neighboring wall were showing some impressive displays of skin. The room wasn't cold enough to warrant the winter gear, but it sure as fuck wasn't eighty-five degrees in there either. He didn't want to see their cleavage—they were barking up the wrong tree.

Sorry, ladies. He was *happily* taken.

Not that they knew that.

"All right, all right. Let's all back up and give Mr. Daniels some space. Zane? Want to grab him a water bottle over from the table? Annaliese, do you want to take his jacket and put it with the others?"

At once, the kids rallied, all shouting out offers to help him with various items. One kid even started to try to untie his boots.

Ashley's gentle hands paused the almost-still-a-toddler's movements and pointed over to where the four-year-old's family was standing against the wall. After an exchange of quiet words, the kid sprinted over to his family and Ashley stayed squatted for a moment more to redo the double knot on Ty's boot.

What a view.

As if sensing his thoughts, she looked up and Ty cursed himself for the direction of his thoughts.

By the teasing in her eyes, she knew exactly where his thoughts had gone while she kneeled before him.

Minx.

Ashley stood and efficiently wiped her hands on her jeans while looking around at the various people mingling around. Quickly, she gave him the rundown.

"Okay, so I want to make sure that every kid gets a photo with you, including the parents. We can't share any on social media because of the confidential nature of our clients but Babs worked so hard this week to help me get the right protocols in place to make this possible. I just want—"

Ty reached out and snagged her tiny hand in his. Slowly, he brought it to his lips and gave the back of it a soft kiss. "Ash, Princess. I know. You've been living and breathing this for a week. I know all the rules and requirements. Just...sit back and relax. The hard part is done. Let me do my thing and let someone help *you* for once."

Her dark eyes were glued to his lips and when he was done talking, she gave a small shake of her head and blinked three times in rapid succession. After shaking off her daze, she looked around as well.

She took a big breath and on the exhale, a big smile spread over her dark lips. "Okay then. I release you to the wild ones. Go be free."

With a final kiss to her hand, that he still hadn't let go, Ty walked over to the nearest family where they were sitting at a small plastic table with matching plastic chairs around it.

He lowered himself into the chair—and so it began.

Family after family, Ty made his way around the room, taking tons of pictures, breaking out his favorite stories, and trying to pinpoint the exact pain points of each family. If there was a comment made about how they had never seen a game, he made a mental note to get them tickets. If a family wanted jerseys, he would pull out his phone on his walk to the next table to leave himself a note to have some sent.

He wasn't Santa and this wasn't December, but he could do his fucking best.

He made sure to treat the adults with as much care as he did the kids. Over the years, he heard the same stories again and again: *I would have gone pro but...I dated a pro hockey player once...I bet Wayne Gretzky couldn't compete with today's style of play.*

Same old, same old.

But his job was to make each person feel like their story was the first time he'd ever heard something like that. And for Ashley, he'd be eligible for an Oscar by the time he was done.

"Okay, everyone, for those who are willing, let's gather around for a group photo, just in case people have to leave early. We still have the hall for a few more hours, so no one feel pressured to head out. I just want to make sure we have photos for those who want them," Ashley called out, her voice carrying over the din of laughter and excitement.

The kids scrambled into position, jostling for a spot next to their hockey hero. Ty bent down on one knee, surrounded by grinning faces, his own smile never wavering. As the camera clicked, capturing the moment, Ty knew they were creating memories that would last a lifetime—not only for the children and their families, but for Ashley and him as well.

The happiness on her face would have him giving up his day off to do meet-and-greets for the rest of his life.

The laughter of the children filled the room, creating a warm and lively atmosphere. Ty was drawn into their world, enjoying the attention and engaging in playful banter with them. A small boy with tousled brown hair and freckles challenged Ty to a mock-hockey showdown, using makeshift sticks fashioned from rolled-up magazines.

"All right, champ, let's see what you've got!" Ty grinned, crouching down to the boy's level and brandishing his own magazine-stick. The child lunged forward, and Ty easily parried the move, winking at Ashley as she watched with an amused smile.

"Mr. Ty," another child piped up, tugging on his sleeve, "how do you shoot so fast?"

"Ah, that takes a lot of practice," Ty explained with a gentle chuckle. "You have to find the right balance between power and accuracy. Practice makes progress."

"Ty," a tiny girl with glasses asked shyly, "what's your favorite part of playing hockey?"

“Man, you’re going right for the deep stuff.” While the girl giggled, he thought on it. "I think my favorite part is being part of a team," he finally answered. "There's something special about working together towards a common goal, supporting each other both on and off the ice. Trusting that your teammate has your back and them trusting that you have their backs too."

"Like a family? Like when you love someone?" the girl ventured, her eyes wide.

"Exactly like that," Ty affirmed. Without meaning to, his eyes drifted to Ashley, who was standing nearby.

Exactly like that.

As the afternoon wore on, Ty answered every question the kids threw at him, never once losing his enthusiasm or warmth. He spoke to them about teamwork, perseverance, and the importance of believing in oneself—lessons that resonated not only on the ice, but in life as well.

With some of the stories Ashley had shared with him about the older kids, he might have shown his hand a little too much on the ‘sticking with their education’ advice, judging by how they rolled their eyes at him—but if something stuck, it was worth it.

"Thanks for doing this," Ashley said, her dark eyes shining with gratitude as Ty leaned against a wall to catch a quick sip of water and a moment of silence. "It means a lot to them. And me."

"Not a problem at all," he replied. "This has been awesome. They're all great people. If this can bring them a little light in a world that has been tough on them...it's all worth it to me."

As they locked gazes, a current of electricity passed between them, a potent reminder of their magnetic connection. But it was more than just physical desire; it was a bond deepened by shared laughter, playful banter, and the mutual joy of making a difference in the lives of others.

As families started serving themselves dinner and things quieted down, Ty found himself sitting next to Ashley at a small card table. They watched the kids play while the parents made their plates, and chuckled under their breath at the older kids that were in the corner gossiping and playing it cool.

"Today was amazing, Ashley," Ty said softly, his gaze lingering on a small boy who was talking eagerly to the man who was still bundled up in the corner, still avoiding the others. He thought he remembered the boy being paired up with the man and a woman who were sitting by the window table. But maybe he was getting the kids mixed up. He turned to Ashley. "The impact you have on these families is incredible. They really love you."

Ashley blushed, her cheeks turning a lovely shade of pink as she stared at the assembled families. "Thank you, Ty. But it's not just me. It takes a whole community to make a difference in their lives."

"Still," Ty insisted, "I think it's you. They trust *you*. It's really something else. I'm glad I got to be a part of this."

"Me too," Ashley agreed, her dark eyes meeting his for a moment before she looked back at the families.

Ty was hit with a wave of peace and contentment that he hadn't felt in years.

Damn this felt nice.

This was more than just a shared experience; it was a glimpse into Ashley's world and into what truly mattered to her. All afternoon, as he watched her cheer on the kids, her face alight with joy, he wanted to learn even more about the woman who had captured his heart. Whatever her responsibility was at home...they could fix it. Together. Somehow.

Because...

She was *it*.

She was his forever.

"Hey, Ty," a young boy sidled over to them, interrupting his thoughts. "What do you do when you're not playing hockey?"

Ty ruffled the boy's hair playfully. "Well, buddy, I love spending time outdoors. Hiking, fishing, camping—you name it."

"I like camping," the boy said tentatively.

"Maybe one day Ashley can get an outdoor adventure going for you guys," Ty suggested, grinning at the prospect. The boy's face lit up before he scampered back to his friends, leaving Ty and Ashley alone once more.

"Ty..."

Shit.

He turned to her, "Ash, we can—"

"No. No, we can't. Don't pull that shit. Not with my kids. You can pretend that this can last all you want when we're together, but *don't fuck with my kids.*"

Ty swallowed and cursed himself.

"Fuck, Ash. I—"

"Don't say anything. That's all. I'm willing to pretend with you, but I've been upfront all along about the reality. You can fantasize, but don't play with my families' hearts like that. They don't deserve that."

Ty's heart squeezed and he cracked his knuckles as he stared at the ground.

Fuck. She was right.

"Sorry." He glanced up at her from where he was leaning forward, his elbows on his knees. Her face was pinched and had an odd color to it. He stilled when he saw the tears in her eyes. *Fuck.*

She rolled her lips together and looked away.

As if by magic, Ty watched her take a couple of deep breaths and—*poof*, there it went.

All emotion wiped from her face and a plain blatant expression took over.

What the fuck had her life been like to have warranted such an aptitude to closing herself off like that?

Absently, Ashley nodded, still not looking at him.

Ty nudged her gently with his shoulder. "Forgive me?"

Ashley gave a rather unladylike grunt.

He couldn't stop his grin as he nudged her again.

"I noticed a coat closet on my way in."

Her lips twitched as she continued staring straight ahead.

"Maybe we can slip away for a few minutes?"

Her lips turned up even more.

"I can show you what I can do in limited space and what I can do with your mouth to force you to be quiet—"

She turned and covered his mouth with her small hand. "Will you behave?"

"Oh, how the tables have turned," Ty smiled big at her, and her expression turned soft.

Softer than it ever had been.

"I think your fan club would miss you."

"Feeling jealous?" Ty arched his eyebrow, and she shook her head with a smile.

"Maybe a little." The small bump of her shoulder against his revealed her fib.

She loved it possibly even more than he did. She just wanted her people to be happy, healthy, and safe.

"I'll try to be less awesome," Ty responded, feigning arrogance. "I'm just a natural with kids. Don't even get me started on how good I am with their moms." He blew out a low, long whistle.

Ashley rolled her eyes but couldn't suppress the smile that tugged at her lips. "I wasn't expecting the moms today. Some of them are happily married for Pete's sake!" she ended on a high-pitched giggle.

Over the course of the afternoon, some of the moms had certainly made their interest well-known if the number of crumpled phone numbers he had squirreled away in his pockets were any indication.

One woman had been so bold as to grope his ass during a photo op.

Ashley would rip that woman's head off if she knew.

Thankfully, Ty had been able to extract himself from that particular lady easily enough.

After the shitty start to his hockey season, Ashley's imminent doom and gloom departure, and now being called out for potentially promising something that he might not be able to fulfill? He was more than ready to drop the somber mood and get distracted by some adorable kids. He had been doing a pretty good job of not letting the roster rumors circulate in his head when he was around Ashley, instead choosing to live in the moment and even try to optimistically plan for a future together...but that was definitely getting harder and harder to block out.

"Time for us to grab dinner?"

After Ashley gave him a nod of agreement, he waved a hand toward the buffet table and invited Ashley to lead the way.

As he pushed up to follow her, he cursed himself out for giving the boy from earlier any false hope. Ty was a grown man, he could deal with the ups and downs and wondering what was going to come. The kid? He'd already suffered his fair share of life's blows.

After grabbing his own plate, he found an empty seat at the table where the bundled-up man and little boy were seated and shook off his self-chastising.

It was time to turn on the charm and make this an experience of a lifetime.

After all, he'd bet anything this was the kid that Ashley was talking about the other day. Therefore, the boy could use a win. And maybe so could his dad.

CHAPTER TWENTY-THREE

November 1, Monday

Ashley

Ashley watched Ty from an opposite table, her heart singing at Ty's easy rapport with the families. His bright blue eyes crinkled at the corners as he joked and listened to them intently. Under that pretty, handsome exterior was a kind heart.

But she knew that already.

Ty met Ashley's gaze, his expression softening as if to say, "Not too bad for being a rookie with kids, huh?"

She smiled back, falling for him a little more in that moment.

Damn, he'd be a good father. One day.

With someone else.

Ashley swallowed hard. Why did that make her want to cry? Or punch the unnamed and far-off future bitch in the throat?

As her own table fell into a lull in conversation, she heard Ty patiently field a barrage of questions from the kids.

"How fast can you skate?"

"About 25 miles per hour at top speed," he replied.

"How hard can you shoot the puck?" Connell joined in.

Ashley's stomach tensed at the appearance of Connell's dad. She had invited him and was hoping he'd come. But she was hoping he'd look better than he did.

He was obviously off the wagon.

Nausea bubbled up.

Was her proposal of signing over rights to Connell to the Jenkins what had pushed him completely over the edge?

Or had it been coming regardless?

"I can rocket it off at over a hundred miles per hour if I really wind up."

The kids oohed and aahed.

Ashley's own eyebrows shot up as she scooped some more food into her mouth. Damn. One hundred? How did she not know that?

Some of the adults around her started asking her questions about her future plans and the food spoiled in her mouth and stomach. Ashley lowered her utensils and dabbed politely at her lips.

What should she say?

"I, uh, I have to finally help take over the family business with my brothers. I'm hoping I can still continue some work similar to what I do here, but the odds aren't looking great."

As in, there was no way in hell her father would allow her to work.

"What does your family do?"

She hated that question.

"It's like a small empire. Lots of deals and trading. Little bit of everything." Not quite a lie.

Apparently, they also had stonewalled her boyfriend's passion nonprofit and its well-intentioned pursuit to protect sacred land from oil drilling. She had asked her brother about it randomly on one of their weekly phone calls, and he admitted that he had heard rumblings, but didn't know the details. Afraid to push further, she let it drop. She'd push more once she was back in Dariqat, but until then, she needed to coast under the radar.

"That sounds intense."

"You have no idea." She looked up when she felt movement beside her. Ty was pulling up a seat. He was like a bloodhound when it came to sniffing out information about her life in Dariqat.

"And you, Mr. Daniels? How do you feel about us losing our lovely Ms. Winters?"

He gave the interfering, but well-meaning, mother across the table a kind smile. "I'm not so convinced that we've lost her yet. I know it's a done deal on her end, but I'm doing my darndest to find a way to keep her here. Completely off topic—but if you see any sales on handcuffs, make sure you let me know?"

The tablemates chuckled as he had intended, and he tucked a piece of hair over her shoulder.

Ashley closed her eyes.

Fuck, she would miss him.

How was she going to survive losing him?

"And you, Ashley? Your family doesn't care that you have someone like Ty here in the States?"

Ashley froze. As did Ty next to her.

Woodenly, Ashley turned her head to face another mother, one of the ones who had gotten a little too close and personal with Ty earlier—they'd have to have words about that.

Ashley shook her head as she answered. "My father doesn't care about anything I have here in the States. He views it all as a rental experience, not actual, worthwhile life experience. As for my brothers, I think they would very much care that I was losing Ty, but unfortunately, in my country, we are not afforded the freedoms that people here in the States, and many other countries, are allowed. In fact, women are very much subservient in the family unit. The fact that I was able to get a degree or even have this small dose of freedom is frankly unheard of. So no, no one back home cares at all that I'm going to lose Ty." Ashley bit her tongue and pulled out her phone, desperate for a way to pretend to avoid the eyes converging on her. Both the sympathetic and envious ones. She could already see the woman counting down the days until she could track down Ty to heal his broken heart.

"Hey, who knows. Maybe I'll get a great deal from a hockey team in Europe. Give that a try. After all, there's lots of wilderness out there to hike as well." Ty chimed in on a chuckle, raising his bottle of water in a toast to the nosy women.

Ashley's heart jumped in her throat and she looked up at him. He gazed down, a soft look in her eyes.

"What do you think? If I'm ever in your neck of the woods, should I forget your number?" He asked it quietly so no one around them could hear it.

"You should absolutely forget my number," she whispered back, her heart rate increasing in fear for his safety should he try to track her down in Dariqat. Especially after she was already married.

"Do *you* want me to forget your number?" His voice was low and grumbly, just the way she liked it.

"I want you to be safe and—"

"Not what I asked, Princess." He gave her a long look. "Do *you* want me to *forget* about you?"

"Never," she gasped out on a whisper, staring up into his bright blue eyes and feeling the burn start in her throat. "I don't ever want you to forget me."

Ty leaned forward and swiped his nose against hers, his faint pine-fresh scent assaulting her senses. "Good. Because I won't. Ever."

He didn't add what they both knew he wanted to tack on at the end, which was 'and I'm not so convinced that this is goodbye.'

Foolish man.

Handsome, kind, wonderful, optimistic, foolish man.

Fuck, how she loved him.

Ashley closed her eyes tight and used every ounce of willpower and training to wipe her face clear.

After all, crying in the middle of a social event with a famous hockey player wasn't a good look.

Chapter Twenty-Four

November 1, Monday

Ty

The event was winding down and the sun had all but vanished, leaving behind a sky painted with hues of pink and orange that burned brightly through the aged windows. The small event hall needed a serious upgrade—he'd have to talk with his accountant about where they were regarding his donations for the year.

Perched on a worn bench under a tired corkboard full of flyers, Ty watched as Ashley helped some children gather their things as they got ready to leave, her gentle smile never faltering even as she bent down to tie a little girl's shoe. There was something almost ethereal about her in that moment—like a siren come to life, with her long hair glowing like a halo in the fading light.

Ashley finished up with the small group across the room, and made her way to Ty, plopping down on the bench next to him.

Her face, usually so animated and expressive these days, now seemed blank. In recent weeks, she had become open, generously sharing her thoughts and letting her emotions play across her features. Her expressions, once guarded, were now vivid and alive. But it was like they were transported to when they first met; her liveliness had faded, leaving an unusual stillness.

Ty gave her a searching look. "Everything okay?"

Ashley nodded, giving him a tight smile. "Yeah, just tired, I guess."

Ty studied her face, noting the faint lines of worry etching her forehead.

Was it the way that the bundled-up dad had hugged his little boy goodbye as he'd left with his foster family?

Was it all the talk of moving back home?

Something else?

Fuck, he wished she was a little more open with her family life issues.

Maybe then he could help rather than floundering around on his own.

"Well, for what it's worth, this was amazing. If...Babs does this again, have her reach out and I'll get more guys to come. I'm sure they'd love to."

He almost said, 'If *you* do this again.'

Ty was getting better about catching those faux pas before they happened, but it was still pretty fucking hard.

Babs had her own connections to the Cyclones' organization and her own friendships with the players. She was always coordinating events between the players and the kids in her caseload, so it'd be easy enough for Babs to arrange this on an even bigger scale...but then again...that wasn't the point. The point was that...Ashley would be gone.

Ashley's distant expression softened, barely. "I'll let her know."

Well, now she just looked sad.

Fuck.

"I can see why this work is so important to you," Ty said. "It's pretty clear the impact you have on them."

Ashley smiled, faintly. "That means a lot, thank you. There's always more I could do. And some people who I just can't seem to get through to. But the group we had today is a pretty biased group. They're my 'success'. My 'failures'...the ones who I failed...they didn't want to come. So, it was a biased representation of my impact."

Ty waved that nonsense away. "I doubt you *failed* anyone, Princess. I don't think you'd recognize failure if it came up and hit you in the face. It's not in your DNA. So don't take on their burdens.

It's not fair to you. I see how hard you work at this job and your clients see it too...if they're aware enough to look."

She let out a pained, imitation of a laugh. "It sucks to think about leaving when I now finally feel like I'm *doing* something though. You know? I'm finally connecting with people. I finally know who to contact for what. And when. For example, did you know that Judge Burroughs is a night owl and is awake till 3 am every morning? He's never grouchy when I have an after-hours call." Ashley gave a weak chuckle. "His wife gets a little peeved though." Ashley looked down at her cute, pink sneakers as she rubbed the side of the rubber on a scuff mark on the worn tile, essentially erasing it from existence. "I have phone numbers for different agencies and officers memorized. I have contacts, resources, and favors owed to me. And...it's all going to waste." Ashley let out a ragged breath and stopped her movements, intently staring at her shoelaces.

Damn.

Well, when put like that...

Ty blew out a breath and leaned forward, resting his elbows on his knees as he stared at his own shoes.

After a month of drowning in each other, Ty understood that sometimes Ashley just needed someone to *listen*. It wasn't about fixing things; it was about letting her unload the weight from her chest, to voice her frustrations without expecting him to swoop in and save the day or offer judgment. Ashley didn't need him to say anything. Ty's role in these moments was simply to be a supportive presence, absorbing her words without the need to respond with advice or reassurances that might ring hollow.

"I wonder if they'll find someone to replace me. Quickly, I mean. I work for pennies because I didn't need the money thanks to my inheritance from my mom. I did the caseload for two employees. I'm not sure if their budget is ready to bring on enough staff to properly allocate the clients in my files." She sniffed and looked up at him, her big eyes watery and vulnerable. "What are those people going to do if the agency keeps them in limbo or bounces them around?"

Her voice was high and tight, and it ripped out his fucking heart.

"If you need me to do anything—anything at all—you know I will. Just say the word."

Ashley's shoulders slumped as she slid back on the bench, her hair perilously close to tangling with the tacks on the cork board behind them. She drew her knees up to her chest, her heels teetering on the edge of the bench, and wrapped her arms tightly around them. With a blank stare, she fixed her gaze straight ahead.

The oddly vulnerable pose was completely wrong for a *conqueror* like Ashley.

She was a *champion.*

A warrior.

A queen.

No *queen* should ever look so lost.

Especially not his.

He reached for her, gently turned her head, and promised her, "Everything will be okay. *You* will make sure of it." He paused until he saw her lips twitch and her face soften. "And when you're gone, *I* will make sure of it."

Then, figuring that it was okay to kiss her now that most of the guests were gone, he leaned in and pressed his lips to hers.

The kiss was a promise, a moment of perfect, painful beauty.

It was a vow to her that he'd take care of her treasures and what she held dear. And it was his pledge that he would remember, and celebrate, what they had, no matter how fleeting.

Ty felt the bittersweet tang of reality waiting just at the edges of their cocoon.

After they separated, they sat curled together in silence for a few moments, until Ashley was able to finish shaking off the melancholy.

"Okay, come on," Ashley said finally with a soft sniff, tugging at his arm. "Let's help clean up before we head out—you have film tonight and need to get going."

"Lead the way."

As he followed her back down the hall, he slung his arm around her shoulders and pulled her close, loving how she fit right into his side.

He pressed a soft kiss to her hair, promising himself that he would love her as if each moment together was eternal, and vowing that there was no way in hell he was letting go of this incredible woman without a fight.

Her father could go suck one.

Ashley was Ty's and he was keeping her.

Together, they made their way back to the gathering room, where Babs was ushering people out the door and starting the clean-up process. The once-raucous room now echoed with the comforting sounds of methodical cleaning and Babs' intermittent, hilarious grumblings. Dwindling light from the windows glinted off half-drunk glasses and plates smeared with remnants of food.

As Ty picked up a broom and Ashley gathered discarded napkins, the mood shifted palpably. The simple acts of tidying and moving chairs created a rhythm of work that was both mundane and intimate. Every sweep and fold seemed to underline the silence growing between them—a silence filled with secrets and sadness about their future. Despite the uncertainty that loomed ahead, Ty's resolve hardened; he was determined to find a way to keep Ashley from being forced to return to Dariqat. Watching her, her face a mask of concentration as she worked, he silently vowed to do whatever he could to give her a *choice*.

A chance.

After saying goodbye to Ashley and watching her safely drive off, Ty spotted the figure of the bundled-up father from earlier, lurking against the side of the building. The man was huddled, trying to protect himself from the biting November chill.

Ashley was steadfast in maintaining her clients' confidentiality—rightfully so—but one night, she had broken down in Ty's arms, sobbing more about the father and kid duo that had her heart in its tragic grip.

Given that the boy who kept running back and forth to the man earlier was named Connell, this had to be his dad.

Garrett Baylor.

Ty approached, feeling the man's heavy gaze on him. "Want a ride?"

"I'm fine."

He wasn't. Ty didn't call him out on it though.

"I'm probably driving past it anyways to get back home, might as well hop in rather than continue to wait for a cab."

They both knew there was no cab coming.

Garrett nodded and Ty led the way to his Explorer.

As they drove across town, their conversation was stilted and filled with awkward pauses. Ty tried talking about Connell and the guy didn't bite. Apparently, Garrett wanted silence.

That was fine too.

Eventually, they arrived at a shopping center known for having a homeless community in its back woods.

Garrett adjusted his clothing, bracing for the cold, but before he could leave Ty couldn't help from asking, "Do you need money? I can bring you somewhere. Pay for a room for a bit while you work things out..."

Garrett stiffened and stared out the window. He didn't look like he was even breathing.

"I'm happy to help, you just have to let me..."

Again, the man said nothing, instead he grabbed the handle and pushed the door open.

The wind howled through the opening and Ty felt the chill bite at his cheeks. It made him sick to think of the nights that Connell had been living out in this with him.

How many other kids were back out in the homeless camp?

Ty made a mental note to talk to someone about it to see if the team could do something.

Garrett's gruff words caused Ty to pull his eyes from the dark opening at the edge of the woods. "We're fine. We have some fires going, a couple generators. We get by."

"Dude."

"We're fine."

"Even the kids?" *Shit.* He was crossing all sorts of lines, but damnit, he couldn't stop himself.

Ashley was going to have his balls.

"The kids are fine too."

Ty frowned at the man. "Really? You really think so?"

"They're with their family. That's all that matters." Garrett looked toward the woods like he regretted accepting the ride.

"Is that true? Is that all that matters?" Ty asked it quietly, not really expecting Garrett to answer. "A friend of mine was kept with his family, even after multiple reports of abuse. It was important to 'keep the family unit together' and they needed to work toward 'reunification.' Trust me, it would have been better if he had been taken out of there." Ty swallowed and soldiered on, "I love Ashley. I love how big her heart is and what she does to try to make the world a better place. But I gotta ask you, man, is being with family *really* all that matters? Did that help you? Or the others back there?"

"The system sure as fuck didn't help us when we were in shitty fucking homes!"

There. A reaction. It was something.

He wasn't a therapist, so he was out of his league on what type of reaction was positive or negative but the thought of this man convincing the courts to give him back his son, just to bring him back here...

Especially when the kid was clearly adored by his foster family.

"No. You're right. Shitty homes...I have some friends who were in a shitty home growing up. But I also have friends that provide the most incredible foster homes." He paused and leveled a hard stare at Garrett. "Homes like the one Connell has now. Warm, safe, secure, loving."

"They're strangers to him!"

"They were strangers to him years ago. Now? Now they're part of his family, too. Always will be, one way or another. Just like you always will be, one way or another. Even if you go back out in those woods and use whatever it was I saw sticking out of your pocket when you moved to get out the truck."

Boom.

Garrett's eyes turned haunted. "It's cold out."

"Fuck yeah, it is. Imagine how a kid feels. Fuck, how I wish I could fix it all for all of you. I wish I could cure all of this. But I can't. I can try to help, but people also have to accept the help. You willing to accept help? You willing to enter a clinic, get sober, get out, stay in a place that I pay for while you get on your feet, and turn your life around? I'll do it. I'll drive us straight to the nearest clinic and write the fucking check. You can take charge of your future and your son will be spending next Christmas home with you in a safe, warm house with brand new Paw Patrol sheets on a brand-new bed."

Ty watched as Garrett's hand went into his coat pocket and pulled out a couple of needles. Did he pick them up from someone he met at the event hall, or did he have them right there the whole time?

"Addiction is a disease."

"Not saying it isn't. Just asking if you want help."

"It's not a choice."

"I'm not saying anything one way or another. I'm just asking if you want help?"

"I want to be free."

Fuck.

"So, does that mean you'll take my help?"

Garrett closed his eyes for a moment, letting the door close slightly.

Ty held his breath, praying the guy would say yes.

"You pay for that clinic or for a home for me, then you're a fucking moron."

"Not what I asked."

"I'll just be using again, first night I get out."

"It's an investment. I've got the money. *You're* worth the chance. *Connell* is worth the chance."

Though, depending on how long it took for Garrett to get clean, it sure as fuck wouldn't just be easy money. It's not like hockey players were paid MLB money for Christ's sakes.

"Can I have one more night?"

"One more night to use that up?" Ty nodded at the needles in Garrett's hand.

Garrett's lips thinned and he looked away.

No, no he couldn't do this. He thought he could, but fuck. This was a mess.

"No, man. You don't get one last ride. You make the choice now, for you and your son. I'll take care of it all. I promise you man, a life is waiting for you. Just let me help you."

"Yeah, help on your terms." Garrett mumbled.

Like a fucking child.

Okay, Ty was done.

"Disease or not, make a choice. Either shut my truck door so I can drive you to a center or get the fuck out. But make the *fucking* choice."

Garrett's face turned into an awful sneer, his lip curling as he inspected Ty like he was the biggest piece of shit in the world. "You don't know—"

"Nope. Not doing this. I'm not your therapist and I'm certainly not trained in this shit. So, listen to me closely. If you think for one minute, a life with you out here is better than the life your son has with the Jenkins right now...then you've fried all your fucking brain cells. I'm trying to be a good person here, to give you a chance at being a better parent to your son. So, it's now or nothing, dude. Either stay with me and get healthy or be man enough to sign over your parental rights – because your son deserves better than this shit for the rest of his life."

Garrett threw open the truck door, burst out, and slammed the door hard enough to rattle the windows.

Ty grit his teeth as he watched Garrett stalk toward the back woods.

Fine.

But Ty wasn't giving up; he'd try again next week. And the week after that. Maybe one of those times, the man would finally take Ty up on his offer.

At least, Ty hoped he would.

As Garrett disappeared from sight, Ty threw it in drive and sped away.

Holy fuck, how did Ashley handle this heartbreak every single day?

Chapter Twenty-Five

November 4, Thursday

Ashley

Ashley stepped into the roaring hockey arena, the deafening cheers enveloping her. She blinked against the bright lights, nerves and exhilaration churning in her stomach. This was all so new—the chill of the ice-rink, the fervor of the crowd, the sticky floor beneath her feet.

A little gross.

A lot of *life*.

Perfection.

She spotted Lexie waving enthusiastically and made her way over, giving her new friend a quick hug before sitting down in the empty seat waiting for her.

It was a risk to be blatantly out like this but as long as she could get lost in the crowd with the rest of the fans, Ashley figured the risk wasn't that big.

"Hey, chickie. How's it hanging?" Lexie beamed, her pitch-black hair in ridiculous pigtails with bright pink dyed chunks in it.

Ashley shook her head. This chick was a nut. "A little to the left, I guess."

"Good woman," Lexie grinned. "I'm so glad we're doing this! I haven't seen you since the auction. Text updates just aren't the same as getting together in person."

"For sure," Ashley agreed.

Lexie leaned back and waved to the two women on her other side. "Ashley, meet Kira and Kayla. They're my puck bunny bitches!" Lexie shouted over a sudden roar of the crowd.

Kira flashed a wicked smile, her Cyclones crop top with long sleeves and ripped jeans at odds with the preppy pink cashmere sweater Ashley wore. Kayla offered a polite nod, dressed in a much more sensible oversized generic jersey with non-holey jeans.

"We're not actually puck bunnies," Kira clarified with an eye roll. "We're just the ones she calls when she wants to crash a hockey game because she knows we're already here. And the cheap bitch knows we can get her a free ticket."

"Millionaires don't become millionaires by being stupid with their money," Lexie declared with a wise expression on her face.

Kira smacked Lexie's arm and laughed hard, leaning into Kayla on her other side.

Kayla leaned forward and added, "You didn't become a millionaire at all. You were born into that shit." Kayla leveled Ashley with a tired but amused look. "She really is freaking cheap."

Lexie rolled her eyes. "Hey, I got you the beers!"

"No. You didn't. You flirted with some guys, and *they* got us the beers."

Lexie shrugged. "A beer's a beer."

Ashley smiled at the women, wondering how Lexie's relationship with Jen and Megan from the auction fit in with these women.

Fuck, the destruction that all the women would cause when all together.

It would be glorious.

She'd invite Ty and they'd kick back with some wine and watch the wreckage.

Or....

She *would* have.

If she were staying.

Fuck.

A booming voice echoed across the arena and the lights dimmed. Singers tiptoed out on the ice, being sure to stay on the narrow carpet, and performed the anthem. Ashley's eyes scanned the ice, desperate to catch a glimpse of Ty's number.

There.

Ty.

Ashley couldn't stop her smile from spreading.

There was her guy.

As the team took their spots on the ice, Lexie and Kira joined the entire stadium in cheering like absolute nuts. Ashley and Kayla made matching expressions of fond exhaustion at their friends' antics.

The puck dropped, and the girls dived into a playful debate about the players—especially Ty. Kira laughed about her brother Ilya's obsessive pre-game rituals, while Kayla spilled all the dirt on the guys' nastier rituals. Same underwear, same socks, had to kiss the Zamboni, had to have a raw fish on the bench in the locker room. The stories had Ashley gasping and massaging at a stitch in her side.

"As their therapist, are you technically allowed to share this?"

Kayla waved Ashley's concerns away. "I never share their private information. This is all what they've shared at various team events over the years."

Eww. Ashley grinned and turned back to the ice. Just in time to see Ty's line pop back out.

When Ty hit the ice, Ashley gripped her seat, transfixed. His fluid speed, his ruthless checks, his unyielding efforts—she'd never seen this intense, aggressive side of him. A new thrill coursed through her as she watched him dominate the rink.

Fuck, he was fast. And his stick skills.

Damn.

The crowd exploded when Ty scored off a blistering one-timer. Ashley leapt up, clapping and yelling in spite of herself.

"That's your man!" Lexie shouted as she grabbed Ashley's shoulders and gave her a weird hug, shake, jump combo.

Heads turned to them and Ashley fought her blush but failed in hiding her smile.

Yeah, he was her man.

But Lexie needed to dial it down *just* a notch. It's not like Ashley could afford to broadcast it.

Even though she didn't want to, she slid back down into her seat and pulled Lexie with her. She issued a quick instruction that people couldn't know that Ty was her boyfriend or very bad things would happen, and Lexie's face got scary in how serious it was.

The vapid, rich girl facade slipped right off, and a mama tiger stood in its place.

Oh, wow.

"I've got it handled, mostly, but for now, I can't really be...publicly shouting that we're together. Okay?"

Lexie gave her a dark, assessing look before giving a short nod. "Bitch, should have said that a period and a half ago."

And that was that.

Lexie turned forward and focused back on the game. But not before a "and don't think for one minute that we're done talking about this."

No, Ashley didn't think they would be. Lexie was not the type to let things go.

But at least she let Ashley enjoy her first in-person hockey game in peace.

Her heart swelled with pride every time Ty was on the ice.

The speed, the skill, the determination. God. He was so *good*.

At everything.

Ashley watched with rapt attention, wincing each time he took a bruising hit against the boards. Whenever an opposing player cross-checked him, she'd gasp, her hands clenched tight over her mouth.

As the final period ended, Ashley felt dizzy with the speed and violence of it all. She'd been somewhat removed from Ty's passion before, watching him play from a screen, distanced from the rawness of action. It was a completely different world being at the game versus watching it on TV.

Now she understood it viscerally.

As the women filed out into the crisp night air, they chatted and rehashed the highlights of the game.

"That last goal of Ty's was insane!" Kira exclaimed, reenacting his quick deke around the defender. "I don't know how he pulled that off, but damn was it impressive. Tell me he has equally suave moves in bed."

"I was raised to never kiss and tell," Ashley declared haughtily, earning herself some playful shoves and squeals.

There was talk about a party that Lexie wanted to hit up. But Ashley's mind was still on the ice with Ty.

"Sorry, ladies. I think I'm gonna just go home and wait for a post-game call from my guy." Her heart fluttered when she called him that and she felt a giddy smile rise to the surface.

Shit, when had she turned into a twelve-year-old again?

She was a grown ass woman and here she was...getting butterflies.

Over a man she was going to leave.

Fuck.

Lexie nudged Ashley playfully as they made their way through the parking lot. "We'll talk more later about your 'issues' but first, no hard feelings about my *slight* manipulation at the bachelor auction? I had good intentions."

Ashley laughed and pushed her away. "Slight is a 'slight' mischaracterization. You straight up lied. But absolutely no hard feelings—he's perfect."

Ashley felt the familiar pang in her chest remembering that her time here was limited. She would miss moments like this—laughing with her new friends, feeling part of something bigger.

Kayla seemed to sense the shift in her mood. "Everything okay?" she asked.

Ashley paused, debating how much to share. "I guess I'm just realizing how much I'll miss this place," she admitted. "My visa is up soon, so..."

"What? You're leaving? Bitch, that's not an end-of-the-night truth bomb you drop before going home! That's a...I don't know what!" Lexie exclaimed.

Ashley winced, shrugged, and gave her a sorry attempt at a smile.

"That sucks," Kayla said sympathetically while watching her closely. "But hey, we'll just have to make the most of the time we have left together. In fact, why don't you come over to my place for the next game? We can order takeout, pop open some wine, do our nails. Live it up."

"That sounds amazing," Ashley said, genuinely touched by the invitation. She felt lucky to have found such welcoming friends in her short time here. "But it's going to have to be soon. I'm gone at the end of this year."

They all arrived at Kayla's beat-up car first.

Apparently Lexie's car was in the shop again. Another fender bender.

They all exchanged hugs and plans to meet up again soon.

When Ashley got in her car and pulled out into the long line of almost standstill traffic of the arena's parking lot, she felt bolstered knowing she had more memorable nights to look forward to. This place, these people—they had truly made an impact. And she wasn't ready to let go just yet.

Back in her apartment, Ashley sank into the couch, closing her eyes as she replayed the game in her mind. The deafening roar of the crowd, the heart-pounding action, the graceful power with which Ty commanded the ice...it had been an adrenaline rush just to witness.

She thought about the way he'd glided and spun, utterly focused, as if the rest of the world melted away when that puck hit his stick. Hockey was clearly more than just a game to him—it was a passion that ignited his soul.

Would he be able to play in Europe?

Did she want that?

Well, that wasn't even the question—of course she wanted that.

Her heart wanted that desperately.

But was it safe for him?

Absolutely not.

Caught up in the fear of losing him, she grabbed her phone, and on impulse, texted him:

"Hey superstar, just wanted to say congrats on a killer game tonight. The way you handled that breakaway in the third? Unreal. You've won me over. Next game I'll be rocking a Daniels' jersey."

She hit send before she could overthink it, then hugged a pillow to her chest. She was only setting them both up for heartache, but even she couldn't prevent it at this point.

She was in too deep.

And so was he.

However fleeting their time together might be, she wanted to make the most of every moment.

Ty's reply came quickly, the ping of her phone piercing in her quiet apartment.

"Hey, Princess, appreciate you coming out to cheer me on tonight. Means a lot that you took an interest in my world. Gotta admit, the crowd energy was next-level tonight. I think it was you that got them going."

Ashley smiled, picturing the sweet and teasing grin she knew would be plastered on his face as he'd typed the message.

Immediately, her phone started vibrating in her hand. She answered the call with a smile so big her cheeks were hurting. "Hey, 'Thoughtful' Daniels. Lovin' those assists, baby. Very generous and on-brand of you."

"You dork." His deep chuckle vibrated right through her. "You up for some company tonight?"

Her heartbeat quickened.

"Depends on who's asking."

"Tommy. He needs to get over a forbbiden-love, so I told him you'll cure his broken heart, and make him forget she exists."

Ashley chuckled. "Well, when you put it like that...Of course. Send him over."

Ty's deep, chuckle rippled into her ear and her toes curled in her warm socks.

"On second thought, nah. I think tonight will just be you and me. We'll let Tommy's broken heart stew a little longer. It will be good company for my own here, soon enough."

Fuck.

Ashley closed her eyes and tipped her head back against the leather couch. "Ty..."

"Nah, no worries, hun. We got this. You and me. We're gonna figure somethin' out. It just might take a minute. Just don't go marrying some other dude or something when you get back home. I need time to strategize an insane attempt to impress your family and convince them that you belong with me...wherever that ends up being."

"Ty..."

What the hell could she say to that?

That she wanted that more than anything in the world?

Because she did. She wanted it *so bad.*

Ashley wanted it so bad, that a tear rolled down her cheek and onto her lips. She licked the saltiness away and then rubbed roughly at her face with her hands.

She didn't *get* emotional.

But with Ty?

She was an emotional train wreck.

Absently, she wondered if that rawness—that *feeling* of feelings—would go away once she was back in Dariqat. Would the switch turn back off? Would the ice re-enshrine her heart and protect her like before she met him?

Ty gifted her with a life-changing love. A perspective-shifting love.

A love that made her want to risk it all.

What would happen if she didn't go back? What would her father do? Consider her a lost cause?

Send someone to kidnap her?

Go after Ty?

No. Unacceptable.

She could get hurt. But not Ty.

Never Ty.

He was too special. Too precious. His life wasn't worth her happiness.

It was so much more.

Therefore, she wouldn't waste the days they had left pining for a future that was doomed. She would embrace each moment with Ty, make the most of every smile, every laugh, every stolen kiss.

This was her chance to live out the love story she'd dreamed—no matter how fleeting. She was determined to hold on with both hands.

And she'd remember it fondly when she was old and gray.

CHAPTER TWENTY-SIX
November 4, Thursday
Ty

Long after Ashley fell asleep in his arms, Ty lay awake, staring at the ceiling, trying to keep his body from tightening with the tension coursing through him.

The game earlier...

Everyone played fantastically—well, except for a few guys—but they still secured the win. There were no angry visits from the general managers, no threats to Coach Montgomery to change up the lines, no apparent interference from management at all...

Then again, how would Ty know? The only reason he even knew what he did was because he caught sight of those little moments here and there. Coach Montgomery certainly wasn't sharing what was going on, leaving everyone worrying in the dark. The coach couldn't be so oblivious that he didn't notice their distraction and concern... right?

Ty stiffened, the movement causing Ashley to mumble something in her sleep and curl deeper into him.

He forced himself to relax, but the frustration of feeling powerless gnawed at him. He had asked Coach Montgomery whether his place on the team was safe, and the coach had simply congratulated him on a great game, told him to keep it up, slapped him on the shoulder, and turned to talk to another player.

What the hell was he supposed to do with that?

In retrospect, Ty *probably* should have asked him in private, but it felt too...whiny and insecure to admit to how much the rumors were affecting him. Certainly, no one else seemed to be as bothered by them as he was...then again, he was the main target of the rumors now.

Ty's abs tightened again as another wave of frustration coursed through him. Why wasn't anyone approaching him and telling him if there was any validity to the rumors? He was playing great—totally kicking ass out there with Bobby and Ian—and management still wasn't happy?

It didn't make sense.

If he was going to be uprooted again, he'd prefer to know sooner rather than later so he could at least mentally prepare.

Why couldn't anyone just tell the fucking truth?

Ashley mumbled something again, her words incoherent. Ty pulled her closer, taking a deep breath of her soft, rose-scented hair. Worried not only about his future in hockey but also his future with her, Ty lay there and soaked it in, imprinting the feel of her in his arms to memory.

Sleep was a long time coming.

Chapter Twenty-Seven

November 7, Saturday

Ty

Ashley's laughter echoed through the neon-lit mini golf course as she enthusiastically high-fived each Girl Scout after they sank a tricky putt. Her dark eyes sparkled under the blacklights, matching the megawatt grin on her face. This was her happy place.

Ty hung back, content to let Ashley take the spotlight. He couldn't take his eyes off her as she celebrated each small victory with the girls, her joy infectious. She was a natural with kids in a way he'd never seen before.

However, a pang of sadness pierced through him. If they couldn't figure out a way to keep her here…they'd never have this: kids of their own.

He knew it was a touchy subject for Ashley; she had mentioned several times that when she returned to Dariqat, she'd be expected to get married and churn out kids—something she was vehemently going to refuse apparently, if her furious rants were anything to go by.

Maybe she was afraid of having a daughter and trapping her to a similar fate? Or marrying someone like her father? Though she rarely spoke of her family, Ty sensed a deep hurt there.

Ashley seemed to love kids, so he had to believe that if she wasn't stuck in this crossroads of losing all autonomy…maybe she would have wanted children…with him.

He sighed. No use feeling sad about it now. Not when she was trying to create a memorable experience for this Girl Scout troop.

For now, he was happy to play the role of adoring spectator. Seeing Ashley so carefree and in her element brought a smile to his face. He sent up a silent prayer of thanks for this remarkable woman who had burst into his life.

Ty meandered over to where Ashley was watching a young girl line up a tricky bank shot. He came up behind Ashley and wrapped his arms around her waist, pulling her in close. She leaned back into him, the floral scent of her shampoo flooding his senses.

"Having fun?" he murmured, his breath warm against her ear.

"Mm-hmm," she hummed, twisting in his arms to face him, a peaceful smile playing on her lips. Her dark eyes locked onto his, full of warmth and promise. "Especially because Babs just texted and said that Garrett has given his approval for Connell to stay with the Jenkins. Forever. Some days my job...damn. It's hard. But when I get through and can help someone who needs it. Fuck, Ty. It's a beautiful feeling."

Ty reached up and gently tucked a loose strand of raven hair behind her ear, letting his fingertips linger on her cheek.

She didn't need to know about his chat with Garrett. Ever. This win was all hers.

"You're not the only one with good news," Ty said. Ashley blinked up at him, her beautiful face serene and expectant. "Just got a text from one of the heads of *GPANL*—a miracle happened. Someone greenlighted the project. The proposal passed! The lands are officially protected from drilling." He couldn't stop his grin and he swayed them side to side in a display of his excitement. Ideally, he'd pick her up and spin her around, giving lots of whoops and laughs, but he didn't want to cause a scene.

Ashley gave him a tight squeeze, a relieved and surprised smile on her face. "Did they say what changed?"

Ty shook his head. "Nope. They didn't say, but someone, somewhere, just did something incredible. They've helped secure a way of life for the local tribes, preserve the environment for the wildlife, and so much more. It's a monumental win for all involved."

She beamed up at him, shaking her head. "Sounds like someone has a guardian angel."

"Do you happen to know anyone on the environmental council that may have helped speed things along, my little tempest?"

This time *she* shook her head in open disbelief. "I wish I could take credit! I really do. But I swear to God, I had nothing to do with this. This was all you guys. I'm so happy for you." She gave him a big hug. "I have no idea how you guys managed to get it done. I'm somewhat...familiar with the politics over there and what your team had to do to get something like this approved...well, it's...unheard of."

"You know a little about politics, hmm?"

She gave him a teasing shove. "Stop fishing, it's a stinky habit."

He tipped his head back and laughed, before reaching out and stroking her cheek with his thumb. "Fishing's not so bad. I'll get you your own reel. I'll make sure it's pink."

Ashley shook her head and snuggled back into him. "Family connections aside, I really am amazed that your agency managed to get the green light on this project. I've been asking my brother questions about any updates he's heard from his contacts when he calls, and he's been pretty tight lipped about the whole thing." She paused and chewed her lip, still looking like she didn't quite believe that it went through. "The governmental agencies that would have had to approve something like this...The people in charge of those departments...I just can't see..."

At this point, she was really talking to herself. Her eyes weren't even on his anymore but staring off into the distance over his shoulder.

Like she didn't trust the information.

Or that she was waiting for the other shoe to drop.

Once again, Ty was reminded that it was a very different world over there and that her confident disbelief might indicate an actual cause for concern for his friends working on this project.

It was also another reminder that he had no fucking idea what her family did for work in Dariqat and he had no fucking clue how much she knew about the politics over there.

Fucking hell, why wouldn't she just come out and talk about it with him!

Shaking her head once more, she wiped the frown from her face and leaned forward, burrowing her face in his chest and squeezing him in a strong hug. "I'm so happy for you, honey. Truly."

The atmosphere of the mini golf course seemed to fade away, as she snuggled deeper into his body. His arms tightened around her, and he rested his head on hers, closing his eyes as he imprinted the feel of her in his memory.

They'd talk about her family 'connections' later.

When they weren't at an indoor mini golf event for a bunch of kids.

They held each other tight, losing themselves in their own little intimate bubble.

How would he survive losing her?

He wouldn't.

Given her fear about returning to Dariqat–he refused to call it her 'home'–maybe she wouldn't either...

Maybe literally.

Who knew what was waiting for her there...

"Don't go," he blurted, unable to help himself as she started to pull away.

"What?"

"Don't go back to Dariqat. Stay *here*. With me. Stay with *me*."

Ashley opened her mouth and shut it after giving a couple of quick blinks at him.

Ty rubbed her back reassuringly. "I wasn't going to bring it up yet, but I've started asking around to see what sort of asylum rules the U.S. has with Dariqat. One of my lawyer friends is looking into the protection rules and something called non-refoulement. Without knowing all the details, I didn't have much for her to go on, but at least she's looking into it. We might stand a chance."

"Ty!" Ashley pulled her arms out from around him and grabbed at the sides of her head, anxiously threading her fingers into the hair there, her usually warm brown eyes, hard and stormy. "What were you thinking? I thought we agreed that you'd drop this and just accept the time we had left. Don't poke the freaking bear, Ty!"

Ty frowned at her and tugged her hips up close to his again, not liking the distance she tried putting between them—it felt cold. And lonely. "I *am* enjoying the time we have left. But I can't just roll over and let you go without at least asking around about ways to help you. Not when you clearly don't want to go back."

Ashley's tight shoulders lowered, and she slid her hands around to the front of her face so they covered it completely. Ty could hear her deep breathing into her hands, her body rock solid against him.

The defeated pose set every protective instinct in him on fire.

What the fuck was waiting for her in Dariqat?

Ty gave her a soft shake and lowered his voice further, "I don't believe in just *giving up*, Ash. *Not* on us."

"I know you don't," Ashley whispered, her voice strained and croaky.

He made her cry?

Fuck.

She sniffed and sucked in a ragged breath. "And I love that about you. But sometimes, love isn't about fighting the impossible. It's about knowing when to protect the ones you love from the battles they *can't* win." One hand left her face, reached out, and twisted into the shirt at his sternum, trying to convey what words could not fully express.

She loved him?

Good.

Because he loved her too.

Even with the ridiculously compressed time they had spent together.

Ty tilted his head to see behind her other hand, frustration aching in his bones. "And you really believe there's no way? No loophole, no chance of changing things? Come on, Princess, you gotta talk to me. Please."

Ashley sighed, a long, weary sound that seemed to draw the warmth from around them as she removed her hand from her face. She swiped roughly at her eyes, careful to drag her fingers below them to catch the small track of eyeliner that had dripped down. "No. I don't think there's a way." She issued her answer in a harsh, no-nonsense way that was at odds with the devastation on her face.

"But we're talking about your life here, Ash. Your happiness," Ty argued, his voice tight. "Doesn't that count for something?"

"It does," she agreed softly. "Which is why these moments with you, they mean so much to me. They're precious...but temporary."

The way her usually commanding voice had turned small and defeated absolutely ripped his heart to shreds.

His princess was *anything* but small or defeated.

She was an inferno. A typhoon. A tempest.

Fuck, maybe she was a *cyclone*.

What she should *never* be was *crushed*.

Ty's heart ached as he studied her face, searching for a hint of an opening–an agreement to let his contacts continue their work.

He found nothing.

Shit.

"So, what do we do?"

"We make the most of *now*," Ashley said, her voice steady despite the pain he saw in her bloodshot eyes. "Like we talked about before. We create memories that can outlast the distance and the time apart.

We love each other as fiercely and as fully as we can, while we can. And when it's time for me to go..." She paused, her voice faltering for a moment. "*We let go*."

The silence that followed was thick, heavy with the unspoken fears and the harsh realities of their situation. Ty leaned down and rested his forehead against hers, closing his eyes for a moment as a wave of hopelessness washed over him. Her weight against him calmed his racing heart. At least, for now, she was here. She was *his*. "I'm not good at letting go," he confessed, his voice low.

"No. You wouldn't be," Ashley replied, her own voice broken and stuffy. "And I love that about you, too. But sometimes, the best way to love someone is to let them go, to hope for their happiness, even if it's not with you."

"And that's what you'll be? Happy?" Ty asked, the strain evident in his voice despite his efforts to mask it.

"Oh, my sweet, *sweet* Ty," Ashley breathed out in a pain-laced whisper. She lifted her chin enough to give him a soft, gentle kiss. "You really are too good for me, you know."

"We'll agree to disagree on that, Princess."

A flicker of a wince danced across her face but it was so fast that he wondered if he misread her reaction.

She resumed their earlier position, foreheads resting hard against each other as they absorbed the weight of the future. "My happiness," she addressed his question from earlier, a tear slipping down her cheek, "is right here, r*ight now*, with you. And I will take it with me, wherever I go. Forever."

Ty stared into her soulful and vulnerable brown eyes, memorizing every nuanced fleck of color.

He'd never seen more gorgeous eyes.

He'd never seen a more gorgeous spirit.

She belonged here. With him.

Living her life on her terms.

Ashley didn't want to leave at all.

Her father probably wasn't the all-powerful mafioso that she painted him as, but she clearly believed that she had no choice and was scared of the repercussions.

She was wrong to be scared. Ty would hire 24/7 security if it meant she could rest easily at night.

It's not like he couldn't afford it.

He'd table the discussion for now, there was no rush to really get into it–especially not here at her event–but they absolutely would be getting to the bottom of this before her time was up.

In the meantime, there was no harm in letting his friend keep running with her asylum search. If she could find a loophole, then great, he'd present it to Ashley.

If she was pissed he continued to *try*... then she didn't know him very well.

And really, what was there to lose?

She was leaving anyway.

And if he presented her with a loophole that she didn't want to take and left anyways?

Well, at least he tried.

He was brought back to the moment by Ashley's cold but soft hand resting on his cheek.

"My sweet, sweet Ty," she repeated the words earlier, her soft minty breath dancing across his lips.

She had also used the L word a lot earlier in her rant.

He loved her too.

Now wasn't the time to tell her that though.

Roses. Thousands of roses.

And the biggest diamond ring she had ever seen.

Or maybe all of her 'success' story clients, holding a letter each, asking her to marry him at a hockey game.

Or displayed on the wall of a coat closet somewhere.

Or painted in their tiny shack at the paintball course.

The possibilities were endless, and he couldn't stop his smile.

He'd find a way. *They* would find a way.

Ty twisted his neck and pressed a sweet, chaste kiss to her lips, savoring the moment.

The flash and click of a camera shattered the moment. Ty's head snapped up to see a sleazy tabloid photographer circling them, snapping photo after photo, the flash nearly blinding him.

Ashley turned solid in his arms before whipping away from the photographer and covering her face.

Shit.

"Hey, back off!" Ty barked, immediately shifting to shield Ashley from the intrusion.

How had this vulture found him? It's not like he was a news-worthy player on the team for Christ's sake!

He hiked and did charity work in his free time! Not lines of coke and hookers!

Why the press periodically decided to hound him, he could never figure out.

But at a place where there were fucking kids hanging around?

That was low...even for this particular vulture.

His protective instincts flared.

As Ty marched toward the gossip monger, the photographer scurried away; his invasive shots secured.

He turned to find Ashley leaning against the wall in a more private part of the large room, chest heaving, eyes brimming with tears. She looked utterly panicked and distraught.

Shit.

He was used to random moments of the media catching him unaware, but he never even *thought* to prepare her.

He should have thought about preparing her.

Fucking shit!

Ty walked over and frowned as he took in the severity of Ashley's shaking form.

Jesus. She was really rattled.

Way more than he would have thought she'd be...

Slowly, so as not to startle her, Ty gathered her in his arms. "It's okay. He's gone."

But Ashley only trembled harder, the encounter triggering something deeper he couldn't understand. Ty held her tight and gently rubbed her back.

What the hell was happening?

Was she okay?

Was this a trigger of something that happened in Dariqat?

Ty gently guided Ashley around a corner, away from prying eyes, knowing she wouldn't want the kids to see her like that. He found a dark, quiet corner where she could catch her breath. Her cheeks were flushed. Ashley's brown eyes were dilated to the max and wide as well, darting around like a frightened doe. She was hyperventilating, her breath coming in short, sharp gasps.

"Hey, just breathe. Look at me," Ty murmured, cupping her face in his hands. Ashley's gaze continued bouncing around before finally focusing on him.

Fuck.

He certainly never expected her to react like this to a little tabloid photo-grab. And this one was fairly benign: there was no shouting at him, and the photographer went away fairly quickly.

"That's it. Deep breaths," Ty coached.

Slowly, her frantic wheezing evened out, though her slender frame still trembled. Ty smoothed back her hair, his brow furrowed in concern.

"What happened? Talk to me."

Ashley bit her lip, dropping her eyes. "I...I can't really get into that right now," she whispered.

Ty sighed, trying to hide his frustration.

There it was again – that wall she threw up whenever she got a little 'too emotional' – her interpretation, not his.

The fear in her eyes made his heart ache. What was she so afraid of?

His stomach flipped.

Maybe her dad really *was* that terrifying...

Ty's muscles tightened at the thought.

"Please, just trust me," he begged, tipping her chin up to meet his gaze. Ashley wavered, a wave of emotions washing across her delicate features. For a moment, it seemed she might open up. But then she leaned back against the wall, hugging herself tight.

"I'm sorry, Ty. I just...need to get home. I need some space," she murmured, not meeting his eyes.

His heart sank as she retreated into herself, slipping deeper behind those walls he just couldn't seem to breach.

That she wouldn't *let* him breach.

He raked a hand through his hair in agitation.

What was going on with her? Why did the idea of them being seen together spark such a panic?

Unbidden, a memory of his slew of exes assaulted his mind.

Fuck.

Time and time again, they all ended up having other men in their lives.

Ashley wouldn't do that...right?

He would have noticed...right?

Historical evidence would suggest...no. No, he wouldn't.

Fuck.

No...it couldn't be.

Ty gently grasped her elbow and leaned down enough to pull her eyes to his. "Ash, hold up. We need to talk about this. This is a part of my life. I'm sorry I didn't think to prepare you before now—"

She moved her gaze back to a nearby emergency exit sign, her posture tense. "There's nothing to talk about. It's fine. I just need to go once I get my shit under control," she said quietly.

"Yes, there is, and no, you're not fine," Ty insisted. "Clearly something freaked you the fuck out. I want to understand and to explain. This is just...normal life for me. You just kind of get used to the media attention. They remember I exist every once in a while, but then they move on and forget me again. It's cyclical but never anything too bad compared to what other guys deal with." He stroked her soft arm with his thumb—something that always seemed to settle her—but was shocked when she stiffened and pulled away from him. Looking at her in confusion, he tried again, "We're together, we love each other, there's not really anything we can do about it, Princess. They're going to take pictures; we just have to ignore them and move on."

Ashley hesitated and turned her eyes on him.

Yeah, he'd just admitted he loved her.

So, what?

She basically had admitted it already anyway.

Ty stared down at her, challenging her to get sassy about it. At least then he'd know she was slowly getting back to normal.

Instead, Ashley refused to acknowledge his statement—which caused dread to pool in his gut.

Fuck.

He cocked his head in confusion, trying to beat back the growing sense of panic. "Ash?"

"It's...complicated and I don't think I can explain. Not without ruining everything. So, let's just keep pretending that I'm just Ashley and you're just Ty?"

Nope, she didn't get to pull that right now. Not when she had a full-on panic attack a minute ago. He needed *something*. Anything.

Throw him a bone here!

Ty set his jaw. "I have a little more faith in us than that. Try me. What's so bad that you don't want to be seen in public with me? Is it your fear of some Dariqat secret agent in a ski mask chasing after me? Or is it something else?" Ty paused, his body getting colder at the fear he didn't want to voice. "Is there *someone* else?" The words felt like they were ripped from him.

Ashley's eyes blew wide. "What? Ty, no, it's not like that. I'm not embarrassed of you at all!" Ashley opened her mouth to say more and then hesitated, a look of discomfort crossing her pretty features.

Fuck, what did that mean?

She reached for his hand imploringly. "I'm just–" Ashley swallowed and looked around, once again changing what she was about to say. "You're just not taking the risk seriously and you need to." She was subtly trying to pull away again, trying to stop them from touching and put more space between them, something that made his chest feel even heavier.

Then she dropped the bomb. "I just can't be seen, and photographed, in public...with you."

Time stood still and Ty was battered by memory after memory of women who let him down.

Woman after woman who lied to him. Manipulated him. Used him.

He thought he was something more to Ashley.

But maybe he really was just the hooker she picked up at a charity bachelor auction.

His mouth was barely able to move enough to form the words, but Ty managed to ask. "I'm not sure I understand. You can't be photographed in public? Or you can't be photographed with me?"

Ashley pulled her bottom lip into her mouth and her pretty white teeth started nibbling at it.

A nervous habit that he used to think was adorable.

But when it was used to not answer a seemingly simple question? He hated it more than being scored on while on a power play.

A total fucking disaster.

He rallied and pushed again. "I don't get it. Why all the secrecy? What are you so afraid of? Is it being seen with me in particular that is so abhorrent or just with any guy in general?"

He hated the pleading note that crept into his voice.

Ashley kept biting at her lip but now she was blinking back tears as Ty finally let her break off all contact between them. "No, it's not just you. It's with anyone. I'm sorry. I wish I could explain more, but...I just...it's not safe for you to be seen with me and I'm just not ready to get into all the details right now...I just need to go home...and process. Or something..."

Ty took a small step back and exhaled heavily, raking both hands through his hair in frustration. "Not ever, more likely. Can you see my confusion here? You have all these sexual fantasies–all these crazy places you want to get it on...but...what if we were caught? Would *that* be okay? You didn't seem to care about being seen with me at the auction. Or at ice skating. Or at dinner? Or at the countless other places we've been together. You've sent me enough fucking nudes to populate a fucking porn site for a year but to be *seen* in public with me? *That* is the problem? Jesus Christ, Ash!"

Ty swore under his breath. He was trying – God knows he was trying – but she continued to shut him out at every turn. He didn't know how much longer he could chip away at those walls before they collapsed on top of him.

"All of those dates were in private locations where media wasn't allowed." Her voice was small. Weak. Tired.

And infuriating.

Where was his tigress?

She needed to fight back!

She needed to fight *for them!*

"Oh, that's nice. Can't be seen with the lowlife, stupid jock? Not as sophisticated as all the rich businessmen of your past?"

That got her attention. Ashley whipped her eyes to him, narrowing them on his face, an angry scowl wrinkling the smooth space on her forehead that he loved to place kisses to.

"Ty! Of course not–"

"Can you see where I'm coming from? What makes me so absolutely *embarrassing* that it literally sends you into an all-out panic to be seen with me? To be *associated* with me?"

"Ty–"

"I know I'm not some genius finance guy, or some creative entrepreneur. And hockey players certainly don't get paid the same salaries as pro football or baseball players, but I think I do all right in the scheme of things. Sure, I love spending my time outdoors. And no, I'm not dramatic. But just because I'm not giving speeches at college graduations, doesn't mean I'm fucking stupid."

She took a small step forward and raised an arm as if to touch him. Ty jerked out of reach, unable to handle her touch right then.

"You didn't answer my question from earlier."

Silence fell.

Ashley wrapped her arms around herself, shoulders hunching as she retreated further into her own world. Ty could see her visibly withdrawing, the light in her eyes dimming as she locked her secrets away.

"I noticed."

She said nothing but stared up at him, terror in her face.

"Is. There. Another. Guy?" He said it in such a slow and even voice that anyone overhearing them would have no doubt about the importance of that question.

The light in Ashley's eyes officially went out as he waited for his answer.

Yeah.

Fuck.

His heart felt heavy and hard in his chest.

He was too young for a heart attack...right?

"Should I ask again? Or do I have my answer?" His voice was wooden and he felt his shoulders collapse in the barest amount.

Ashley took a small step forward, erasing the distance that he had put there when he jerked away.

"It's not like that. I love *you. I love you.* This is not about you. This is about my family and–"

"And how it's not safe for me?"

She blinked in surprise.

"Yeah, you've said that one before. Not sure how much to believe of what you've said. Maybe that one was a truth. Maybe it wasn't. I guess it doesn't really matter, right? I mean, I *tried*. I wanted to be there for you, Ash, I did. But you needed to meet me halfway and you couldn't even do that." Even with the finality of those words, he couldn't help from adding, "I can't keep hitting this wall again and again, give me *something*."

Ashley flinched at his harsh tone, fresh tears spilling down her cheeks.

For a moment, it seemed she might relent, might open up. But then her expression shuttered, lips pressing into a thin line as she stepped back, turning away. "Don't worry. There will be no more 'wall hitting' soon enough."

Fuck.

Well, that was that then.

"Message received. Loud and clear."

Ashley's breath hitched, a muffled sob escaping her lips.

But she didn't call out to stop him as he strode for the nearby door.

Luckily, there were a few of his teammates here at the event —so the kids wouldn't miss *him*. Not Ty.

Apparently neither would Ashley.

He was *just Ty* after all.

Ty paused with his hand on the door, heart hammering against his ribs. "I love you, Ash. More than you will ever know." His voice cracked on the last word. "I hope you find happiness."

And just like she asked, he let go.

Chapter Twenty-Eight

November 7, Saturday

Ashley

After Ty left, Ashley crumpled to her knees, finally letting the tears flow freely, wrapping her arms around her middle as if to keep from splitting apart.

She longed to run after him, to pour her heart out, and end this torture. But the words were lodged in her throat, held back by years of conditioning and expectations.

So, she wept on the cold floor, trusting the parents to keep their kids away in case they rounded the corner and saw their troop leader's heart completely self-destruct.

After fleeing from the 'Mini-Golf with the Hockey Stars Extravaganza' she had meticulously planned and championed, Ashley wandered aimlessly through the park, her heels clicking against the paved path. The sun filtered through the treetops, dappling the ground with shards of light, but she barely noticed the nature around her. Her thoughts were consumed by Ty—his smile, his laugh, the feeling of his strong arms around her.

What she wouldn't give to be with him and not worry about what her father would do in retaliation.

The popping of camera flashes played over in her mind.

She remembered Ty's protective stance in front of her, shielding her from the invasive lens. Her pulse quickened as she imagined the photos being published and landing on her father's desk back in Dariqat. She could practically hear his booming voice berating her for being so careless, threatening to drag her back, and making it his life's mission to ruin Ty in his quest to exact retribution for her risking her marriage to the foreign prince.

Ashley's breath grew ragged. She couldn't lose Ty—not when she finally found someone who saw her as more than just a princess. He encouraged her fiery spirit in a way no one else did. He...calmed her fiery spirit in a way no one else did.

He gave her peace.

Acceptance.

Bliss.

She shook her head bitterly. If only her father cared about how Ty made her *feel*, how he filled the longing in her soul. But the king only cared about duty, propriety, and keeping up appearances. He would never approve of his daughter slighting a neighboring prince. Not even for love.

Ashley kicked at a rock and watched it sail away under a bush.

Fuck her fucking father.

She never got a *choice*.

Her autonomy was taken from her the moment she was born.

Her agreement to marry Prince Tabir was coercion at its finest.

She didn't consider herself engaged.

She didn't consider herself yet another awful woman who made Ty feel like he was the 'other man.'

Ashley was not engaged to someone by choice.

She did not cheat!

And Ty *of all people* should know that she wouldn't do that.

"He should *know*," she sobbed in a broken whisper, angrily wiping the deluge of tears from her face. "*He* should know."

Ashley tilted up her face to the sky, letting the chilly breeze bite at the wet streaks on her face.

What if...she refused to go back?

What if Ty really could find a way to keep her here?

Her heart stuttered and she felt lightheaded.

Could she do it?

Scorn her father and her duty like that?

All for...Ty?

For *herself*?

Fuck, *that* felt good.

The thought of taking back her *choice*?

Of living to *live*, not just to obey...

The thought of reclaiming her agency, of making decisions based on genuine desire rather than mere oppositional defiance, felt liberating.

Ashley lowered her head and straightened her shoulders, chest blazing with heat and nerves.

She prided herself on not letting men control her. Well, one more just got added to the list.

Her father.

She had to tell Ty the truth about her royal heritage, no matter how terrified she felt.

This was *her* life, and she would fight for the man she loved.

And Ty...he'd forgive her for the lies.

He'd understand.

Wouldn't he?

Holy shit.

Was she really doing this?

She'd never see or talk to her siblings again.

Never be able to grab her things from her bedroom in the palace.

Never be able to pull her mom's favorite clothes from the trunk in her closet in Dariqat and hold them up to her nose in an attempt to smell her sweet, rose smell.

She'd lose everything.

Well, not *everything*.

What she'd gain was pretty incredible.

But could she actually do it?

Ashley's steps slowed as she reached a quiet grove of trees. She sank down onto a bench, heart pounding.

Where would she even begin?

She watched a pair of pigeons peck at an abandoned piece of trash, both quickly darting their beaks at the food that had stuck to the plastic. "Hey there, so you see," she pretended to explain things to them as if they were Ty. "I'm not actually *just* a social worker. Surprise! I'm actually a princess. Funny nickname you chose when you met me, huh? And the reason I had to go back to Dariqat? Well, there's this royal wedding my controlling father keeps pressuring me about. Funny thing—it was supposed to be mine. So, yeah, it's an arranged marriage thing that neither of us wanted, and truthfully, I thought that I could maybe talk him out of once I got back to Dariqat. Or maybe I was hoping that Tabir would find love before my time was up here in the States and would cancel on me...But the arrangement was supposed to save lots of lives, or strengthen our economies, or something that I was never actually important enough to know. Why would *I* need to know what my marriage was for? I'm just a silly, little female who let my 'foolish and insane mother pollute my mind.'" Ashley bit off the last part in a sour, low-pitched voice, trying to copy her father's disparaging tone whenever he was forced to bring up one of his deceased wives. "So, I don't know why he's so intent on having me marry Tabir. He never felt fit to tell me; I'm just a woman, I don't need to know; I just need to show up, say I do, and pop out heirs. Sounds like a dream for someone with my personality, right?"

Ashley dragged a hand through her hair. "Oh, and those pictures, they can't get posted because it would cause an international scandal if my ever-so-beloved fiancé and his family found out his future queen was in love with someone she met in the States and publicly shamed their 'engagement'."

She let out a shaky, somewhat insane, laugh.

It all sounded so ridiculous when said out loud.

Ty was going to think she was fucking delusional.

Ashley pictured his bright blue eyes gazing at her with that mix of desire and tenderness that made her weak. She thought of his strong arms around her, his breath warm against her neck. Her heart ached at the possibility of never feeling his touch again.

She had to try.

What did she have to lose?

Resolved, Ashley stood and continued down the path. She'd get a cab to his place, hopefully he was there. And then, before her courage failed her, she would bare her soul completely.

Her future hung in the balance, but she was ready to fight for it—*for them.*

Chapter Twenty-Nine

November 7, Saturday

Ty

Ty's phone buzzed with notification after notification.

Jesus, the guys were incessant.

After he'd stormed out of the mini-golf event, they started shooting him texts and calling him every six seconds. Ty had fired back some quick "I'm fine" texts and headed home. He'd been back for all of thirty seconds and here they were starting in on him again.

"Fuck, guys. Just give me some fucking space." He mumbled as he glanced down, expecting to see a bunch of worrywarts texting him to make sure his feelings were okay.

Instead, his eyebrows furrowed at the barrage of headlines flashing across his lock screen.

Local Hockey Star Dating a Real-Life Princess!

Princess Ashira's Secret Love Affair with Hockey Hunk.

American Athlete Wins Heart of Dariqat Princess.

Dariqat Princess spurns fiancé, a Prince from Meridel, with her American fling.

European Prince scorned after his fiancé had an affair with a hockey player—what does it mean for their countries' alliances? Who will pay the price for the princess's lack of restraint?

Curiosity piqued, Ty tapped on an article, eyes widening as he was faced with Ashley's true identity.

Princess Ashira Wazir of Dariqat.

Engaged to some prince from Meridel.

Ashira Wazir. Not Ashley Winters.

Fuck.

How had Ashley kept this from him? All those vague comments about family expectations and pressures.

He scrolled further, pulse quickening at the photos of Ashley in elegant gowns and tiaras—a far cry from the jeans and sweaters she wore around him. Was she just slumming it with him like the article said? Using him for a thrill before her royal duties consumed her? Was this her way of getting an adrenaline kick before it was all tea parties and galas?

His grip on the phone tightened, jaw clenching. Betrayal and anger simmered within him. He'd opened up to Ashley, let her in. And she'd kept this massive secret. Played him for a fool.

He'd actually believed she loved him. God, he was fucking stupid.

No wonder she kept stonewalling him when he was trying to brainstorm ways to get her to stay.

There was no fucking way she'd want to stay with a nobody like him when she had a fucking prince waiting for her back home.

Ty hit pucks for a living. He was a low life compared to a fucking *prince*!

With a growl of frustration, he tossed his phone onto the couch, raking both hands through his hair.

What now?

Confront her?

Avoid her?

Give a statement to the press? That's probably what the Cyclones management would want.

His heart and head waged war as the truth shattered the illusion of the pedestal he had placed her on. Ty paced his apartment, emotions churning as he tried to process this bombshell.

Had he really meant nothing to her?

He thought of the easy way she was able to wipe the emotions from her face.

Yeah, she was a good actress. He witnessed it firsthand time and time again. Somehow, the naïve part of him had him convinced he was seeing the truth as it slipped through—not a second layer of acting so she could get her rocks off with a stupid jock.

He recalled their first meeting at the auction, the easy banter and their undeniable chemistry. The late nights spent tangled in each other's arms. Her melodic laugh, the way she scrunched her nose when she smiled.

Had it all been part of an act? Just a princess playing commoner and slaking her rebellious streak?

The more Ty thought about it, the more he believed it. God, how could he have been so blind? All along he had wondered what she saw in him. Now he knew...nothing.

She had used him.

Anger and hurt roiled inside him, causing his jaw to tighten.

A knock at the door jolted him from his brooding. Ty stomped over to it and swung it open, giving a small start when he found Ashley on the other side with creases of worry lining her face.

"Ty, I know you must have questions," she began, words spilling out rapidly. "I wanted to tell you, truly, but it was too risky and—"

"Save it," Ty snapped, grabbing her arm and yanking her inside. The last thing they needed was another paparazzi shot. "Was this all just a game? Slumming it with a dumb jock before you got to marry some fancy, foreign prince?"

Ashley flinched, looking stricken. "No, Ty, please..." She reached for him but he recoiled. "It's complicated, my father, the marriage...I never meant to hurt you."

Ty's laugh held no humor. "Was anything you ever said true? Or was it all just royal lies?" He forced himself to turn away before he started to really light into her about her betrayal.

The woman he thought he knew had vanished, leaving only disillusionment behind.

Ashley's breath hitched, tears welling in her eyes. "My feelings for you are real, Ty. The time we spent together...I've never felt so free, so alive." She moved closer, voice dropping to a desperate whisper. "I don't want to lose this. Lose you."

Ty stiffened. He wanted to believe her, and yearned for things to be as they were. "Oh yeah? Why the sudden change now? You've been adamant this whole time that you needed to go back home. I see why now. He's handsome for sure. Rich as fucking God, if the news articles are correct. You've made it abundantly clear this whole time we had a deadline. I didn't understand then. I do now," he rasped out. "Problem solved, *Princess*."

She flinched. Then she inhaled shakily, moving tentatively towards him. "I know. And I'm sorry. Let me explain..." She reached for his hand but he pulled away once more. Her face pinched with the pain of his rejection. Swallowing hard, she persevered. "Back in Dariqat, my life is not my own. I'm a princess first, a person second. Every choice is made for me. It's suffocating." Her eyes misted again. "With you, I can just be Ashley. Not royalty. Myself. Just me." She searched Ty's face beseechingly. "I never meant to hurt you. And I want to try. All I want is a chance...for us."

"Did you agree to the marriage?" he asked, his voice low.

Ashley hesitated, dropping her gaze.

"Look at me," Ty said sharply. "Did you agree to marry him?"

Ashley's shoulders slumped in defeat. "Yes," she whispered. "But only because it was the only way I could get out of the country. It wasn't a real engagement or anything. I was told of it by my father when Idris and I were negotiating my trip here. I was hoping he'd find the love of his life while I was here and call it off. Or that I could renegotiate with my father...or something. I never thought I'd find someone like you. That I'd...fall in love."

"So, you're engaged."

She wrinkled her nose and looked like she was going to deny it.

"I don't want the sob story. Yes or no, are you engaged?"

Her face paled as she stared at him. "Are you even hearing what I'm saying? I'm trying to open up. Like you asked me to. I'm trying to–"

"Yes or no?"

"Ty–"

"Yes or no, *Ashira*?"

She stepped back as if she'd been struck, raking a hand through her hair. "Yes. Yes, I guess by your standards I'm engaged. Happy? Is that all you want to know? Is that all you care about?"

"So, this whole time...you've just been playing me for a fool. Cheap–sorry, *expensive*–entertainment?"

"No, that's not true and you know it."

"Isn't it?" Ty fired back. "Slumming it with a hockey player while you keep your royal fiancé on the side?"

"Are you not listening to me? I'm going to find a way to get out of it! And I haven't even spoken to Tabir in *years*! It was arranged by our parents, not us!" Ashley stepped forward, her face wrecked and desperate. "I want to be with you, Ty. *You*."

Ty's huffed out a dry laugh. "Huh. Weird. Cuz I feel like I tried to get you to stay with me. Again and again, actually, and you kept saying no. Earlier today even." He gave her a dark look. "Or am I remembering that wrong?"

"No, but—"

"And I feel like I kept trying to get you to share more with me and you kept your little secrets close to the chest. And when I told you about those women using me...you didn't even blink." He rubbed his face with his hands. "Well, it's not like it's a surprise. I have a fucking, Goddamn, type."

Ashley reached for him. "Please, you have to understand. I was trapped, I felt like I had no choice—"

"Stop." Ty held up a hand. "Please." His voice broke. "Please stop with the lies and excuses. As I've told you before: I've heard them all and I'm just so...tired. So, please...as you once so perfectly recited, *let me go*." Each breath was a struggle, as if the air itself became thick and resistant.

He stepped around her and went to his apartment door, pulling it open.

Ty used every ounce of willpower to not show just how utterly destroyed and betrayed he was.

It was easy to tell when a couple was toxic...when it wasn't your own relationship.

He was thinking that once he told this to Bobby, his friend would give him the hard truth, that some things were just too broken to fix.

And some betrayals were just too big to forgive.

With tears streaming down her face, Ashley walked slowly to the threshold. She paused, searching Ty's stoic expression for any flicker of warmth, but he gave her none.

He'd taken a page out of her book and made certain his face was as empty as possible.

As empty as her soul. And now, his too.

His chest tightened, a relentless vice squeezing until his ribs felt as though they might crack under the pressure. The pain was not just emotional but physical, a deep, gnawing ache that resonated through his very bones.

With shoulders hunched in defeat, Ashley slipped past him and out of his life.

Good.

But if it was so good, why did he feel as if he had just watched his last chance at pure happiness walk out of his life forever?

As he tossed on his rose-scented pillows that night, the echo of her laughter, the fire in her eyes, and the heat of her soft skin was a haunting echo that replayed mercilessly in his mind.

Chapter Thirty
November 7, Saturday
Ashley

Ashley rushed away from Ty's apartment, her cheeks flushed with anger and dejection. She had never felt so conflicted in her life.

Probably a bit how Ty was feeling....

The air outside was crisp and cool, doing little to calm her racing heart as she made her way through the streets to her apartment. Her mind was a whirlwind of emotions.

She wanted Ty. She wanted to support her family—her country. She wanted to continue to make positive impacts on the community around her. Though her heart felt torn to shreds, there was at least one tiny bright spot that burned hot—her success with Garrett and Connell. Because of her, Connell would never have to spend another night homeless. Because of her work with Garrett, and his recognition of her good intentions, she had been able to get through to him. Maybe with a little more time, she could even help him help himself.

But to do all that, she needed to be *here*. *Not* in Dariqat.

Ashley and Ty's apartments weren't even close to being in the same part of the city but the cold barely registered. It didn't matter, anyway. She needed to walk this out. A cab would bring her home much too fast. She needed...time.

Story of her fucking life.

Once she finally got back to her building, Ashley dragged herself up the stairs and shuffled down the hallway, her vision blurred by tears—brought on by not only sadness, but the freezing temperatures.

The confrontation with Ty kept replaying in her mind on an agonizing loop. She had never seen him look so cold, so closed off. His bright blue eyes that usually shone with laughter had been hard chips of ice. Damn, is that how she looked when she closed off her own feelings from him?

Her heart squeezed.

Shit.

As she reached her apartment door, Ashley paused, trying to steady her breathing and gather her thoughts. She leaned against the door, attempting to find some semblance of balance amidst the chaos in her heart. With a deep breath, she fumbled with her keys and finally unlocked the door.

She stepped inside the darkness and didn't bother with flicking on the lights. Despite the gloom, the walls were vibrant with photos and decorations collected during her time in the States. This had been her home. The only place she'd truly felt comfortable.

Dropping her purse on the floor, she went to the kitchen and slid into one of the dark, wooden dining chairs. Finally, she let the sobs overcome her.

She had lost him—the only man she had ever truly loved.

The vision of Ty's face, alight with passion, swam before her eyes. The feeling of his strong arms wrapped around her, the brush of his fingertips against her skin, were sensations she would likely never experience again.

Wiping her eyes, Ashley glanced around the beautiful kitchen. This had been her haven, a place where she could pretend the crown waiting for her back in Dariqat didn't exist. That she was just a normal woman free to live and love as she chose.

Ashley closed her eyes tight.

But the fantasy was over. Reality was crashing down around her. Her father and the royal council were expecting her back in Dariqat soon, where she would marry the stupid prince as they had been arranged. Her time was almost up, closing the window of freedom she had carved out for herself.

Could she leave everything behind and stay for Ty? Renounce her family, her country, and give up her royal title?

It was the choice she desperately wanted to make. But the consequences would be severe. Not just for her, but for her family and her people.

Getting up, she grabbed a tissue from the box on a side table and made her way into the living room, where she stopped dead.

Her heart plummeted into her stomach.

Sitting on her living room couch, looking stern and serious, were her father and older brother.

Ashley's blood ran cold as she realized that the stakes had just become much higher.

"Father...Idris," she managed to stammer, her hands shaking slightly. "What are you doing here?"

"Oh, good. You're finally done with your blubbering?" Her father's expressive dark eyes bore into hers, making it impossible for her to look away. Beside him, her brother, Idris, sat silently, his worried gaze flicking between Ashley and their father.

"Of course. I'm sorry you had to witness that," she replied quickly, trying to regain some semblance of composure. "I wasn't aware that you were here. I wasn't expecting you."

Fucking lockpicks. Her door *had* been locked. She was sure of it.

"Ashira. We're *always* here. One way or another," her father scolded in a tone that sent shivers down her spine.

What could she say to that?

Nothing really, so she positioned her hands neatly in front of her like her mother had taught her and assumed a posture that indicated subservience—a disgusting show of respect.

"Moving on," her father said, his voice dripping with disapproval. "We're here because we need to discuss some important matters with you. You've clearly enjoyed your visit here, but it's time for you to come back and fulfill your responsibilities. We were present well before the media frenzy erupted, so the timing is fortuitous. We can depart this evening, and this incident will fade into obscurity within a mere week. It will all be forgotten. Not by Prince Tabir or his parents, I'm sure. But the US outlets will move on. If not, I'm sure your brother can find something else for them to focus on."

Idris nodded, his face tight, yet somehow, she thought she detected a sadness there.

For dragging her back to Dariqat? For cutting her time short? Or for the fact that she selfishly risked her entire nation's security?

Ashley's heart raced, her mind screaming at her to find a way out of this impossible situation, but she couldn't get her brain to work right. She just kept hearing herself screaming internally.

Ashley's heart pounded in her chest as her father rose to his feet, the regal bearing and stern countenance she'd always associated with him making her feel like a small child again. The air in the room seemed to grow heavy, suffocating her with the weight of unspoken expectations.

"Father, please—" she started, but he cut her off with a dismissive wave of his hand.

Ashley's stomach tightened into a knot, her mind racing with a hundred different thoughts and emotions.

"Enough, Ashira. You've had your chance to explore this country, to experience its culture and its people. But now it's time for you to stop this foolish rebellious streak and start thinking about your duty to your family and your country. Your work here was touching, quaint, and you can do much more once you return home. You'll see. The children you and Prince Tabir will have will form a strong alliance between our countries and I know you don't agree with a lot of our customs, this is what you agreed to when Idris negotiated this...sabbatical."

His words stung like a slap to the face, and Ashley felt her cheeks burn with a mix of shame and indignation. Her father had never been one to hold back his opinions, but hearing them now, after already being slaughtered by Ty, was almost too much to bear.

"Sabbatical? Vacation? Is that really all you think I've been doing?" she snapped, the anger bubbling up inside her finally breaking free. "Just taking a walk on the wild side? One last hurrah? I've been working hard, trying to make a difference in the lives of people who need help. I'm not just some frivolous girl on a wild adventure!"

"Enough!" her father bit out, his face turning a deep shade of red. "I will not sit here and have my daughter speak to me so. Remember your place, Ashira. You know as well as I do that your place is in Dariqat, fulfilling the duties you were born to carry out. That has never wavered."

Tears pricked at the corners of Ashley's eyes, but she refused to let them fall. She took a deep breath, trying to steady herself, and met her father's fierce gaze head-on. Her father's words hung heavy in the air, like a storm cloud ready to burst.

Ashley clutched her hands together, trying to control their trembling.

He continued, "You know as well as I do that your place is not only in Dariqat, but by the side of your future husband. You are to marry and strengthen the alliance our family has built. And, *Ashira*" – he emphasized her true name, a reminder of the weight behind it – "you are to produce heirs."

The mention of producing heirs struck Ashley like a punch to the gut. She knew this had been part of the deal when she'd left for the United States, but hearing it now made it all too real. The thought of being trapped in a loveless marriage, her life dictated by duty, turned her blood to ice.

Having children with someone she didn't love...Someone who wasn't Ty...

She wanted to vomit. She wanted to run.

"Father," she began, her voice barely above a whisper, "I've tried to make something of myself here, to be more than just a princess waiting to fulfill her duties. Can't you see that?"

Her father's voice thundered through the room, causing Ashley to flinch involuntarily. "You've had your time here, pursuing your interests and indulging your whims. I even let you dally around with your useless hockey player out of honor for the deal that you and your brother struck." Beside him, Idris flinched. "But now, it is time for you to return home and do what is expected of you. The advisors are getting restless...and with your lack of communication with us...we felt it was time to cut this vacation short. Maybe if you had made yourself more available to our summons, we wouldn't have had to resort to this."

Ashley stared at her father, her heart pounding in her chest, her eyes wide with shock.

He had come all the way to the United States just to confront her like this?

What the hell was happening back in Dariqat with his 'advisors' to warrant this personal trip? Idris alone would have sufficed.

Though he would have had to drag her by her hair to get her to board their plane.

"Father, I have one more month," she said, desperation creeping into her voice. "Give me the rest of my time. I still have so much I want to do here. You have repeatedly reminded me that my foolish and rebellious 'degrees' will be wasted as soon as I return to Dariqat and marry. Let me transition my clients in a healthy way, let me finish my time here." She ended her plea in a small, tight voice. "I'm not ready to say goodbye yet."

"Time is a luxury you no longer have, Ashira. You made that decision when you brandished your fling for everyone to see. At least your previous dalliances were able to be kept discreet and hidden from the media...despite your apparent *insistence* on having many of those odious affairs in public locations. It was your *dear* brother's responsibility to keep tabs on you here and make sure that you were adhering to the terms of our agreement. Idris was also responsible for ensuring discretion from those who might be tempted to share information on those romantic liaisons. He proved himself incapable of handling such a simple task." He shot a scathing look at Idris, who failed to hide his wince. "There will be consequences, I'm sure, but we'll deal with that when we get home." His tone was final, leaving no room for argument.

But the photos were *just* barely released...

And he said that they were here before that.

It wasn't adding up.

She opened her mouth to ask, but snapped it shut at the steely light in his eyes.

It didn't matter.

She needed to remember her place.

And it wasn't questioning her father.

Already he had allowed her more than was normal for their interactions. Any more and she was pushing it. She would be leaving the States, and nothing she said could stop it.

He probably had security stationed somewhere in the building, just waiting for the word to bodily remove her from her home.

And they would, too.

Kidnapping his daughter wouldn't even be close to the worst thing he had done.

As reality began to sink in, Ashley's emotions threatened to overwhelm her. Her thoughts raced, trying to find a way out of this impossible situation. She couldn't deny her father's demands forever, but the thought of leaving everything behind – especially Ty – filled her with dread. The love and passion they had shared felt like a cruel joke now, a beautiful dream that was quickly turning into a nightmare. They couldn't end things like this.

"Father," she said, her voice shaking with suppressed tears. "I know my duty, and I will do what is required of me. But please," she hesitated, struggling to find the right words, "please give me my last month."

"Things have changed in your time away. The landscape of our politics has shifted. Yours and your mother's silly dreams are not worth the future of our family or our country," he replied coldly.

Her feelings meant absolutely nothing to him.

His steadfast conviction left her feeling small and powerless, her hopes and dreams crumbling around her. As she looked into his iron gaze, she realized just how much she stood to lose. He would do whatever was necessary to ensure her return...including hurting Ty.

Her brother, still seated on the couch, cleared his throat and shifted uncomfortably. Idris glanced between their father and Ashley, anxiety etched in the lines of his face. "Father," he began cautiously, "perhaps there is a middle ground we can reach. We all know how determined Ashira can be, but she has also shown great dedication to our family and our country. What's one more month?"

Ashley looked to her brother with a mix of gratitude and hope.

"Compromise?" her father scoffed, his eyes never leaving Ashley's face. "This is not a matter of negotiation. It is her duty, her responsibility. There can be no compromise when it comes to our family's legacy. And, as if I would entertain another idiotic compromise with *you*. " He spit out the words like they tasted sour.

Damn, what had happened when she was gone?

Ashley's heart sank. He wouldn't budge and he expected nothing less than her complete obedience.

"I have worked hard here," she said, her voice trembling. "I have made a difference, and I have found happiness. Isn't that worth something?"

"Your happiness is important, yes," her father admitted, his eyes softening ever so slightly. "But you must understand that your duty to our family and our country comes first. You cannot put your personal desires above the needs of your people."

Her brother chimed in again, attempting to mediate. "Perhaps we could find a solution that allows Ashira to fulfill her duties while still pursuing her dreams. Surely there must be a way for both worlds to coexist."

The atmosphere in the room grew heavier and Ashley could feel the weight of her father's gaze as he considered his son's words. She knew that she was trapped between her love for Ty and her sense of duty to her family. The thought of losing either one left her feeling gutted.

"Please," she whispered, barely able to meet her father's eyes, "let me find a way to do both."

Her father's silence hung in the air like a thick fog, making it difficult for Ashley to breathe. She could see the worry in her brother's expression as if he were holding his breath along with her.

"No. I've been patient with you, but I can no longer stand idly by while you continue to disgrace our family and your country. The bodyguards..." He cast a sour look at Idris who was now standing stiffly, eyes straight ahead. "The *bodyguards* that your brother *hired* to monitor you here have...." Her father's face darkened and he stopped talking to visibly control his anger. "Well, that's *another* thing your brother and I will be *discussing*. Apparently, your brother's standards for what is acceptable are much different than mine."

Before Ashley was allowed to come to the States, Idris had contracted with a local security company for high-level protection. She knew she was monitored, but not to the extent her father would have demanded. Ashley had met with the agency's owner after arriving, pleading for more discreet monitoring. Eventually, they monitored her from afar, giving her a semblance of privacy, especially during her dates. While they were 'close,' she mostly forgot they were around since they didn't interfere or hover—an approach vastly different from her father's expectations outlined in the contract. She was unsure what was in the reports the men submitted to her brother for the council's review, but they had promised her again and again not to worry about it and that they would support her. She felt a wave of guilt at possibly getting the security agency in trouble with her father, but then again, maybe it wasn't that big of a deal... The owner had looked heartbroken for her as she begged for some freedom, and afterward, he was *very* confident in his promise of giving her an opportunity to experience *life*.

"Your *mother* and brother put this trip to the States in motion, in a way that I couldn't stop, but I at least thought I had a trusted team here to monitor you and make sure you didn't...debase yourself and Dariqat," her father's voice grew louder, faintly trembling with the rage he was trying to control. "And to get news that you were sleeping around and dallying with a public figure..." He shook his head, his disapproval almost tangible. "To shame your husband—and me!—by acting like...a...a *slut!*"

Woah. Ashley recoiled at his horrible words.

Oh God.

She sucked in a ragged breath and tried to maintain the calm, poised expression that was always expected of her. Despite Ashley's best efforts, her lips trembled, and tears threatened to spill from her eyes as she looked at her father's disgusted face. She darted a quick look at Idris and found him wearing his own disappointed expression. Fighting to maintain a steady voice, Ashley began, "I never meant to hurt anyone..."

"Your actions say otherwise," her father retorted, his regal air making him as unapproachable and as untouchable as ever. "You have all but rubbed your dalliances in Tabir's family's face. We all are deeply insulted by your blatant disregard and disrespect."

Her relationships were private and nothing like this had ever happened before. Honestly, she was surprised it hadn't, and looking back, she should have been much more concerned about the fallout if it had. The tabloids today had been a blindside. What had prompted it? Why had someone recognized her now?

And why was her father here *personally* to deliver this message?

He continued speaking at her, completely oblivious to her inner turmoil. "Ty Daniels was part of the Council's plan to keep you safe and distracted, and to prevent you from engaging in yet *additional* relationships with *numerous* people."

Ashley rocked back, shock ripping through her, tearing every single muscle to shreds in the wake of its violence.

"The fool was *supposed* to be a *temporary* distraction—not someone you'd fall for. He was aware of this expectation and breached his contract as well. We'll see how much he values his idiotic nonprofit soon enough—we'll be visiting with him while you pack."

The words hit Ashley like a physical blow, knocking the air from her lungs. She sat frozen, her eyes wide and unblinking as she tried to absorb the revelation. A rush of conflicting emotions swept through her—anger, disbelief, and a profound sense of betrayal. Her hands shook uncontrollably, and her heart hammered against her ribs. The world seemed to tilt, leaving her feeling disconnected and lost. It didn't make any sense...Ty wouldn't do that...would he?

"Wh-what?" Ashley whispered, her chest aching. A roaring sounded in her head. Her hands started to shake, and she couldn't feel her legs.

"Tyler Daniels." Her father said his name with disgust. "He was to keep you occupied as your specialty visa expired, not to show you off to the world. Your relationship was to be kept quiet, out of the spotlight. Silly ice skating, stupid hikes, and private events. He broke his end of the bargain when he started taking you out in public places. That was *completely* unacceptable. It prompted our visit. Among other things." Her father turned and glared at Idris, which elicited another flinch from her brother. Their father just shook his head in distaste, like a business partner had just let him down.

Her chest felt too tight.

Ty?

Her Ty?

He wouldn't have played her like that.

The thought of Ty being part of some elaborate scheme to keep her entertained was... impossible.

Right?

Ashley was reminded of Ty's land project in Dariqat—the one that meant so much to him.

Oh, God, please no.

Her hands trembled at her sides, and she fought the urge to scream.

"I don't understand..."

Her father looked down his nose at her, "Nor would I expect you to."

Ashley shook her head, trying to clear it. "Leaving Ty aside...my work here—"

"Your work here is a joke. A specialty visa and job placement were a favor from one friend to another. Your responsibilities to Dariqat—and Meridel—are actually important. That is where you belong: fulfilling your duties and keeping your promises."

At the look on her face, the king frowned and sighed. Reaching to his side, he pulled out a thick folder from the edge of the couch. He tossed it on the coffee table between them with a decisive flick.

Ashley hesitated before she reached for it, her heart pounding in her chest.

"Fine. See for yourself."

With trembling hands, she opened the folder and scanned the documents inside. Case files, detailed reports, and photographs—all related to her job as a social worker. As she flipped through the pages, one thing became painfully clear: her family had been pulling strings behind the scenes to resolve many of her cases. The realization felt like a slap in the face.

"Idris?" she whispered in disbelief, tears stinging her eyes.

Her brother swallowed hard, indecision creeping into his expression. "We keep tabs. We ensure cooperation in cases where a little...extra motivation...is required. When you spoke of the young boy weeks ago...we already had an entire file on him. You were right: his father should have trusted others to his care. Now he did. *We* solved your problem. *That's* what family does. We help each other and do what is best for our family."

"Help each other?" She slammed the folder shut, her tight voice rising with every word. "You...You..."

But words failed her.

Everything she had thought she had achieved had been linked to her family's interference. Right down to Garrett and Connell Baylor. She never could have imagined that her periodic phone calls to her brother were being used against her like this.

It might have been to the benefit of some, but what sort of coercion had her clients been forced to endure?!

"You're telling me that everything I've accomplished here was...because of you?" The words burned coming out. Actually, everything inside her burned. "I've...done...*nothing? Accomplished nothing? Helped no one?*" Her voice was small and high, a mockery of her usual confident and modulated tone. A pressure in her chest had her sucking in deep breaths.

She had done *nothing* while she was here.

All that work. All those hours. All the heartache and sleepless nights.

All for nothing.

She was nothing.

How could this be happening?

Had Babs known?

Ashley's heart raced as her emotions threatened to spiral out of control.

Her family, the people who she was supposed to trust most, had lied to her about so much.

Even Ty, the man she had grown to love, was somehow entangled in their web of deceit.

"Control yourself," her father commanded, slamming his hand down on the armrest of the chair. "It's time for you to return to Dariqat, Ashira. You must fulfill your obligations as a member of our family and as the country's princess."

The conclusiveness of his tone left Ashley feeling hollow.

She had always known that her duty would come before her desires, but she had never imagined that it would tear her heart apart like this.

Not only was her time here a complete farce. A child's attempt at autonomy....

But the 'great love' she found?

The one she wanted to risk everything for had been a farce as well.

She closed her eyes and tried to suck the tears back in, knowing her father would hate seeing them.

"Very well," she whispered, her voice barely audible as she tried desperately to clear her expression...and failed.

Her eyes flickered to her brother, the crowned prince, who still stood like a silent sentry.

The unspoken plea in her gaze begged him to refute their father's words, to tell her this was all a terrible joke.

Her brother winced, his eyes filled with guilt and reluctance.

Ashley closed her eyes again, swallowed another gulp of air, trying not to succumb to the sob making its way through her chest.

As much as she wanted to fight, to scream that she would not be forced into a loveless marriage, Ashley knew there was no escaping her responsibilities. Both her country and her family demanded it of her. And perhaps this was the only way she could truly make a difference in the lives of those she cared for.

"Fine," she whispered, her body trembling with the weight of her decision. "I'll go back. I'll marry the prince."

Her father nodded, a look of satisfaction on his face, while Idris' expression remained conflicted.

All she felt was an overwhelming sense of loss.

She had given up her dreams, her freedom, and the man she loved—all for a duty that had been thrust upon her from birth. And as she stood there, surrounded by the shattered pieces of her once-hopeful life, she couldn't help but wonder if she would ever truly find happiness again.

Chapter Thirty-One

November 7, Saturday

Ashley

Ashley's father summoned his security and left the apartment with little fanfare.

Apparently it was time to exact his vengeance on Ty 'the liar' Daniels.

How could she have been so foolish?

All those one-on-one dates. All those private, secluded moments.

How could she not have suspected something like this?

Especially after Ty's land protection campaign had been so miraculously green lit. She would bet anything that the campaign had been his bargaining chip. Sure, he'd keep her busy if they approved his nonprofit's big proposal.

Ashley ground her teeth in a desperate attempt not to dissolve back into tears.

Her brother lingered; his face indecisive as he glanced around the apartment she had made her home.

"It's a completely different vibe in person than in pictures."

Then he needed better spies.

"It's...*you,*" Idris said, his eyes locking onto her.

They both stood there in their respective silences.

Softly, she cleared her throat and dared to ask, "Was Ty really a part of this?"

She needed to know.

She saw the struggle within him, but when he finally spoke, his voice was steady. "Yes, Ash," he admitted. "Ty's involvement was part of the act to protect you and ensure that you stayed out of trouble.

We enlisted him after the auction. Our contacts had informed us of the events and they...*we*...made decisions."

The air seemed to evade her lungs. For a moment, she couldn't breathe.

How could a person take this much pain and still be standing?

She rubbed at her chest – it ached – like she herself had just been checked into the boards at one of Ty's beloved hockey games.

"How could *you*?"

How could Ty?

Her brother flinched at the accusation, but he didn't back down. "We did what we thought was best for you and Dariqat," he said quietly, his voice thick with emotion. "I'm sorry you feel betrayed, but our intentions were never to hurt you."

"That doesn't feel even remotely true," she shot back, tears brimming in her eyes.

As she stared at her brother, memories of their shared childhoods and secrets flooded her mind, only to be tainted by the realization that even he had kept something so monumental from her. It felt as though the very ground beneath her feet was crumbling, leaving her grasping for something – anything – to hold onto.

Her once-strong bond with her brother was broken, leaving her feeling more alone than ever before. The sting of treachery coursed through her veins, hot and sharp like a poison.

"Ty..." she whispered, her voice breaking as she thought of their recent fight. The hurtful words they had exchanged now took on an entirely new meaning, and she couldn't help but wonder how much of it was real and how much of it had been part of this twisted plan. Was he supposed to end it nastily to make her departure to Dariqat easier? Or had he truly been heartbroken?

Fuck! Why was no one being honest with her!

It was probably a situation of 'Pot meet Kettle,' but still!

"Please, Ash," Idris implored, reaching for her hand. "We did what we had to do. You know how Father can be. We can work through this together. I'm still here for you. Everything will be fine once we get home, and the marriage is finalized. Everything will get better."

Ashley yanked her hand away.

He didn't get to fucking touch her.

She needed time to think, to sort through the lies and determine where she stood in this mess of deception.

"Right now," she said, her voice cold and distant, "I'm not convinced anything will *ever* get better."

Ashley looked one last time at the quaint apartment, the room feeling smaller than ever, and retreated silently to her bedroom.

She had a suitcase to pack.

It was time to move on.

Chapter Thirty-Two

November 8, Sunday morning

Ty

Ty's phone spent the night receiving ping after ping of media coverage updates talking about his fling with Ashley. The news outlets dissected everything: guesses on how they met, how they were going to make it work *when* he was traded, what her family must have thought, and what Dariqat was like.

Frustratingly, each article or sports talk show seemed to have countless *unnamed* 'sources' who *promised* that Ty was on the roster chopping block.

Then, after receiving a 'goodbye' text from Ashley, Ty gave up on sleep and headed into the practice facility. Her message was short and to the point—she was flying out later that afternoon and wished him all the happiness in the world. The words stung like a slap, and he rushed to the arena for a pre-practice workout, desperate to burn off the excess...everything...he was feeling. Plus,

The lights from the parking lot cast long shadows against the walls as he entered the building, his sneakers squeaking on the polished floor. His mind buzzed with thoughts of Ashley's deception, intertwined with the uncertainty of his career.

Ty already lost his girl. Now, with no distractions left, the gnawing uncertainty of his job security loomed over him. The threat of losing his home, the bonds with his teammates—some of whom he considered family—and his sense of belonging, were fading away.

What chain email from middle school had he ignored to deserve *this* level of bad luck?

He felt a knot of anxiety tie in his stomach as he walked through the doors of the deserted facility. The scent of fresh ice and cleaning products swirled around him, usually a comforting aroma that now only heightened his unease and loneliness.

Navigating the corridors, Ty spotted Coach Montgomery in one of the side classrooms, his gaze fixed on a screen dominating the wall. Despite the coach's outward calm, the tension in his shoulders hinted at the stress he was under.

Well, he could just *join the fucking club.*

Ty paused in the doorway, observing Montgomery hastily scribbling notes on a nearly filled-up paper.

Demanding the truth from Ashley while keeping his own secrets...fuck, he was a dick. Ty had expected complete honesty from Ashley, a woman he had only known for a few weeks, without considering her feelings, history, circumstances, or the risk to them both. And then...he'd unapologetically shut her down when she tried to explain. The memory of her hurt expression lingered in his mind.

His heart squeezed with a mix of anger and regret. He grabbed tight to the betrayed outrage...that was weakening by the second. But if he didn't hold onto his anger, he'd drown in the despair of losing the woman he loved.

Taking a deep breath, Ty resolved to confront his own hypocrisy. He'd told Ashley that he'd wait until she was comfortable to share, promising to work through whatever it was with her...and then broke that promise immediately. But, he'd at least given her the benefit of the doubt up until then. Ty hadn't extended that same courtesy to his coach. He needed to know what was going on; Ty couldn't keep living like this—his anxiety was choking him.

What do they say about conflict? That it's a momentary discomfort needed for long-term growth?

Well...here it goes, watch him grow.

Squaring his shoulders, Ty stepped into the room. “Coach, can we talk?”

Coach Montgomery jumped slightly and glanced toward the door, his eyes widening at the sight of Ty standing there. "Of course, Ty," Coach Montgomery replied, his brow furrowing. "Come on in."

As they settled into the small room, Ty's heart pounded on the wall of his chest as hard as a puck slamming against the boards. He stared into the coach's eyes, forcing himself to embrace the discomfort.

"I need to know what's really going on with these trade rumors," Ty started, his voice wavering slightly. "I've been hearing things, and it's messing with my head. Blaine’s interference, the changes to the lineup... it’s all too much. I need to know if there’s any truth to the rumors about a roster shake-up."

Coach Montgomery's eyes bore into Ty's, clearly searching for the right words to explain the chaos that had engulfed their team. "Ty, it’s complicated," the coach began, slumping his weight forward onto his forearms, leaning against the table. "I’m not sure how much is circulating and how much isn’t...” His voice was tentative like he didn’t know how much to divulge.

"I need to know if there is a real chance that I might be traded. *I don't...*" Ty swallowed hard, trying to not let his voice crack. "*I don't have anyone here.* Not like the guys with families and stuff. But...this team...these guys...I've felt at home here in a way I never have. I don't want to leave, but I also know it's part of the gig. Regardless, I need to know. My brain is fried and it's totally fucking with me...and I know that sounds weak and shit, but I don't care. *I'm...floundering, Coach.* I really just need someone to give me a heads up here." Ty's throat tightened, "Please."

As Coach Montgomery took in Ty’s ravaged and exhausted expression, the older man blinked and sat back. Something like surprise rippled down his hard features. After staring into Ty's defeated eyes, Coach Montgomery took a deep breath and rubbed at his face, a small look of grief and shame ghosting across his features.

He closed his eyes for a moment and then, when he looked back up at Ty, there was a new steely resolve in his face.

Whatever internal realization or debate he had just had with himself…the transformation now was…

Yikes.

With a determined look, the coach leaned toward Ty and clasped his shoulder tightly, his hand firm and warm. "Blaine has been causing a lot of problems in the office. He's trying to undermine Sam and take over. He wants more control over the team and is using these rumors to destabilize things. He was seriously pissed when a *woman* got the GM position over him and has rallied the 'old guard' within management to destabilize her efforts for the team. I *believe* he's trying to set it up so that he can come in and save the day."

Ty's gut twisted.

Fuck.

Coach Montgomery's grip on Ty's shoulder tightened. "I was trying to play the game. Keep both sides happy. But all that I ended up doing was screwing over everyone. This shit has reached a breaking point. I've had enough of this manipulation. My job is to coach my guys, not to be a pawn in some power struggle. You all deserve better than this."

Ty felt a weight *partially* lift off his chest. "Oh."

Coach Montgomery nodded, his expression resolute. "I'll clear the air with the rest of the team too. You guys deserve to know the truth. I should have put my foot down weeks ago. I should have realized that this was what was bothering some of you—I sometimes forget that not everyone processes the media dialogue and rumors in the same way. Because I was always able to ignore it, I tend to assume that everyone processes it similarly. I forgot that that's not the case. I should have taken more care with you all."

They chatted until they started hearing people start to move through the halls outside the classroom. Coach Montgomery walked

Ty back out to the hall, apologizing and promising to address the rumors before practice later.

Now that his work concerns were *somewhat* addressed, Ty made his way to the locker room obsessively thinking about Ashley.

Had his worries and stress about his spot on the team made him more trigger-happy, contributing to his intense reaction to Ashley's revelation?

The thought hit him hard, nearly choking him with the depth of his heartbreak and the pain of regret.

There were so many unspoken apologies and questions festering inside him. He had let his past betrayals taint his response and allowed his stress to boil over into his relationship with Ashley. The fear of being cast aside again had consumed him, and he had struck out, reacting without taking the time to hear her...or...like he always tried to do, 'read' her—not just hear her words, but her intent and emotions behind them. One simple blindside and he'd closed her down. Like an asshole.

The memory of Ashley's tear-filled eyes and her cracking voice as she said goodbye haunted him. Despite their different backgrounds, she had been the one person he truly connected with, and now she was gone.

With a heavy sigh, Ty acknowledged that the damage was done, and all he could do was move forward, which meant focusing on the team and helping them navigate the Cyclones' management struggles.

If he could just make it through practice and lunch with the guys, perhaps he could go home, crawl into bed, and find a way to process his feelings without spiraling into a depression. He had lost something incredibly precious...and there was no way to retrieve it.

CHAPTER THIRTY-THREE

November 8, Sunday

Ty

The smell of frying bacon and his teammate's banter filled Victor's Diner as Ty slouched in their red, leather booth. He stared at his half-eaten burger, unable to manage another bite.

"Man, I can't believe you were dating a real-life, fucking *princess*. Looking back, I can't believe we didn't see it. She's well-bred, poised, sexy, intelligent—" Tommy hissed when Bobby elbowed him.

"Dude, just shut the fuck up," Bobby slid his eyes to Ty's mopey form.

"'Princess,' I can deal with. Being engaged to another guy? Cheating? That's my line," Ty said with a nod to Bobby. He looked around at his teammates, who had been trying to cheer him up since they'd sat down for lunch. "She texted me goodbye this morning and wished me a good life, said she was flying out this evening out of Logan. Guess she didn't want to stick around any longer."

Unable to stop himself, he pulled out his phone and opened the message from Ashley. Yup, still stung.

"That's it?" Bobby raised a dark eyebrow.

"Well, there was some shit thrown in about how she hoped I'd find someone who could be honest with me and give me the life I wanted but didn't think you guys needed to know that part," Ty bit out, taking out his frustration on his friend.

Bobby gave him a tired look and shook his head, going back to his sandwich.

"Does she have some ritzy private jet taking her back?" Ilya took another bite of his grilled chicken.

"How am I supposed to know?"

Ilya shrugged and Tommy shook his head.

"Nah, the Dariqat royal jet is gone. Caused a real ruckus for air traffic controllers this morning when he gave a thirty-minute departure notice due to an 'emergency'."

All their heads swiveled to Jason who was making finger quotes in the air. He shrugged at their shocked expressions. "Got a...friend...who works over there. She was pissed and wanted a rich person to bitch at. Woke me up at the ass crack of dawn with her rant."

Ty scowled and turned to look out the window. The raindrops on the window made the parking lot blurry and unwelcoming.

Like his entire mood.

"For what it's worth, she wasn't on it."

Ty couldn't stop his head from whipping back and looking at Jason.

Jason shrugged. "Apparently it was just 'his royal highness' and a couple of his scary-as-shit security men. While she was bitching about his bad attitude and blatant misogyny, I snuck in a question about Ashley. Guess she heard him saying that Ashley was flying back later today on a commercial jet with her brother. She overheard him on the phone talking to someone about how he was making his foolhardy daughter and his incompetent son slum it with the civilians on the way home if they loved commoners so much."

"Sounds like a real Scrooge," Bobby mumbled.

"Worse than that," Jason added with an eyebrow raise, looking around. "Because I couldn't get back to sleep, I spent the rest of the morning researching the charmer. How Ashley turned out even remotely normal is a miracle." He gave Ty a serious look, "How you didn't end up in a body bag at any point during the last month is an act of God. From what I read, I wouldn't have put the removal of your existence past him and his cronies. That he allowed you to be a distraction for as long as you were..." Jason didn't finish.

A wave of ice washed over Ty.

"Damn, bro. That's nuts," Ilya muttered, shaking his head.

“And to think Ashley grew up with that,” Bobby wrinkled his nose and frowned at Ty’s shell-shocked expression.

"So, maybe there's more to it than you realize," Jason offered, attempting to soften the blow.

“Do they execute women over there? Is she at any risk?” Tommy muttered his question to Jason. Jason sighed heavily, shaking his head and staring at the placemat in front of him.

Ty’s stomach rolled and started burning with acid.

Fuck.

Ty thought back to Ashley's fierce nature, her passion, and her desire to experience life.

Even so, behind that confident exterior was a woman who struggled—clearly torn between her desires and the expectations placed upon her. She had spoken of her father's pressure to fulfill familial duties, but she had never gone into specifics. She had never *lied* about the royalty piece.

Lied by omission, maybe.

He mentally cursed himself for excusing her actions. Again.

But she certainly didn’t mention having a fiancée!

She should have fucking told him!

Then again...given what he was learning about her dad...maybe she was afraid of the...risk.

She was always telling him about the risk ‘to him.’ Seems like it was warranted.

But what about *to her*?

Was she going home to be punished? Was her family forcing her home early to demand some pound of flesh?

Ty was growing nauseous at the idea of anyone hurting her, while he tried to balance his own heartbreak.

There were too many emotions bouncing around inside of him—he didn’t know what to think or feel.

"I don't fucking know anything! And I don't know, because she never fuckin' told me!" Ty dragged his fingers back through his short hair, frustration mounting. "But it doesn't change the fact that she's leaving. It was going to happen sooner or later and with how things ended...sooner was probably for the best."

"Unless they behead her," Tommy chimed in, under his breath.

"Dude, just shut the fuck up!" Bobby looked at their friend in horror.

Tommy grimaced.

"You can't just leave it like this, Ty. You guys have no idea what's going on with each other. Too many lies. One freaking conversation could straighten all this out. Just fuckin' talk to her before she leaves and you can't see her again. It's not like you're ever going to be allowed to set foot in that country at this point." Jason placed his drink down on the table between them a little rougher than was necessary.

"Oh, and you're the king of being honest and open with people?" Ilya raised his brows at Jason.

"No, but—"

"She could have told him the truth right off the bat. Ty's the most even-keeled guy in the fuckin' world. He would have been fine with it." Bobby added.

"Actually, pretty sure he would have bailed as soon as she mentioned that she was already engaged," Tommy said in a distracted murmur, his eyes scrolling along a trivia card that was stationed at all the tables.

The men grunted in acknowledgment of that point.

"We could have been friends..."

The guys all laughed outright at that one.

Ty felt his cheeks burn.

"Yeah, so I would have jumped ship. So what? It would have been the right thing to do. I'm not doing that to anyone else, no matter if I know them or not. I'm never going to be the *other* man."

"You already have been. Several times." Tommy added, turning the card over to look at the back.

Ilya leveled Tommy with a stern look. "Are you helping?"

"Tryin' to," Tommy said without looking up and taking in Ilya's chastising expression.

"This is stupid. You both love each other. Just go to her and talk it out." Bobby turned his whole body to Ty. "This is one huge comedy of errors and for fuck's sake, a conversation could have prevented it all! Do you recognize how frustrating this all is to sit and watch?"

Jason scoffed and turned to Bobby. "Mighty rich, coming from you. How long did you harbor a secret love for Thea?"

Thankfully, at least *that* story had a happy ending.

Bobby rolled his eyes and looked by at Ty.

"Do you realize how many times I asked her, begged her, to open up to me? To share? To give me *something*? Anything?"

Tommy jumped in again, "And do you realize that she spent her entire life probably being told that sharing emotions, feelings, and secrets would be used against her, her family, her country? Or worse yet, how sharing those things could even result in death if she shared too much with the wrong person?"

All eyes turned to Tommy and he shrugged. "What? Have you never watched *Banaz: A Love Story*?" At their blank looks, his handsome face turned horrified. "It won a freaking *Emmy*, guys!"

Still, they gave him nothing.

"Jesus Christ, you Neanderthals, expand your palates, you uncultured swine." And with that, Tommy went back to his trivia cards.

Ty looked around at his friends, their words sinking in. He thought back to the many times Ashley had hesitated, her eyes filled with emotion as she grappled with an unseen burden.

"Okay," Ilya gave Tommy a confused look before turning back to the others. "So, if nothing else, you really should probably talk to her. Clear the air."

"Otherwise, you might spend the rest of your life regretting it." Jason finished for him.

Ty paused, considering the advice.

He turned to Bobby. "You really think so? We're not...toxic?"

"Do *you* think you're toxic?"

Not in the slightest.

But the cheating...

At his silence, Bobby tried again. "Is this about the royalty thing, lying thing, or the cheating thing?"

"Cheating," Ty bit out.

"She wasn't cheating. There. Problem solved. Go get the girl."

Ty blinked at Bobby. "What?"

"She wasn't cheating. She was coerced, threatened and manipulated into agreeing to marry some other dude. It's not like she was doing it by choice. You don't judge a vegan for eating meat if they've been kidnapped and the only food they've been provided is veal. Move on, dude."

Ty jerked. "Are you serious?"

"Dead serious. Quit with the pride and judgment. You're always saying you can read her beyond her words. Do it now. Think about what she really means and feels, not just what she says or said. You *know* her. So *read* her, damnit."

He'd had the same castigation of himself earlier. Hearing his friend repeat it back to him? Yeah...he dropped the ball. He could almost feel Ashley's soft touch on his cheeks, the way her body fit against his—their shared affinity for rough and passionate encounters that left them both breathless.

The connection they'd had almost immediately, both emotionally and physically, was undeniable.

And now...

Now it felt as if a piece of him was being ripped away.

"Yeah," Ty finally admitted, a fire burning in his gut. "Yeah, I need to talk to her."

"Better hurry, then," Ilya said, clapping him on the shoulder. "Clock's ticking."

Ty glanced at his watch, swearing under his breath when he saw the time.

He needed to get to Logan Airport before Ashley disappeared from his life forever.

Could Ashley have been shielding him from her complicated life, despite her own desires?

The image of Ashley, her dark eyes brimming with unshed tears as she fought to maintain her composure while he cursed her out, flashed through Ty's mind.

"Thanks, guys," Ty said, his voice filled with gratitude as he pushed up from the table.

"Go get her, man."

“I’ll text my friend and let her know yet another rich man needs a favor. She’ll get you fast through security. I’ll shoot you her number now.” Jason pulled out his phone. Then he added in a mumble, his chin down, “Maybe comment on how grateful you are, will ya? I think she needs a win.”

And as Ty left the diner, his steps quick and purposeful, he thought of all the things that could go wrong. An accident on the highway, arriving at the airport too late, getting held up by the media, fans, or security, the list was endless. He had a small window to reach her. He needed to make the most of it. Needed to make this moment count.

He *couldn’t* let her go.

Chapter Thirty-Four

November 8, Sunday

Ty

"Come on, come on!" Ty muttered under his breath as he navigated through traffic on the Mass Turnpike, every second feeling like an eternity.

The image of Ashley boarding her flight and vanishing from his life forever forced his foot a little firmer on the gas.

Why was everyone on I-90 driving like they were out for a Sunday stroll?!

"The speed limit is 65, not 60!" He shouted at a car who was dallying in the left lane. "Fucking hell."

As the car finally pulled to the right, Ty zipped up to take its spot. He had to resist the urge to flip him off as he drove by, it wasn't very Canadian-like, and his mother would have chewed him out if she could have seen how he was driving.

'I can see why they say people from Massachusetts drive like Mass-holes,' he could almost hear her say.

Just under an hour later, he roared into the Logan drop-off terminals. Not caring about whether or not he was in the right place, he parked his truck, turned it off, practically jumped out of his car and raced inside. Ty bounced lightly on his feet as his eyes scanned the departure board for any sign of Ashley's flight to Dariqat. Jason had called him with the deets while he was driving so he knew what to look for.

Frantically, he clicked on Jason's lady friend's contact info and bounced on his feet as he waited for her to answer. It didn't take long. After a short ten second chat, the angel swooped from the shadows, dragged him through a security bypass lane, handed him a ticket to Dariqat, and pointed him in the direction of Ashley's departure gate.

With thirty minutes to spare before her flight was set to board, Ty snatched the boarding pass and took off toward her gate.

Would she board first?

Would she have security?

Would he find her?

What if he actually flew to Dariqat? Would they...detain him when he was there for 'risking' their princess?

Please, let me catch her in time, Ty silently prayed as he sprinted down the concourse to Ashley's terminal.

Thank God, Jason's girl was high up, or else Security would have been tackling Ty to the ground.

Up till now, Ashley hadn't lived like a princess, but with the news being out about her...she might have boarded early?

Fuck, he hoped not.

Ty charged into her terminal, eyes scanning the sea of faces for the woman who held his heart. Each step brought a mix of hope and despair, as he wondered whether he would find her in time.

He couldn't lose her now, not when he'd finally realized just how much she meant to him.

The clock was ticking, and every second counted as he searched desperately for Ashley, for the chance to set things right, hoping against all odds that he wasn't too late.

The tension and anticipation built with each step, his mind racing as fast as his legs.

Now that she was this close...

He couldn't let her slip away like this, not without fighting for what they had together.

"Come on, where are you?" Ty muttered, his breaths coming in short puffs. Yeah, he was a professional athlete, but even so, he was winded as hell.

Just as he rounded a corner, Ty spotted her and slid to a halt.

Ashley stood in a line near her gate, her dark hair cascading down her back as she conversed with a man next to her. A man who shared the same skin tone and beautiful wide eyes.

Relief washed over him, followed by a surge of determination.

He couldn't waste another second. It's not like they'd delay the flight so they could sort out their shit.

"Ashley!" Ty shouted across the crowded airport, his voice bellowing with desperation. Startled passengers turned to look at him as he barreled towards her, his athletic frame cutting through the throngs of people like a freshly sharpened skate on the ice.

"Ty?" Ashley's eyes widened in surprise, confusion etched on her face as she watched him approach.

"Wait, please," Ty panted, finally skidding to a halt in front of her. "You can't get on that flight. We can't just let it end like this. We need to talk it out. You can't just run away."

People around them began to gather, drawn to the drama unfolding before their eyes.

"What are you doing here?" Ashley asked, her voice wavering with some mysterious emotion. Ty could see the uncertainty in her eyes but couldn't read the other feelings floating around in those dark pools.

"Look, I know you're scared," Ty said urgently, his hands cupping her face, "and I know you think you need to do this alone. But you don't. I'm here, and I'll do whatever it takes to make this work. We can face your father, your responsibilities, everything—together. We can keep you protected. I promise you."

Ashley blinked and pulled back from his hands.

"What are you talking about?" Her voice was raspy, as if she had spent the entire night sobbing.

Fuck.

"You and me, Ash, we're solid. The real deal. Those rare, once-in-a-lifetime kinds of love. We can't toss that away over some dumb misunderstandings or family drama. Deep down, we're still us. We've gotta fight for that. And hey, you've got so much more to give here. If not for me, do it for the families you're helping."

Okay, so apparently his race to the airport had converted his brain from thinking 'let's talk it out' to 'let's get her back.' As he stared into her gorgeous eyes...he was okay with that switch.

She was *his* Ashley.

And fuck, who hadn't made mistakes in a relationship?

As tears welled in her eyes, he thought maybe she agreed.

Until she put two hands on his chest and shoved him away.

Chapter Thirty-Five

November 8, Sunday

Ashley

It wasn't a big shove, just a slight rock to his upper body, but it was like her hands were possessed. The thought of him being that close to her made her want to stab him in the eye with the pen in her purse.

Ashley stared down Ty, the man who had stolen her heart and refused to let it go. "How could you do this? What the fuck are you trying to pull? Why are you *here?*" She ended on a hiss, the anger threatening to explode from her in a way that would make airport security antsy.

Ty's expression broke, "Princ–please, Ashley, just listen to me for a minute. I'm so sorry. I just...had a lot of big...feelings, and I...felt like I didn't have a choice. I felt backed into a corner and manipulated."

"You felt manipulated? You!?" Ashley was trying to keep her voice down but judging from the looks around them, she really was not doing a great job.

Ty's brows furrowed. "Yeah. I mean...you lied to me. Like it was nothing. Multiple times, I might add." He said it like she was dense for not understanding.

Ashley's fingers curled and she felt her perfectly manicured nails bite into her palms.

"Are you *joking* right now?" She leaned in, her voice sharp and high. "*I* lied to *you*? That's where you want to go with this?"

Ty's head cocked as he stared at her, taking in her murderous expression and the way her hands fisted. "Uh...I don't think so?"

"Ya think?"

He frowned at her, leaning back a little. "I'm just saying, I felt a little betrayed. Like what we had was a lie and it pissed me off. I'm not saying I handled it well – I didn't – but I'm here, trying to fix things. What exactly are you doing?"

"Going to Dariqat to get married."

Ty's face hardened just a bit. "Yeah, let's talk about that. That's a terrible fucking decision and you know it."

"Why? You think he'll lie to me? Not be honest about his interference in my life? Because damn, Ty, you sure had me fooled."

He blinked and widened his stance, staring at her with a perplexed expression. "When did I ever lie to you?"

"Oh, please, you hypocrite" Ashley couldn't stop her eyes from rolling and she shifted to turn away. But before she could take a step, Ty's hand shot out and held her shoulder, keeping her in place.

She hated the fucking tingles that shot through her body at the contact.

"You're mad at me for lying to you?" Ty asked, incredulously.

She chewed on her lip. "Well, I guess I never explicitly asked about conversations you had concerning my life when I wasn't around, but yeah. I'm pissed that you manipulated and affected my life and didn't even have the balls to come to me about it. Then you had the nerve to get mad at me about secrets? Psh!"

Ashley felt her stomach drop out at the wave of understanding that washed down his face.

There it was.

So, everything her father had told her about Ty had been true after all...

Ty sighed and rubbed his face. He took a deep breath and his chest moved visibly under his coat.

Yeah, buddy. You fucked up. Big time.

"What do you want me to say? I'm sorry? Because I'm not. I'd do it again. I was just trying to help and my intentions were good."

Ashley stiffened, biting her tongue from ripping him a new one right then and there.

"I didn't know what else to do. It felt like the safest option. Who knows what kind of shitheads are out there? He could have been hurt. I offered to help." Ty's wide shoulders gave an inelegant shrug, and he shared a sad smile. "I'd do it again. It worked. It got the job done, for the most part. Still working on the other half of the equation."

Wait, what?

She had been following most of what he was saying until that last part...

The other half of the equation?

Ty shifted and kept talking, unaware of her confusion. "I told him I'd pay. I told him I'd do whatever it took. But he didn't want it. Too prideful." Umm, what the hell was he talking about. "But Connell is safe and that's all that matters. I have someone looking into things a bit, to see if there's anything the team can do to help going forward. But it's not safe out there, Ash, you know that. I couldn't just *not* say something."

Chills broke out all over Ashley's body.

Holy fuck.

A small tremor started in her hands and she moved them together, locking her fingers in front of her to hide the movement.

Holy fucking shit.

"You're talking about Garrett and Connell?" She croaked out, unable to form a more coherent thought as it all just pummeled her in waves.

Ty became very still and stared at her, his forehead wrinkling. "What? Yeah, of course I am. What did you think I was talking about?"

"You talked to Garrett and got him to sign over Connell?" Again, words were failing her, but the shaking was increasing in intensity.

Ty reached out a hand and then pulled it back before touching her, not able to read the expression on her face.

Hell, she didn't even know what she was feeling.

"Yeah," he said slowly. "I gave him a ride to the encampment after the meet and greet. We had some...choice words, but it ended on me...saying some more choice words." He swallowed and rushed to say, "I know that's totally crossing a line and I'm—"

Ashley reached out and pressed a single finger to his lips.

He needed to stop talking.

Now.

She closed her eyes and counted to ten, trying to wipe the emotion out of her and failing. Shit.

Instead, she pushed through and opened her eyes, staring Ty down.

"This is maybe one of the most important questions I'll ever ask you and you need to be one hundred percent honest and transparent. No lies of omission. No half-truths. I need it all. Please."

At Ty's increasingly concerned look, Ashley's heartbeat thundered louder in her ears.

"You interfered with Garrett?"

Ty nodded.

Ashley took a deep breath and then asked, in a tone as even as she could manage, "Did you, or did you not, communicate with anyone from my family or our advisors about keeping me occupied during my last few months here in the States?"

At the confused expression that encapsulated his face, Ashley's heart ripped wide open.

So.

Who was lying?

The love of her life?

Or her brother, whom she loved so dearly.

Fuck.

Ashley took a ragged inhale.

"Ash? What's going on?"

Something she'd like to know as well.

The line started moving around her and Ty panicked, grabbing at her arm, his voice pleading. "It doesn't matter. Whatever it is, we can make it work. Please, don't get on that plane. Stay with me, and let's fight for us."

The line continued to stream around them, and Ashley looked at Ty, unable process everything—including his increased anxiety and why he looked ready to kidnap her.

"What?"

"Don't get on the plane. There's a whole bunch of shit I need to say. Just...give me a minute to get it all in order. I swear I practiced it in my head on the drive here. I'm just a little thrown right now, I just—"

Ashley furrowed her brow,. "Ty. The flight isn't boarding yet," she said, glancing over his shoulder at the front of the line where a small table was set up beside the boarding area. A local psychic duo were stationed there, flipping cards, reading palms and tea leaves. A line of people had formed to get a turn, many sitting down with their travel companions while waiting for their flights. "I'm waiting in line for one of the psychics, not to board the plane..."

As realization dawned on Ty's face, a flush crept up his neck. He gave an awkward chuckle, relief smoothing over the embarrassment he felt at his dramatic plea.

"Wow, I really thought you were about to leave me forever," Ty admitted sheepishly, running a hand through his hair.

Ashley couldn't contain her own chuckle, the tension eased as she gazed into Ty's bright blue eyes.

"Yes, I suppose I can understand that," she conceded, her heart softening with affection at his wry grin.

Ty nodded as he reached out to take her hand. "You'll talk with me? Get this straightened out? Whatever *this* is." His voice pitched at the end and Ashley realized again that he either was a superb actor or he really didn't have any clue what she was talking about.

Which reminded her that her brother lied...knowing full well it would wreck her.

Had her family even talked with Garrett? Or were all of those case file notes just duplicates of the ones in the system? Had they actually involved themselves in any of it? Or was it just an additional lie to get her back as soon as possible?

Jesus. What the fuck was going on in Dariqat that demanded such extreme measures?

Then again...this was all assuming that her family were the liars—not Ty.

Either brought a slash of pain to her heart.

"You can't leave me, Ash. Not now, not when we've come this far." he said, a determined edge to his tone. Yet, there was a vulnerability in his voice that tugged at Ashley's heart. The weight of his words hung in the air between them, promise and plea wrapped into one.

She needed to know the truth—and she wasn't going to get it from him.

Chapter Thirty-Six

November 8, Sunday

Ashley

Ashley stood at the crossroads of her life, her heart pounding in her chest as she looked into Ty's bright blue eyes, trying to find even the hint of a lie.

As she breathed in his familiar pine scent, a wave of desire and peace washed over her. *Home.*

"Ashira?" a deep voice demanded, cutting through the charged silence.

Idris stepped closer, puffed up with an aura of arrogance and authority. He was tall, regal, and every bit the embodiment of Dariqat's royal expectations. His dark eyes narrowed as they took Ty in. He gave a small grunt, clearly unimpressed.

"Ty," Ashley began, her voice shaking slightly in anticipation of a blow-out, "this is my brother, Idris."

"Idris," Ty said, extending his hand. "I've heard a lot about you. I'm Ty Daniels. Nice to meet you. Thanks for all you did to get Ashley over here and allow her to live her dream."

Damnit—why did he have to be such a good guy all the time! Her family would rip him apart! He needed some thorns!

Idris eyed Ty's outstretched hand for a moment before reluctantly accepting it. "So, you're the hockey player," he said, dismissively, his voice dripping with disdain. Ashley whipped around to face her brother.

What was up with the douchebag act?

Idris didn't bother looking at Ashley, choosing instead to continue sneering at Ty.

As she glanced from Ty to Idris, the weight of her decision bore down on her.

Her duty as a princess and as a daughter of Dariqat battled fiercely against the love she felt for Ty. She thought about two lives, neither one yet hers. The life she was given, back in Dariqat with her family or the life she could have with Ty—filled with laughter, passion, and adventure.

A burning sting started spreading through her sinuses.

She was leaving this airport today, by car or plane...but either way, she would be losing one half of her heart.

Her Ty...or her family.

"Idris, I'm glad you're here. I was hoping you could clarify something..."

Idris lowered his eyes to her, and his face softened—just barely.

"I think there has been a misunderstanding." There was no fucking misunderstanding. "Yesterday, our father seemed to imply that he was the reason that my work here was successful. That all my clients achieved positive results because of some sort of interference by the council. Did I understand that right?"

Ashley heard Ty's sharp intake of breath and sensed the sudden stiffness of his muscles as he coiled with irritation at her words. She felt his heavy gaze on her, but she refused to look at him.

If she did, she knew that she would break down.

The thought that her brother and father had made her feel this way on purpose just to manipulate her...it was inexcusable.

She channeled every ounce of willpower into blanking the emotions from her face. Again, she failed, but she was in more control than she had previously been for the last twenty-four hours.

Idris remained very still. He watched her with a somber expression. He didn't even tip his head to look at her straight on. Instead, he chose to mimic their father's favorite pose of disdain; and the evidence of the changes she was seeing in her brother made her heart hurt for an entirely different reason, now.

"There may have been some involvement. Since escorting you out of the country years ago, dynamics have...changed. I'm no longer privy to a lot of information and I no longer have a seat on the council."

Ashley gasped.

They could do that?

Kick her brother out?

Because of helping her escape to explore the world?

As she took in his hardened gaze and changed persona, she recoiled. Yes, they certainly had...and by the looks of it, they'd stripped her brother of more than just that. How exactly had they exacted their retribution for helping their prized broodmare leave the sanctity of their homeland? What price had her brother had to pay? She thought back on her father's words from yesterday.

"Idris?"

He shook his head, his eyes darting at the people standing at the gate around them, gawking and snapping pictures.

Fuck.

"Okay," Ashley said slowly, still trying to come to grips with everything. "Did the council reach out to Ty and ask him to keep me occupied for my remaining time here in the States?"

At that, Ty jerked. Immediately, he stepped toward Ashley, crowding her.

"Ash," Ty said in a panic, "I swear to God, I—"

Ashley gave a small shake of her head to silence Ty, and turned back to her brother expectantly.

"Idris?"

If he said 'yes,' then he was sticking with his story from yesterday and she had to decide who to believe.

If he said 'no'...

Then he was contradicting what he said in front of their father yesterday and...

Well, she didn't quite know what would happen then either.

Idris gave Ty the quickest look, the sour look on his face slipping for just a second. He focused on Ashley, speaking tentatively. "Little sister, I'm not privy to all that Father does, nor the council. After Father left for Dariqat this morning, he simply tasked me with bringing you home. That is what I'm doing."

"Bringing me home?"

Idris nodded.

"So, you know nothing about Ty's recruitment?" She pushed again.

She needed to fucking know, damnit!

She needed to hear the words come out of her hero's mouth.

The brother who convinced Father to teach her to shoot. The brother who would sneak her down to the kitchen for snacks if dinner was gross and she didn't eat. The brother who bought Ashley her first pair of jeans and snuck them into a drawer in her bedroom.

She needed to hear him say it.

"Please," she whispered.

Idris closed his eyes and deflated in front of her.

Ashley's chest cracked open.

"Father said...a lot of things yesterday...Things have...*changed* in Dariqat. Not for the better." Idris winced and looked away before making eye contact with her again. "Like the copies of your client files. If you had looked closer, you would have seen that most of it was garbage. I kept an eye on you here and made sure my contacts were keeping me informed of any more...dangerous...cases. We intervened only twice, and that was simply to prevent...planned acts of violence against you. We didn't meddle in your cases...that I know of," he tacked on as an afterthought.

Ashley's heart hammered hard in her chest and her head felt like it was going to explode.

"And Ty?"

“Father says they made a deal with him...” Idris opened his eyes and turned to look at Ty, shooting him an apologetic expression. “I have my doubts.”

There were a few moments in Ashley’s life when she felt like she lost all sense of time and space.

When she was told her mother had died. When she was told that she could come to the States if she agreed to marry Tabir. And when she had fallen in love with Ty.

Finding out her family had outright lied and manipulated her...it made the list, as well.

Ashley woodenly stared at him, sucking in fast, quick breaths.. What the fuck was happening?

Ashley rubbed the fingers of her right hand across her lips.

The sensation felt odd. Like her hand was disconnected from the rest of her body.

Ashley's eyes shimmered with unshed tears as she looked at Ty, feeling the pressure of the revelation weighing down on her.

What was she supposed to do now?

"Ty, I..." She faltered, unable to find the right words to say.

“It’s fine. We’ll work it out. I’m sure they had their reasons. But they can have their reasons from their home, and you can have your reasons from ours.”

Ours? That felt...beautiful.

And heartbreaking when she considered the cost.

"Look," Idris interrupted, his tone haughty and cold, "This isn't just about what she wants. It's bigger than that. It’s about what's best for her and our family. My job is to bring her home."

"Idris," Ashley said softly, her voice wavering, "please let me handle this."

Her brother gave her a curt nod, stepping back but remaining close, like a silent guardian watching over her. Ashley took a deep breath, turning her attention back to Ty.

"Ty, I love you more than anything," she whispered, her dark eyes pleading. "But I have duties I can't ignore. I wish I could just walk away from it all, especially now...but I can't."

"Then let me help you," Ty said, his voice thick with emotion. "We can figure this out together. I won't let you face this alone."

"But what if I can't have both? What if I have to choose between my duty and my love for you?" Ashley asked.

"Then choose me," Ty said simply, his blue eyes blazing with conviction. "Choose *us*."

Ashley's heart pounded in her chest, her emotions swirling in a tumultuous storm. She glanced at her brother, who stood stoically nearby, his expression revealing nothing of his thoughts. He was the embodiment of her royal duty, a constant reminder of the expectations she had been born into.

“Ashley?”

"Ty, I—" she began, struggling to find the right words. But before she could continue, Idris interrupted.

"Can't you see what’s at stake?" he snapped, his dark eyes narrowing as they bored into Ty. "Do not pressure her into something she will regret. A knee-jerk decision now will affect the rest of her life. The life with Tabir will provide her with something you could only dream of. Tell me about all the pet tigers you will buy for her, the gold you will drape her in, the rose gardens that will be built in her name. You’ve known each other all of twelve minutes—she’s known Tabir since we were children. You’re so certain that you’re a forever kind of love that you’re willing to risk her entire future?"

Ashley looked at Idris in shock. When had he started talking like a formal robot?

When had he started to care for such frivolous things?

"Let her speak for herself," Ty retorted, his gaze never leaving Ashley's face.

A mix of fear and admiration bubbled within Ashley as she watched Ty stand up to her brother. He was willing to challenge the very foundations of her world for the sake of their love. And now, it was up to her to decide whether she was willing to do the same.

Ty's voice, barely more than a whisper, cut through the mounting tension. "Ashley, please," he pleaded, his eyes shimmering with desperation. "Don't leave."

The raw vulnerability in his gaze sent shivers down her spine. She could feel the weight of his love and the depth of his fear as he laid himself bare before her—and her brother.

"Ty," she breathed, her own voice wavering with emotion. Her chest ached with the turmoil of conflicting desires.

Could she really give up her entire family just at a chance at love with Ty?

What if they didn't work out in the end?

They had only known each other for two months. Not even.

Her eyes flicked to her brother.

His presence was both an anchor and a chain.

As much as she longed for freedom and a future with Ty, another part of her was anchored to the traditions and expectations that had shaped her entire existence up until now.

"Please," Ty whispered, his thumb stroking her cheek as he searched her eyes for an answer. "Don't let this be the end of our story." His voice was gaining strength.

She closed her eyes, letting the cacophony of voices, the camera shutters, and the muted hum of the airport fade away. She searched deep within herself, wrestling with the desire for freedom and the duty that had been ingrained in her since birth. The choice was hers—and she knew the consequences would be profound.

The loudspeaker crackled to life, jolting Ashley from her thoughts. "Flight 2090 to Dariqat is now boarding," the flight attendant announced in a cheery voice that seemed to mock the heaviness of the moment.

Ty's sapphire eyes locked onto hers, pleading and vulnerable.

Ashley hesitated, feeling torn between the two paths before her.

"I'm sorry," she whispered, her gaze drifting to her brother. "I can't do it."

Idris's shoulders sagged in what seemed like relief, and a small smile tugged at the corners of his lips before he wiped it away. He stepped forward and pressed a gentle kiss to Ashley's forehead. "Thank God," he murmured, only loud enough for her ears to hear.

Just like that, gone was his stilted, proper speech in an octave too low.

This was the brother she adored.

Idris looked down at her, his expression still blank and Ashley became aware of what sort of failure this was for her brother who's one job was to bring her home to secure the future of their small nation.

“Idris?”

What would his latest price be?

Could she let him pay that?

Was it her choice?

Idris pulled her into a tight hug and kissed the top of her head while squeezing her tight. “Let's get you home, Ashley. That's my job, after all.”

Chapter Thirty-Seven
Epilogue: June 18, Saturday
Ashley

Seven months later...

A warm, early summer breeze ripped through the park, bringing with it a warm, delicious mixture of all the food spread out on the various picnic tables.

Ashley stood with her hands on her hips, surveying the welcoming scene. Colorful decorations adorned the picnic tables, and families from her social work community mingled with some of the Cyclones players and their loved ones, their faces alight with happiness. The laughter of children mixed with the excited chatter of adults, creating a lively atmosphere that swelled Ashley's heart with pride.

"Looks like you've outdone yourself again, Princess," Ty said, coming up beside her and wrapping a strong arm around her shoulders. His bright blue eyes shone with admiration as they took in the festive scene before them.

"Thank you," she replied, leaning into him. "I couldn't have done it without everyone's support."

"Hey, you're the one who brought us all together," Ty said, planting a tender kiss on her temple.

"*Do you see how many people actually came*?" Her voice was high and breathy and did nothing to hide her excitement and wonder.

"More than double from the last time we did one."

Ashley stared at the mingling guests.

How had she amassed such a network?

Ty gave her a small nudge. "Embrace it, Ash. These people love you. Your 'successes.'"

Ashley squinted and blinked fast, trying to dispel the tears that had gathered.

“I called a few of them my ‘failures’,” she admitted in a guilty whisper.

“I know.”

“They weren’t my ‘failures’.”

“Nope.”

“It just...took a minute...”

“Some people get there differently.”

Ashley sniffed and looked over at Garrett Baylor who was tossing a football with Connell and Mr. Jenkins. The trio made an awkward triangle as they tried to not throw into any tree branches in the small clearing off to the side.

Ashley’s heart squeezed at how healthy Garrett looked...and how happy Connell looked.

Fuck.

She swiped at the one tear she couldn’t stop from falling.

"You need a moment, or do you want to mingle?"

Ashley took a steadying breath and centered herself. “Mingle,” she declared while lacing her fingers in his.

Hand in hand, they wove through the crowd, greeting whatever guest they came across.

As she caught up with familiar faces–both clients and players–she felt a surge of pride for the home she had created for herself.

Laughter flowed freely, and the joyful buzz filled the air, setting a cheerful tone for the afternoon.

She absently watched Lexie roar and stomp after some kids over on the colorful play structure. The children shrieked with delight and scattered, climbing up the playset, sprinting to the swings, scrambling up the enclosed slides.

Lexie fit right in.

Ashley couldn’t stop her smile.

As they continued to mingle, Ashley felt a renewed sense of belonging. The connections she had made, both in her professional life and personal, were more than she could have ever imagined.

Despite the losses she endured to get to this point.

She glanced up at Ty, who was gazing at her with a soft smile of wonder on his face.

He pulled her close, pressing a firm kiss to her hair.

Ashley gave a quick peck to his cheek, and nestled into his side as they watched their friends approach their small cocoon.

Jason, Tommy, and Ilya gathered around them, their laughter mingling with the chatter of the families around them.

"It's good the agency was willing to keep you on after everything. I doubt they would have found someone to replace you, someone who would have been capable of something like this."

"Thanks, Jason," Ashley replied, trying to ignore the twinge of discomfort at the mention of what her familial drama had caused.

"This park is freaking dope. Did you see the splash pads they had over by the entrance?" Tommy ripped Ty away and tried tucking him under his big arm, manhandling Ty's body with the practice of an older brother.

"Dude, you're not kidding.. I was checking out the pond earlier and had never seen water so clear. They even have a few benches and gazebos for people to relax. I can picture settling in a hammock, listening to the murmur of the little rivers and waterfalls, and losing myself in a good book. I'm totally giving it a try next week." Sure enough, an ever-present book was poking out of Bobby's back pocket, proving his claim.

Ty preened and admitted in a shy grin, "This park is one of ours."

The men swiveled to look at him.

"What?"

"It's one of the parks we bought and restored. We have some clean energy initiatives we've been working on, and this was a place close to home that I could be more involved in while the Dariqat stuff was going down."

The guys all stared at him, and Ashley felt a rush of pride for her man.

Her nature-boy.

Saving the world.

After a round of macho teasing and shoving, Tommy turned to Ty and demanded, "Actually, what's the latest on the Dariqat project? GPANL takes my money easily enough every month, but you guys are total garbage at sending out newsletters and updates. Are we still making progress over there?"

Ashley hid her grin at the 'we' reference. The man could be rough but there was nothing he wouldn't do, or adopt, for his friends.

"Still going strong, surprisingly. Not sure what Idris did but we haven't been blackballed yet."

The friends collectively sighed in relief, nodding with a mixture of admiration and reassurance.

"Speaking of the hero of the hour, how is your one decent relative? Have you heard from him yet?" Jason asked, a small wrinkle between his brows.

Ashley pursed her lips, feeling a cold shiver of dread trickle down her spine. Her throat felt tight. "No news," she managed to say, her heart sinking with each passing moment of silence-they all knew what that might mean..

Since Idris had taken her back to her apartment, then flown back to Dariqat without her, she hadn't heard a peep.

That was months ago now.

Ashley frequently searched for news online, photos – anything – to catch a glimpse of what was happening. To see that he was okay. Nothing.

Her brother was nowhere to be found.

Even his phone was disconnected.

She wet her lips, which had suddenly gone dry, and started wringing her hands together, the twisting of her rings becoming almost frantic. "But he said that might happen. Told me to be patient, that he'd reach out when it was safe."

Who was she trying to convince? Them or herself?

The silence from Idris was deafening, a void filled with the worst scenarios. What if he was in trouble? What if he was being punished and couldn't reach out for help?

Her thoughts tormented her at night, causing countless nightmares, each more unsettling than the last.

Bobby gave her a sad but supportive look, his face shadowed with understanding. "I'm sure *someone* will find him and let you know. We certainly have enough people working on it."

Ty, his friends, and *all* their contacts were working double-time trying to find Idris.

In desperation, she reached out to the owner of the security team tasked with keeping tabs on her in the States and inquired about Idris. The man's expression turned deadly serious as she explained the situation. Calling in his team, he reminded her that he was once the elite of the elite in black ops and promised to find her brother. His vow left her both relieved and feeling sorry for the men in Dariqat who were about to face an entourage of American ghosts in the dead of night.

Even Lexie had placed some rather expensive calls.

Ashley forced a small, brittle smile, her eyes glassy with the effort of holding back her fears.

Her gaze drifted off, her heart weighted with worry, weak hope mingling with fear.

Sensing the mood shift, the men quickly changed the subject, bickering about some inane thing. Ashley tuned them out, choosing to focus on Ty's warm hand rubbing comforting circles on her back.

While she worked on recentering herself, Ashley noticed Bianca–Ty's lawyer friend–arriving at the picnic tables across from them. The poised attorney caught Ashley's eye and offered a charming smile before depositing several containers of various ice cream flavors on the dessert table.

"I brought some treats to help us all stay cool in this heat," Bianca announced cheerfully, waving to the group.

"Thanks, Bianca!" Ashley called back, raising a hand in greeting. Her heart swelled with gratitude as she thought about how instrumental Bianca had been in helping her resolve her visa situation. Without the combined efforts of Ty, Bianca, and their well-connected friends, Ashley might have been forced to leave the life she'd built here in the States and risk the wrath of the Dariqat council.

Bianca wandered over to where Babs, Kira and Kayla sat, giggling conspiratorially about something scandalous. As the women exchanged whispers and laughs, Ashley felt a surge of affection for the small community that had become her support system.

Just then, Ashley caught Tommy and Jason shooting narrowed glances at the women, curiosity and suspicion etched on their faces. Despite the intensity of their gazes, there was an underlying playfulness that hinted at the strong bonds there. Ashley quickly looked away, trying to suppress the grin tugging at the corners of her mouth. She didn't want to draw attention to the men's scrutiny or spoil the fun for her friends.

But when she looked away, she caught Bobby staring intently over at a small circle of members from the Cyclones Ice Crew, the Chill Chasers.

The love on his face...it warmed her defrosted heart. Actually...it mirrored the devotion on Ty's whenever he looked at her.

Love.

Home.

The rest of the afternoon passed in a flurry of games, pictures, and competition. As laughter and conversation flowed around them, Ashley took a deep breath, savoring the beauty of her life.

As she stood at the edge of the gathering, she took in the scene before her. It was everything she had been striving for – a sense of community, belonging, and purpose.

And next time she did one of these events, there would be even more attendees.

Because Ty was right: she *was* awesome at her job.

Ashley loved her clients and she wouldn't give up on them.

"Hey," Ty murmured, sidling up beside her and staring out at the mingling attendees. "You look like you're lost in thought."

She gave him a wry smile and turned back to people-watching. "Just thinking about how different things could have been if I hadn't met you."

"You'd have a lot more pet tigers," he teased as he watched Ilya roll on the ground with some toddlers.

"Get on that, will you?"

Ty's lip twitched and he scratched at this five o'clock shadow. "Damn, woman. I already have someone custom-making a portable coat closet. Now you want tigers? If I knew you were this high mainten–oof."

She lightly smacked his abs with her noticeably ringless left hand. Ashley then held it up to him in question. "Forget the tigers. When is *this* getting heavy?" She wiggled her fingers for emphasis and gave him a haughty look.

"*Patience*, Princess. I have plans. I've been so busy touring houses with rose gardens that I haven't had time to coordinate the best damn proposal you'll ever get. Don't worry, it's coming, you bossy minx."

"It's not like it's hard to beat the last one," Ashley fake grumbled, her saucy attitude causing him to grin and pull her close.

"For sure. Mine is definitely better. Trust me—when you wear my jersey next season, our names will match. Promise."

"They better," she sniffed, and then burrowed in deeper, unable to stop her smile or the butterflies that erupted in her belly.

Ty *would* be a Cyclones player next season...Coach Montgomery and Sam's executive team had rallied and made sure of it.

They continued to watch the party, cuddling close and basking in the love around them. Ashley sighed, resting her head on Ty's shoulder.

"Thanks for not letting me go," Ashley whispered, unable to look at him.

Ty pulled her close, pressing a firm kiss to her hair and inhaling deeply like he always did.

"Never, Princess," he promised, his voice low and tender.

And while she wasn't a true princess anymore, she'd become something better.

Here, she was *just Ashley* —Ty's Ashley—and that was more than enough.

A bookworm hockey player. A determined best friend. A fake-dating arrangement to get the attention of his rival that will risk not only their hearts, but their friendship. Will they share the truth before it's too late or will they lose it all?

Secret Crushes, Sizzling Chemistry, and a Fake Romance That Feels All Too Real

Click now to see where the series started with Bobby and Thea— https://mybook.to/SCe—**Embellishment:** A Steamy Fake-Dating, Best Friend Hockey Romance

Discover More From Ella Haines

Springfield Spartans Standalone Professional Football Romances:

Crystal Clear: A Steamy Springfield Stripper *Novella*
Offensive Holding: A Forbidden Friends-To-Lovers Stripper Romance *Novella*
Illegal Substitutions: A Friends-To-Lovers Steamy Football Romance
Illegal Contact: A Steamy Workplace Football Romance
Unsportsmanlike Conduct: A Steamy Single Mother Football Romance
Intentional Grounding: A Steamy Opposites Attract Football Romance
False Start: A Steamy Second Chance Football Romance

Springfield Cyclones Standalone Professional Hockey Romances:

Boarding: A Hockey Romance *Novelette*
Embellishment: A Steamy Fake-Dating Best Friends Hockey Romance
Hooking: A Steamy Bachelor Auction Hockey Romance
Interference: A Steamy Best Friend's Ex, Hockey Romance
Misconduct: A Steamy Forbidden Psychologist-Patient Hockey Romance

Tripping: A Steamy Captain's Forbidden Little Sister Hockey Romance

Social Media Information - Ella Haines

Did you enjoy this book?

If so, please visit **www.EllaHaines.com** and sign up for the newsletter to receive additional scenes, freebies, and updates on future releases.

Newsletter signup here:
http://ellahaines.com/newsletter-for-freebies/

Also, if you have an eagle eye and caught any typos that slipped through the rounds and rounds of edits, take a moment and think if you'd like to be an ARC or beta reader for any future releases! If so, drop me an email! I'd love to have you on the team.

If you find any typos, you can let me know here: EllaHaines.author@gmail.com

About Author - Ella Haines

Ella Haines is a lover of all things love. Raised to know that she could be anything in the world, she made the wild and crazy decision to become a neurotic accountant. Balancing trial balances and filing taxes didn't quite fill her bucket, so she started dabbling in short stories. Those short stories evolved into complex storylines with empowered women, their families and friends, and the hunky men who adore them.

Request For Review

If this book brought you a smile and you think others might enjoy it, please review it on your purchasing platform (and copy it to Goodreads if you're willing and able).

This helps to spread the word about the book. Social proof to other readers is important and helps them find their next favorite read.

It also brings me joy and keeps me writing <3

Content/Trigger Warnings

Warning:

This book will contain explicit language, the threat of violence from a trigger-happy father, and sexy times (sometimes in public). It also has a heroine who is learning how to be confident in her sexuality and embrace who she wants to be. Also, you need to be able to suspend disbelief about a foreign princess from a patriarchal society being allowed to live in the US. If these are triggering/bothering for you – here is your warning to maybe avoid this book. Regardless, I promise there will be an HEA.

This book is a work of my imagination and any mistakes are my own. A big thank you to those who helped me craft this story.

Made in the USA
Middletown, DE
13 August 2024

58681561R00179